SANDS OF EPPLA

JANEAL FALOR

For Erik
Because we share a love beyond the senses

MAP OF EPPLA

CHAPTER ONE

For as long as I could remember, I had wanted someone to care about me more than anything else in all of Eppla. But it wouldn't happen. I was blind, doomed to never fall in love at first sight—or ever. If my parents hadn't tried to challenge the way things were, maybe I would still have my vision.

I shivered at the morose thoughts despite the warmth of the day. Tewy, my monkey, brushed against my hand. The sound of the nearby waterfall soothed me. "You're right. Let's get some chores done."

There were traps to check, water to bring in, fruit to gather—none of which I wanted to do, but there was no one else to do it. Leaning down, I felt for my walking stick and straightened again. Tewy jumped onto my shoulder, ready for the ride.

The magic sand lining the riverbank squished between my toes. In the middle of the day, the heat bore down on my shoulders as I tilted my face toward it. Tewy chittered with the other nearby monkeys. Home meant peace, even if it was lonely.

I reached up and stroked Tewy, finding comfort in the softness between my fingers. "Met up with some cohorts today, did you?"

He squawked.

"Ah, a lady friend. Are you falling in love, Tewy?" I guessed. My heart gave a stab of yearning. I should have given up on such things long ago, but I'd grown up with stories of romance from my caretaker. It didn't matter if I'd been abandoned in my world with no one for company except a monkey. Didn't matter if it was something I could never have. I was still in love with love.

Tewy tweaked my nose.

I laughed. "All right, chores it is. No more teasing you."

He continued to chat amiably as I used the tip of my staff to scan my surroundings. Nothing unusual there. The wind rustled the leaves of the nearby trees, and I was grateful when the heat eased as I slipped beneath them. "Coconut, Tewy."

The weight lifted from my shoulder. He'd bring it inside for me. I walked to my house, stepped high enough to cross the threshold, and went in. It was silent—oddly so. Where was the chatter of monkeys and squawks of birds from outside my home?

I went to the area I used as the kitchen, though it was next to my bed too, as it was all one small room. Tewy should be here. I tapped my foot as I waited. Where was he?

The breeze picked up, blowing through my window and open door. The scent of something wafted to me, making me freeze.

What was that? A hint of spiciness. A little sweat.

I gripped my cane. Only one person knew where I lived, and Antonia, my caretaker, had been gone at least eight or nine rainy seasons. Besides, her scent was lavender. Perhaps Tewy had found something new? A different herb to cook with would be nice. Then again, it might not be a good surprise.

With a sure grasp, I swept my walking stick across the ground, hard-packed dirt from years of use. Nothing. Several more steps into my dwelling, the tip of my stick ran into something solid that didn't roll away, so it wasn't a coconut after all. "Tewy, you come out right now. You are in big trouble."

What had he left me this time? Last time, it'd been a dead rat, but this felt bigger. I whacked at the solid thing, trying to figure out what surprise I'd been gifted. And then it groaned.

I skittered back. That sounded distinctly human. "Tewy?"

A familiar squawk came from my left, not even close to where the groan had come from. My little monkey hadn't left me any bad surprises after all. I hesitated.

A hand wrapped around my ankle. I screamed and struck out with my cane, whacking something hard. There was a slurred mumble. I couldn't quite make out the words, but it was much deeper than Antonia's voice had been. But then, who was this new person that had stumbled upon my dwelling?

"Fi..."

A hand gripped my other ankle. I bashed it again, determined to get whoever it was off of me.

The hand released my ankle with a weak, "Ow."

"What are you doing in my house?"

"Find..."

"Find what?" What was going on? I wanted to prod the man further to figure out what I was dealing with, but I didn't want to hurt him either. Unless he wanted to hurt Tewy or me; then, that would change in a heartbeat. Maybe he was trying to find my things? Though that didn't explain why he was on the floor. Perhaps he was injured?

Skin brushed against my calf this time. I slammed my stick down hard, but the grip was tight. Panic flowed through me. As if I wasn't nervous enough, this man wasn't letting go. I wasn't going to put up with it anymore.

With as much force as I could muster, I knocked my weapon into the person on the floor. His hold loosened and there was a soft thud.

I bit my lip. Had I knocked him unconscious, or was he going silent waiting to launch his counterstrike? I nudged at the man on the ground. When there was no response, I went around his entire body doing the same, prodding and poking with the tip of my cane, trying to figure out what I was up against.

The person was huge. Long legs. Thick torso. An enormous man had invaded my space.

When I got to his head, I drummed my fingers across the wood in my hands. Antonia had taught me not to touch people unless I asked first, but this was a different beast altogether. I had to know what I was facing, more than just the impressions I gained from my walking stick.

I bent down slowly, readying to hit him if he moved. When nothing happened, I stretched out my hand. I tentatively reached around, searching for the contact of skin. Nothing. I licked my lips. Should I keep going? Why not? I'd already come this far. But it felt dangerous, like my entire world would change with just one touch.

Not stopping to debate any longer, I hurried forward. There were sharp pricks against my skin. I darted back. What was that?

My monkey chattered from nearby, not sounding the least concerned, but the memory of that rough texture still stung my hand. Not bad, but enough to make me cautious. "Tewy, where are you?"

He hooted amiably. It sounded as if he was perched right on the person who'd been grabbing at me. If Tewy could be brave, so could I.

I stretched my arm back out and inched forward. The scratchy texture was rough against my palm, the warmth of skin beneath it. The man hadn't shaved. He sighed, startling me away. Was he waking?

Fear spiked through my chest. In her stories, Antonia also had cautioned me against those people who came into homes uninvited. Her youthful voice couldn't have been much older than mine, but the warning was clear. Was he here to harm me? I'd have to take measures to protect myself before he woke. "Tewy, rope please."

4

There were light thumps as he moved through my little one-room house. He wouldn't be able to carry the entire coil of rope, but he could bring me the ends. As I crouched there waiting, I held my stick out, ready to slam it against the man, should he attempt to do anything.

Despite my fears, nothing happened except Tewy bringing me the much-wanted rope. Acting quickly, I touched the man again. I followed his scratchy face down the side of his neck, past his shoulder that had something hard on it—armor maybe—until I reached his bare arm. It was warm and alive, something I hadn't felt for years and years.

How long had I been alone? I'd been in this house since I was seventeen and many rainy seasons had come and gone since then. I had to be in my mid-twenties at least. Too long a time to be without human company.

I let myself pause for just a moment before tracing down the rest of his arm and finding his wrist. I wrapped the rope around several times and knotted it before switching to his other side, searching for his free hand.

Tewy made a sad little noise. "I'm just protecting myself. We don't know why he's here." Or how long he'd stay knocked out. Why wasn't he awake anyway? It wasn't normal to be unconscious like this. Whatever the case, I needed to restrain him until I could ask him some questions.

I tied up his other wrist, placing the two next to each other before moving down to his ankles. There was some type of shoes on his feet, sandals with straps that wrapped around his lower leg. I used to wear something similar, but they broke and I didn't know how to make new ones. I had tough feet after living so long without them.

I finished tying him up, leaving him able to move, but not well. At least, I hoped not. It left me wondering if it was a good enough job and I hunched down by him. "What do you think?"

Tewy chattered back at me.

"Sometimes, I wish you'd just use words."

His retort was sharp.

"Sorry. It'd just be easier." I hovered there for a time, the wind blowing in again, making the unfamiliar spicy scent and sweat fill my nose. It was like nothing I'd ever smelled before. Too bad I didn't know his intentions. What he had planned. How he'd found me. Why he was here. I'd question him, threaten him for answers if I had to.

"Did you bring the coconut in?" I asked, not wanting to do my chores with danger about but needing to finish them anyway.

Tewy responded cheerfully.

"Best get to it then. I don't believe our guest is going to wake anytime soon." With one last brush against my prisoner's wrists and ankles to make certain they were still tied together in front of him, I stood, hurrying over to the counter. There, I found the promised item. "More coconuts, Tewy."

Over the next few hours or so, Tewy brought me what I asked for as I took apart the coconut, my mind fixated on the man on the floor. Where had he come from? Was it a coincidence or did he intend to harm me? There were too many questions and no explanation. Should I wait until he woke up or should I try to wake him? The latter didn't appeal to me.

I worried my cheek. There had to be a way to get answers, but without the man being awake, I didn't know how to obtain them. If he didn't wake soon, I'd probably need to give him some water.

My shoulder dipped as Tewy jumped on it. His fingers tugged at my hair. "Not now, I'm trying to think."

"I hope you're thinking about untying me." Weary though he sounded, I tensed at the voice.

I cocked my head toward the man who smelled like spice and felt prickly. "You intruded in my house, why should I let you go?"

"Good question. Can I at least get a drink and some clean bandages?"

That piqued my interest. "You're injured." I had suspected so, but it was good to know for certain. Probably, it was the only reason I'd been able to tie him up in the first place.

"So it would seem." His words yawned out.

I didn't often need to attend to injuries now that my feet had hardened up, just the occasional bruise or scratch. Yarn was running low, and I hadn't made many items of late, but I did have a few strips I'd crocheted that I could undo and do again for practice. That would have to do.

I circled around the room, keeping in mind where he was on the floor, hoping he didn't move and throw me off. There was nothing except his labored breathing. That was new. Before, I'd barely noticed it.

When I got to my stash of materials, I fumbled through them, overly aware that someone else was in the room with me. Focusing was a difficult task when an incident so unprecedented had occurred. What would Antonia have said? A pang of sorrow squeezed my chest. I could have used her as my eyes and wisdom. I'd have to go without and make the best of it, I supposed.

Once I had the strips, I grabbed a bucket of water by the door and knelt close to where I believed the man to be. "Where are you hurt?"

"If you let me go, I can fix this up myself."

Ahh, I'd guessed right. He was close to me, almost too much so. I repeated, "Where are you hurt?"

"I'm the one who can see. I'll take care of it, just untie the rope."

How did he know I was blind? Maybe from watching me? "Arm? Leg? Torso?" I hadn't come across any wounds there, but perhaps I'd missed something.

He grunted. "You're not going to do what I ask?"

"You sound amazed at that fact."

He grumbled something unintelligible.

"Yes, well, that may be, but you're stuck with me," I responded despite not knowing what he'd said. "Where's the damage?"

"Right side of my torso." His words grew weaker as he spoke.

"There, that wasn't so hard, was it? I'm going to touch you now." I stretched forward, not having to go far to find him. I located an elbow, then down his arm with muscles corded beneath his skin. I moved to his side, finding a hard, unmoving form. His armor. The pieces I remembered covered the chest and vital organs and were made from leather, crossing together over the shoulders. It had to be hot and annoying.

Why was he prepared for battle? Had something changed since I'd left the outside world? I ran my hand down until he hissed and my hand came away damp. "We need to get this armor off of you and clean the wound." That was about the extent of my healing knowledge.

"I can if you free me."

"No."

"If that's the case," he said, sounding muddled, "go get some sand from the riverside and place it on the wound. That's my best chance."

The magic spread through Eppla as long as you were near the river, which was the safest place to be. If it didn't, things would be so much different for me. "You think magic will save you?"

"Hasn't failed me yet."

But it had failed me.

CHAPTER TWO

I dipped my fingers into the wet sand, all coarse and thick. Magic. That was what my prisoner said he needed, and so that was what I was giving him, despite my own experience. I gathered it by the handfuls, letting it plop to the bottom of the bucket. Everyone who lived by the river had access to it, so I wasn't certain why he hadn't used it previously. When it felt like I had enough, I reached forward and let the water rinse the excess grains off.

The iciness was a welcome relief, but not a long enough one. It wasn't the time to linger. I grabbed the bucket, stood, and worked my way back to my house.

"Thought you'd left me to die." The man's voice held a hint of teasing and a whole lot of pain.

"It would have been easier, except then I'd have to figure out how to clean you out of my house."

"That would be a problem."

I searched for my walking stick where I'd left it by the door. Usually, I didn't use it inside, but I felt off-kilter with a man here. Extra security was a must.

"Are you going to beat me with your staff?" he asked, like I hadn't done so already.

"Only if you don't behave."

"I'll endeavor to do my best then."

I swiped the tip of my staff along the ground until it bumped against something that shouldn't have been there. The man. I knelt down, keeping my stick close by. "You know this magic may do more harm than good?"

"A skeptic? Just put it on the wound. I'll manage."

I reached my left hand forward, feeling along the stiff armor until I ran across wetness. He groaned. "Sorry."

"Don't be. You'll have me fixed up in no time."

"Do I need to move your armor or, um, clothes?"

"How do you propose doing that with my hands tied together?"

He had me there. "I'm not sure how much sand will reach the injury if I don't."

"Enough."

I wasn't as certain as he was, but if that was what he wanted, I'd give it a try. I really didn't want to have to clean up a dead body off my floor. Besides, if I was honest with myself, there was a glimmer of excitement at no longer being alone and having someone other than Tewy to converse with.

With my left hand on the wound, I reached my right around until the wooden bucket stopped me. I dipped inside, grabbing a handful of sand. The dampness was cool as I stretched out and placed it on the gash. "Is that the right spot?"

"Yes," he groaned.

I patted the grains in, trying to get them down where the magic could touch the damage. Why was he wearing armor anyway? Antonia had read about it, but never wore it herself or made any for me. I had felt it one other time when she'd pulled some out to inspect. I should have asked her where she got it. Too late to do anything about it, and the piece had disappeared around the time she had. Many items of hers had gone the same way.

The leather armor brought a slew of memories trying to flood me, a whole onslaught of sights from back before my vision had been taken from me. Men who worked for Reding, the ruler of the known world. The warriors always wore armor, but then so did others who worked on the river, or those who were personal guards of the upper class, the amant. The upper class meant those who had fallen in love.

What was a warrior doing clear out here anyway? We were at least a day or two from the closest town, not to mention the chasm between my house and the rest of the population. Why had he come here? I needed answers and I needed them now. "What happened to you anyway?"

"What's your name?" he asked.

He clearly didn't want to talk about it, but then we all had things we didn't wish to speak of. "Cassandra."

"Cassandra what?"

"Just Cassandra." He probably wanted my last name, but I'd given that up long ago. "What's your name?"

"Nikon Trimend, but you can call me Nikon."

That was a good, strong name. "I don't believe I should be that familiar with my prisoner."

"I don't have to be a prisoner." His words were enticing.

"And have you steal all my food or murder me? No, thank you." I remembered enough of the world even if I hadn't been part of it since I was seventeen.

"I wouldn't hurt you."

I bristled, though inside I was softening. Was the magic working on me as well as him? "Everyone hurts everyone." And they did, even if they didn't mean to. I patted on the last of the sand. "Is it better?"

"I feel the same."

"Well, Nikon, like I thought, the sands aren't so miraculous. What do you want me to do to help you heal?"

He sighed. "You don't have to do anything unless you want to let me go."

"You want to die? To bleed out?"

"I'm not bleeding anymore. Why don't you believe in the power of the sands?"

I dropped my hand back into the bucket of sand and let it squish between my fingers. I shook it off, picked up the bucket, and stood. It was not that I didn't believe, it was more that I didn't trust it. But he didn't need to know my reasons; I was the one in control here, not him.

Storming from the house, I didn't wait to find out if he was going to try to convince me to stay. I had things to do, and I wasn't going to let some warrior tell me differently.

Tewy chattered from the house. I left him. He could watch Nikon. I didn't need him. Didn't need anyone.

I stomped away on the firm ground until my legs got caught by sharp stabs. Branches. I growled. "Sandblasted berry plants." Not only had I run into what I was supposed to be picking from, I'd forgotten my bucket. This was not the day I'd been expecting when I'd woken up this morning.

Some birds tweeted nearby. They sounded happy and carefree. Of course, they were. They didn't have a stubborn, injured intruder in their house. I scowled and got to work. I felt my way through the bush, coming across more pokey sticks than soft berries, but my fingers were calloused against them. I scooped the bottom of my dress up, placing the berries inside. My dress was probably stained, but it didn't matter when I couldn't see it. If it felt and smelled clean, there wasn't a problem. As I picked, I tried to decide what to do with my prisoner. It was a harder conundrum than I thought.

I popped a berry in my mouth, enjoying the hint of sweetness with the tart. It wouldn't help me make a decision though, and I had more than enough fruit for the moment. I held my lifted skirt to one side so the folded edge brushed my knees as I headed back to my house.

It was quiet when I returned. "Are you awake?"

No response. Guess that answered the question. I moved to my kitchen area where I kept the buckets, something I should have grabbed on my way out. When I got there, I felt around for one. I brushed against the wood, picked it up, and dumped the berries inside with a plunking noise.

My shoulder sunk as Tewy jumped on it. I sighed, moving the bucket of berries to my counter and lifting one up to him. It was snatched from my fingers. At least Tewy would always be on my side, but what to do about the intruder?

I continued through my chores, boiling water, arranging food and the like, while the man never made a sound. I bit my lip, wondering what he was doing. Nikon must have been tired. When I finally finished for the day, I pulled together a few odds and ends of food and a water skin. I took them to the intruder.

It was so silent inside, like it always was. Had the man died? Had my actions killed him? I hoped not. I may have tied him up, but I didn't want to be the cause of anyone's death. Then, a deep breath met my ears. Not dead, only asleep.

"Time to wake up," I said.

"Already did that."

"How long have you been conscious?"

"Long enough to know you work hard."

For a reason I couldn't understand, my cheeks warmed. They'd never done such a thing before, not without the sun on them. I bristled against the unfamiliar. "I do what needs to be done. How's your wound?"

"Hurts."

Hmm. "How did you get it?"

"Doesn't matter. What matters is that I need you to let me go."

13

"Why should I? You invaded my house!" Tewy let out a tirade of hoots and squawks. "See, Tewy agrees with me."

"The monkey has a name?"

"My monkey does. You didn't answer the question."

"That's restricted information." There was an authority in his tone that I hadn't heard in a long time.

"How so?"

"What are you doing living clear out here all alone? I thought no one lived past the chasm."

He wasn't going to answer my questions. What's more, he wanted knowledge about me. There had to be a way to use that to my advantage. Antonia would have done so. "Better question, what are you doing out here?" When he didn't respond, I said, "Your wound is probably going to bleed out."

"I don't think it's bleeding anymore, but it could use more sand."

"If you believe in the magic so much, why wouldn't it work the first time?"

"Because it's having a hard time getting past my armor." His voice was strained.

I didn't think he was right, but if he wanted more sand on it, who was I to stop him? The least I could do was take care of him since I had tied him up. I searched for the bucket I'd left by him that held the sand. When I bumped against it, I reached in and pulled a handful out.

"You need to get fresh sand," Nikon said.

"For a prisoner, you're rather bossy."

"It won't work if it's dried out."

Though he was right, I didn't want to trek back out there. Despite my feelings, I grabbed the bucket and made the short journey outside. The air kissed my skin with a cool breeze. Night was on. When had that happened? I needed to eat more than a few berries, and the intruder was probably hungry as well.

I hurried to scoop up sand into my bucket and get back to him.

When I entered, I went straight to where I'd left him, hand still covered in sticky grains. I knelt and felt my way to his skin, tracing it down until I found his armor and the packed-on sand.

"You'll have to take off the old magic," he said.

I bristled. "I know." I tried clearing the area gently, but he still sucked in a painful-sounding breath.

"This would be much easier if you would untie me." His words were strained again.

"Nice try, but I won't have you stealing from me, murdering us, or doing any other harm."

"You get a lot of thieves and murderers up here, do you?"

He had me there, but I wasn't about to let him win. "I know stories." I remembered a life with others. I scowled.

"I'm nothing like what you may have heard."

"How do you know what tales I've come across?" He certainly was nothing like the hero in a romance just from the way he talked. Didn't matter. I was far too old and blind to still be pining after fictional characters.

"By the tone of your voice."

"Oh? And what does that tell you?" I swiped away the last of the sand, making him grunt. "Sorry."

"Doesn't matter," Nikon said. "I only want you to know that I'm not here to harm you."

"Tewy thinks otherwise." Lie. My monkey had been oddly accepting of this man, not even squawking to let me know he was in the house.

"Well, if I have to earn Tewy's approval, I'll make an effort to do so."

My hand bumped into the bucket in my attempt to find it. I'd never felt so frazzled before. This wasn't going how I wanted it to. Not that I knew exactly how that was. He needed to get out of my house and away from the waterfall back toward civilization, only I couldn't let him go. Not if he was going to do someone harm. I needed a plan, but one wasn't springing to mind. I scooped up the sand and patted it over where I thought his wound was.

"To the right a little."

"Just testing you." I scooted the source of magic to the side and attempted to shove it down past the leather to where the wound was, without hurting him. By his stiff breathing, I was certain I'd failed at that task.

"I've never been this close to someone who couldn't see before," he said, the strain gone from his voice.

I sat straight, slinging the excess sand into the bucket with greater force than necessary. Frustration at my situation built up in me, coming out in an abrupt burst of anger, "I'm blind because of magic."

CHAPTER THREE

Guilt pinched me awake. The anger burning through me was directed more at myself than at him. I couldn't keep my mouth shut, and that was my fault. Him invading my area, well, that was on him. Mix the two together, and I'd forgotten to feed Nikon before huffing to sleep.

Despite Nikon trying to get out of me what I'd meant the night before—about being blind because of magic—I'd climbed into bed and ignored him after dropping a blanket toward where I thought he lay. I wasn't about to explain myself, not when I shouldn't have said anything in the first place. I didn't know anything about this man. I shouldn't have been giving him any information.

The cabin was hushed. It always was in the mornings except for the river, but I expected something different with a man on my floor. I sat up and crept from my bed, wondering if he was asleep as a strong breeze blew into the house. His scent had wafted to me several times in the night, reassuring me that I hadn't dreamed up the entire thing. That and the shuffling around. He'd been awful noisy in the night, though I couldn't fathom why. I hadn't smelled him or heard him this morning. Had he managed to get away?

I stopped just before where I remembered leaving him and dipped my toes forward until they ran into cool skin. Still there.

"Did you need something?" Nikon's voice made me jump back.

"I thought you were asleep."

"Pretty hard to do when you need to use the bathroom."

"Oh. Sorry. I didn't think about that. Is that why you were so noisy last night?"

"Erm...would you believe me if I said yes?"

"Not now."

He sighed. "The truth is, I was testing my bonds to try and get out of them, but you did a better job than I expected."

I tried not to be smug but couldn't help it. He still had to go to the bathroom though. What could I do about that particular issue? I had not a clue other than knowing I still didn't want to risk untying him. That, and I certainly wasn't going to help him with this particular situation. "I can get you a bucket, and I'll leave the cabin to give you some privacy. Will that work?"

He sighed again, this time with frustration, but instead of complaining, he said, "It will."

I hurried to grab two buckets, leaving one with him that I'd never, ever use again, and taking the other with me to the riverbank. When the rough texture of dry sand beneath my feet changed to smooth and wet, I went a little farther before dipping my bucket into the river, the water swirling around my ankles in a cool stream.

Not knowing how long Nikon would need, I stayed there listening to the rush of the waterfall and the cacophony of sounds the morning birds and monkeys made in the nearby trees. "Tewy? Are you out here?" It wasn't like him not to have greeted me yet, but then, maybe it was earlier than I thought. The heat wasn't pressing in on me yet.

Why hadn't I smelled my intruder this morning? Probably because the breeze had blown the scent away, I surmised. It would have been nice to realize that before I'd made a fool of myself.

I gave gave him several more moments while I stood in the river, the tip of my dress sagging under the weight of the liquid it had absorbed. I hadn't changed it the previous night before storming off to bed. That should be remedied this morning. I paused where I was, the longing in my heart confused by the man in my house. What was I to do with him?

I'd probably waited long enough. "Or more like, I don't want to be alone with my thoughts." I growled at the words escaping me, scooped up a fistful of sand from the bottom of the river, and headed toward home.

My mind was full of the map in my head when I entered. "I brought something cool to drink and more sand."

"Why do you continue to bring me magic if you don't like it? If it made you blind?" Nikon asked, his voice coming from near the floor where I'd left him.

"Because you asked for it." I set the bucket nearby and, after taking the waste bucket outside, I knelt down. Fumbling my way forward only took a moment before I ran into the sensation of his skin, something that was becoming all too familiar. I found the last clump of sand and brushed it onto the floor. I was going to have a mess to clean up later. At least it would be something to keep me busy.

After taking care of his wound, I sat back. Tewy yammered, and it was coming from close by. Probably making friends with Nikon. I rubbed my forehead. "Tewy, ladle."

With a squawk, a couple of thumps headed toward my kitchen. "He listens well," Nikon said.

"He's been well trained." For which I was beyond grateful, but even more than that, Tewy was my friend. I might get frustrated with him at times, but I always loved him.

Tewy padded back over, and something fell in my lap. I picked it up to find a fork. I grumbled. "Not so well trained. I'm not in the mood for pranks. Nikon needs some water. Ladle, Tewy."

My monkey made a noise that sounded almost like a chuckle. I shook my head. The creature was incorrigible. My thoughts were still on him when a low, joyous sound came from next to me. Nikon? Was he...laughing?

It was unlike any sound I'd heard in a long, long time, a deep noise I felt all the way to my core, one that left me smiling despite not wanting to a moment ago. Unsure what to do with the feeling, I got up and went to the kitchen, felt my way to a ladle, and brought it back to Nikon. By then, the sound had petered off. Despite that, it stuck with me, filling my chest.

I found my bucket and got a scoop of water. "Are you thirsty?"

"Very."

"Take this then."

The dipper left my grip. Moments later, he said, "I can't reach my mouth without sloshing water everywhere. The rope is too short."

It was impressive he hadn't asked to be let go. "I'll help." I took the ladle from him and reached forward, putting my hand up. "I need you to keep speaking so I can find your face."

"What do you want me to say?"

"Tell me about yourself."

"There's not much to me. I'm Nikon Trimend. I may not love you, but I believe you are the most beautiful woman I've ever seen."

The shock of his words washed through me, leaving my hand frozen in midair.

"Sorry. You're probably not used to such frank speech," he said, his breath teasing my fingers.

"I'm not accustomed to speaking at all." I moved the rest of the way to his mouth, resting my fingertips on his lips. They were soft around the edges but chapped, making me realize I was spending far too much time thinking about his lips and not enough helping him get the liquid he needed.

Lifting the ladle toward my hand, I tilted it toward him and let my free arm fall back to my lap. The handle moved as if someone was putting pressure on it. He was probably drinking. I turned it toward him.

Nikon sputtered.

"Sorry."

He coughed and cleared his throat. "It's fine. It surprised me and my lap is now wet anyway, but it's not a big deal."

"I didn't mean to spill it on you."

"Truly, don't worry about it."

Why'd I have to go and make a mess of him? "Do you need more?"

"I'm drenched enough for the moment."

"Sorry. Again."

He chuckled. "It's not something to stress over. Unless it makes you want to untie me?" There was a note of hope in his words.

"Can't do it." I put the ladle in the bucket of water and stood. I had to shove aside the tender thoughts that wanted to let Nikon go. It was a bad idea, wasn't it? He could rob me. Take everything I worked so hard for. Kill me. I was making the correct decision, even if I had to keep reminding myself of that. I still had to figure out what I was going to do with him.

Nikon said, "I shouldn't push you, it's only that you're in danger here."

I paused in the doorway. "I'm in danger? From you, maybe." And his strange declarations of my beauty without loving me.

"The truth is, I'm being chased." The hesitation in his voice told me more than his words.

Leaning against the doorframe, I asked, "Why is this a secret? Why didn't you say something sooner?"

"I don't want anyone else to get hurt."

I lifted my eyebrows. "Anyone else? Who's been affected already? And why? You're speaking in riddles like a sphinx."

"I wasn't feeling well before. Wasn't thinking clearly, but now that I've rested and my thoughts are coming back, I know I need to leave this place, and you need to come with me."

I crossed to the kitchen, steps stiff. "Neither of us is going anywhere."

"Then you just promised our deaths."

CHAPTER FOUR

"What do you mean, I just promised our deaths? Do you wish to call it down upon us both? You know we don't speak of it." What was I doing even responding? To do so would invite death just as much as he had. Growing up, my parents had always taught that to speak of it was to bring it upon a person.

"I can't tell you more." His tone was guarded.

"If I'm going to be killed anyway, why can't I know?"

He refused to speak no matter how I prodded him, so I ignored him the best I could after his threatening words. That didn't let the hint of death leave my thoughts though. Our deaths. What could be so serious as to cause that? Who could be after him, and why would they want him—and by extension, possibly me—dead? If he wouldn't tell me, how could I believe him?

I hated being in uncharted territory.

"I'm going to be gone for a while. Do you need anything when I return?" I asked Nikon, not trying to keep the annoyance from spilling out into my words,

"You know the answer to that."

I didn't listen to the censure in his tone. He wanted to be let go, I understood that, but that didn't mean I had to like it. "Come, Tewy."

My monkey chattered from where Nikon was, but the thuds of his approaching me and the dip of my shoulder never happened.

"Tewy, now."

He squawked.

"Fine. Have it your way." I marched out of the house, taking my walking stick and a clean dress with me. I grumbled as I headed toward the waterfall.

The humid day pressed in on me, making me ache for the cooling water. I hurried my steps, swishing my walking stick in front of me as I went, so I didn't trip over anything. I wasn't as familiar with this section of the riverbank since I only came this way a couple times a week. I'd tripped over a coconut once. That'd been enough to make me cautious.

When my feet hit the wet sand, I set my stick and dress down and stripped, wading into the water. It was cool, a welcome relief from the hot day. I rubbed myself down with the sand. Magical or not, it still helped clean me.

Once I finished, I floated, listening to the rumble of the falls. It wasn't far, but distant enough that the pool was almost still. I tried to clear my mind, to think of what I needed to do, but nothing came.

Frustrated, I got out, dressed, and headed back to the house. By the time I arrived, my hair was almost dry, the straight locks reaching to my waist. Antonia used to cut it every so often, but I hadn't since she was gone. It needed to be taken care of, but I hadn't been brave enough. Not that it made a difference if I had uneven hair. Nikon was the only one around to see it, and what did he matter?

Still, I didn't make plans to change my hair anytime soon. I went to my house, set my dirty clothes in the corner to be washed later, and faced where I thought Nikon was. "I need to know more about you."

"And I'd like to know more about you. You're fascinating, Cassandra. I've never met anyone like you."

"You've only been here one day."

"Then help me understand you." When I didn't respond, he offered, "What about a question for a question. You ask me something, I'll answer, and then we'll switch."

"I can do that." I settled myself near enough so I could catch that spicy, sweat scent but not so close I could reach out and touch him. At least, I didn't think I could. I didn't test my theory. "I'll go first."

"I should go first. I'm the one that came up with the idea." Despite his words, there was a note of amusement in his tone.

I wasn't letting him get away with that. "It's my house."

"Fine. What do you want to know?"

"Why are you here?"

"I'm...curious."

"About what?"

"Ah, ah, it's my turn," he said. "Why are you living out here all alone?"

"My caretaker brought me out here after my parents died. Of heartbreak, she said." I hadn't questioned that before, but it made me wonder. Could people really die from heartbreak? If so, I'd like to think I would have died when Antonia disappeared on me. "What are you curious about?"

"Right now? You."

I shook my head. "You're infuriating."

"It's the truth. I've never met anyone like you before. You're different in a way I can't put my finger on." A scuffle of dirt came from the floor as I assumed he shifted weight.

"It feels like you're cheating."

"I'm answering your questions honestly. We don't have to continue if you don't want."

"No, I want to know more about you."

"Very well," he said. "Why did you say magic made you blind?"

"Because it did."

He huffed. "That's all you're going to give me?"

I grinned. "What can I say? I learned from the best."

That laugh I'd liked before filled the room. "I'll have to take that into future consideration."

"See that you do." I softened my tone despite my words. "Do you have a family?"

He didn't respond right away. When he did speak, his voice was subdued. "My parents aren't alive, but even before they died, I hadn't had much contact with them for a long time."

"Why?"

"It's my turn. What about you? Any siblings? What happened to your caretaker?"

"That's more than one question, but I'll indulge you. No siblings. My caretaker was just gone one day, along with all her things. If it weren't for her missing items, I'd believe something bad happened to her. Maybe it did anyway, I have no way of knowing if she's wandering Eppla somewhere or if she was attacked and someone came in, stealing her belongings, and that's why she hasn't returned." I sat up straighter. I didn't want to discuss such personal information anymore. "But it doesn't matter. I'm able to take care of myself."

"That much is evident. You managed to capture me as your prisoner, after all."

He was being overly kind, as he had been half passed out when I'd tied him up. "Yes, but you invaded my home so I had to do something against you. Why did you come here? And I don't mean the reason you are avoiding telling me, but the reason why you entered my home."

"Fair enough," Nikon said. "If the truth is to be told, I don't remember much about the few days prior. I was on the run, going so fast that I forgot to put sand on my wound, and it left me delirious. From what my hazy memories tell me, I found a place out of the sun and wanted to take refuge here. Imagine my surprise when I woke to a blind woman having tied me up."

"It must have been quite a shock."

"You have no idea."

I giggled. "You don't remember me tying you up?"

"Only bits and pieces. I know you've got a great swing."

My face heated. "Sorry."

"Don't mention it. I would have been surprised by an unexpected guest in my home too."

Guest? I snorted. "Do you need more sand on your wound?"

"This batch does seem to have dried out."

"I'll take that as a yes then. I'll be right back." I headed out to get a bucket of sand and hurried back. I wanted to finish our conversation, and more than that, I wanted his wound to heal. It was a strange thing, being around a person again. I may have had my reservations about him, but it was good to talk to someone. Better than good, actually.

When I entered the room, Nikon said, "What's that grin for?"

Had I been smiling? I searched my way next to him and took the dried sand off his wound. "If the truth is told, it's nice to have another person around again."

"I'm glad I could give you that, Cassandra."

Hearing my name soothed me. Tewy couldn't say it. Before Nikon came, I couldn't remember the last time it was spoken. But it was strange, this man I'd thought was so dangerous instead conversing with me and giving me compliments. If it weren't for his forbidden talk of death, I'd have thought he had come to be my friend.

I took care of the sand. He'd been wearing the same thing since he got here and who knew how long before that. "You stink."

"Thank you."

"No, I just mean, it hasn't been nice of me to not let you clean up." Come to think of it, he hadn't brought anything with him either. If I was traveling away from home, I'd want to take at least some of my personal effects with me. "Did you bring a change of clothes?"

"No." Though it was only a single word response, it was guarded.

What was he hiding from me? "No? Why not?"

"There wasn't time. And that's two questions I answered for you. Your turn."

"Ah, but you asked me about my grin, so I only owe you one answer."

"Has anyone ever told you how frustrating you are?"

"No, and that's two questions, so my turn." While I tried to think of what I wanted to ask next, he snickered. "It's not my fault if you ask a lot of questions," I said. "Oh, I've got it. What do you believe? I know you believe in the magic of sand. Do you think the Reding is an intermediary between magic and people? Or do you think the High Priest is?" The ruler of the world was typically believed to simply rule and the High Priest was in charge of magic, but not all people thought that.

"I believe that you ask a lot of questions."

A non-answer again, which was like the Nikon I was getting to know. Despite all this talking we'd done, there was still much I didn't understand about him.

There was a scratching sound as if he was shifting his weight. "I'll answer your question, but let me ask you first, when were you last with the people of Eppla?"

It was my turn to shift uncomfortably. "I don't know exactly."

"How can you not?"

"My caretaker never kept track of time out here. After she was gone, I didn't know how to do so. It feels like forever since I've been with another person."

"You don't know how old you are?"

I shook my head.

He remained silent, making me wonder what he was thinking.

When he spoke, his words were soft. "I'm sorry for all you've had to go through. You look like you're in your late twenties to me."

"Then I've been here about ten years. How old are you?"

"I'm thirty-two." He sighed. "I can't imagine how hard it must be for you to understand, when you haven't lived in a city or even around people in so long. I wish I could explain it, but there are certain expectations. Not just laws we have to adhere to, but unspoken rules and customs. If we don't follow them, we could lose our lives. I want you to understand this because I think you need to come with me. Like I said."

"Come where?" This conversation was taking a strange turn.

"I'm not sure where's safe yet, but away from here. They're going to be looking for me here."

"Who is?"

Skin brushed against my hand, and two palms engulfed my fingers that grazed against the roughness of the rope tying Nikon together. I focused in on that touch, the warmth and guidance it was trying to give me as his spicy, sweaty scent moved closer.

He said, "The more I tell you, the more danger you're going to be in."

"Then tell me and surround me with your magic sand. That should be enough to save me. Let me choose for myself."

He gave my fingers a squeeze before pulling back. "You're so different from other people."

And he was unlike any man, but that was probably because it'd been a long time since I'd been around others. "Do you really believe they are coming? And *who* is coming?"

"If they can track me to your home, yes. I'm not sure how well I hid my trail once I started feeling more ill. It may be hard for them to pick up at first, but if they can find it, I probably led them straight here."

"But who is it?"

He didn't respond.

"I need to think." I stood, heading toward the berries I'd picked the night before. "Are you hungry?"

"Famished. If you have any fish, that would help me heal. I need the protein." He hesitated. "Can you fish?"

I bristled. "Just because I can't see doesn't mean I can't do things."

"Sorry. I don't know what you can and can't do."

I let my shoulders slide back down. "I use a net trap in the water. It doesn't kill the fish but collects them for me. I can gather what I need and let the rest go to catch another day."

"Clever."

"My caretaker set it up." That pang of hurt in my chest whenever I thought about Antonia was sharp. Didn't matter if she'd been brusque, she was all I had for a long time. "I'll go get you some."

I hurried from the room, only just remembering to grab a bucket as I went. The breeze picked up. I pulled the back of my skirt up between my legs and tucked it into my front waist so that it wouldn't get in the river.

The monkeys were chatty this afternoon, filling the air with their noises. "Tewy? Are you out there?" Probably out cavorting with his new love.

Moments later, weight dipped my shoulder. "There you are."

He tweaked my nose.

"All right, I might have been hard on you about your lady friend. I think I understand a little better now." Not that Nikon and I would ever have that sort of relationship. He'd already declared he didn't love me, which would have happened at first sight of me if it was going to happen, and I couldn't see. Or maybe he could never fall in love with me because I could never fall in love with him? Whatever the case, we would never have those deep feelings for one another. But we were starting to understand each other at least.

The river was cold, shocking my feet, but I pushed on, heading across to where I kept my net set. I gathered the fish into my bucket and waded back across the water. When I reached the bank, I shook off the liquid and didn't bother untucking my skirt.

My steps were sure as I made my way back, dripping. The moment my soles touched the hard-packed dirt that was my floor, Nikon said, "That's a good look on you."

My face flushed. "It keeps it from getting soaked in the river."

"Many people do that when they visit the river, but you make it becoming."

The feelings flittering through me were confused. I set the bucket on a counter and called out for Tewy while I dipped my hand into a second bucket of seeds. He'd get into them if he was hungry enough, but usually waited for me.

There was a scurrying across the floor followed by him calling out and taking the seeds from my fingers.

"You're welcome," I told him. "Now, I'll get you some fish, Nikon. Cooked or salted?"

"If you have salted, why did you bring in fresh?" he asked.

"To replace it if we use it. I don't want my stores to get low. Which do you prefer?"

"Cooked, please."

"Very well." I turned to my right, feeling for firewood I'd previously gathered, and set it in my oven. Once it was arranged, I added kindling and found my flint, quickly starting a fire.

"I'd be happy to help."

"So I can let you go? I've got this."

"I wouldn't run off on you, at least not right away. You have my food for starters."

I laughed. "That would be enough to keep you around. But no, sorry, I can't let you go." Though I was beginning to feel like he wouldn't rob me of my pots and pans as I'd first worried he would. I got a good feeling from him. Whether it should or not, my trust in him was building.

"Do you have any spices?"

"Just salt."

"Guess I'll resign myself to that then, but it's another good reason you should join me," he said. "You'd be able to try new seasonings and probably a new variety of food. I think you'd like the city."

So, he was going to one of the cities. It made sense as I couldn't see him living in the desert like a marauder, but then why run from it in the first place? I put a pan on the stove and held my hand over it, feeling for heat. While I waited for it to warm, I cleaned the fish in an empty bucket, remembering a faint hint of spices from town from when I was younger. "Why do I hear a note of hesitation in your voice?"

"You're making stuff up."

"Am not," I retorted. "I can hear it even more now, plus you've got some incredulity."

He snorted. "I think I'd prefer it if you could see. Seems like it's easier to get people to believe you when they're not trying to read everything in my words."

"I'd like that as well." My words were sober.

"Sorry, I didn't mean—"

"Don't worry about it. Being blind is a fact of my life, even if it's something I wish I could change. Now, from the tone of your voice, I gathered I wouldn't like the city. Why not?" The pan was warm beneath my hand. I searched for my jar of oil by touch, found it, and poured some in the pan before placing the fish in. It sizzled as I sprinkled it with salt I'd gathered from a nearby salt patch. "I'm waiting."

"Sorry. I would worry about you in the city. You get along better here than I would ever have guessed, but there would be other people to get in your way and things they would say. People can be cruel. I wouldn't want them to treat you that way. Not to mention there are very few blind people. Usually, when one is found, they tend to disappear."

I stopped, cold running through me. The searing of the

cooking fish scent filled the air but did nothing for the churning in my stomach. "What do you mean, they disappear?"

He didn't respond.

"What do you mean, disappear?" My words came out almost hysterical.

His reply was soft. "The Reding and Vading have ordered those who are blind into slavery. Most don't live more than a few months once that happens."

Shock coursed through me. "When did this happen?"

"About six years ago."

"And the Reding, when did he take a wife?" When did the world gain a female ruler to go with the Reding?

"About the same time."

"And you want me to go there?" It was unthinkable.

"It's safer than what will find you out here."

"What's that, Nikon? It can't be worse than being turned into the Reding's slave until I suffer death." My words were sharp, and I hoped they cut.

"I would keep you safe."

"How would you manage such a feat?" When he didn't respond, I turned my attention back to his fish. I hoped it burned.

CHAPTER FIVE

According to his deep breaths, Nikon was still asleep when I woke. How could he have wanted me to go to a place where I would end up a slave? It didn't make sense. He'd never answered my question, ignoring all my attempts to nudge it out of him.

Reminding myself that he'd said we would die if we stayed here, I thought about it. Maybe he'd believed being a slave superior to death? I didn't.

I muttered under my breath and cast myself out of bed, hoping to step on him out of spite. I missed. Taking a large step, I went over him, continuing to grumble. Grabbing my things, I headed out to the water.

I scrubbed my dirty dresses in the river using the sand Nikon thought was so magical. It was better than relying on it for my life and well-being. Besides, it had always cleaned in the past. I didn't expect that to change because he was using the sand on his wound.

The way I scoured, there were going to be holes in my clothes. It was just as well. They were old anyhow, though I hadn't grown in a long, long time. It was time for something new. Or a lot of things. Too bad I didn't have a way to get anything new unless I went to the city.

Tewy screeched, the other monkeys responding in kind. I stiffened, the clothes in my hands feeling bulky.

Someone was here.

I licked my lips, remembering what Nikon had said about death coming to us. Was that what he meant? I wasn't about to find out.

I had brought my cane with me. I could use it as a weapon if need be, but I wasn't sure how well I'd do. Occasionally, I fought off an animal; however, I hadn't done anything more than practice with Antonia. That was so long ago, who knew what I'd remember? Besides, I'd never been very good.

The monkeys quieted, but there was a nearby splashing followed by Tewy chatting wildly to me. He jumped on my shoulder, his words quick, telling me almost as much as if he could speak my language. Danger was near.

I went back to washing my dress, but kept my ears perked for anything that wasn't an ordinary sound. A moment went by. Then another. A crack sounded to my left, far closer than I had expected.

I wanted to jolt to my feet, but instead forced myself to grab my staff and slowly stand. "Hello?"

"Zaykai," a woman said, giving the formal greeting I hadn't heard since Antonia disappeared.

"Zaykai. Forgive me, but what are you doing here?"

"You're right to be cautious. There's a dangerous man about."

She must be one of the ones Nikon said was chasing him. "Oh?"

"Yes. I've been sent to apprehend him. You haven't seen anyone around, have you?" Her voice was melodic. So pretty, I could listen to her all day.

Caution bit my tongue. "I can't see."

"Ah, yes. I thought you were blind." There was censure in her tone. "Have you heard anything out of the ordinary?"

"Besides the monkeys shrieking a moment ago?"

"Yes, they seem to not like me."

Tewy shook on my shoulder as testament to that. He hadn't acted that way around Nikon. Was there something to his fear? Time to trust my little monkey. "I haven't heard anything that doesn't belong here."

"That's good for your safety."

"What has he done anyway?"

"Crimes against the Reding."

I did what I could to let my fear show through. It wasn't hard because I was scared, though more of her than of Nikon. I'd spoken with him, gotten to know him a little bit, and he didn't seem threatening to me—unlike her, whom I knew nothing about other than the creatures around me seemed to dislike her.

What did she mean anyway? Had Nikon really done something against our leader? There were many who'd tried when I was little since the government was still fairly new, but the older I got, the less attempts that had been made. Had things changed since I'd been gone? Were people going against the Reding again, or was it only Nikon? And if so, why?

The woman interrupted my thoughts. "Would you mind if I had a look around?"

Yes, my mind screamed, although my voice said, "No."

"Thank you. I'll scoot right through so you won't even notice me, and then I'll be out of your way."

"I appreciate it." I had to get to the house before she did, but couldn't make it look like I was panicked. I stood, wringing out the dress and wondering where she was and what she was doing. There wasn't a sound to give her away. It made me trust her less.

I bent to find my staff, knowing I couldn't leave it behind and raise suspicion. Besides, it felt more comforting to hold it in my hands, and to know I had some sort of protection should I need it.

Though I had a feeling it wouldn't do me much good against her. People who captured other humans were not known for their kindness. More like they were known for their rough and tough skills.

Once I found my walking stick, I strode quickly back to my house. My nerves were so out of sorts, I almost muttered aloud to myself, but I was trying to keep an ear out for what she might be doing. Despite my efforts, there was nothing to hear except the monkeys that were still shrieking. Tewy clung to my neck.

As I entered my house, I wished I had time and a way to hide Nikon. If that woman came looking for him in here, there was nothing I could do about it. I had to warn him. I walked over to where I'd left him and reached out my foot to brush against his body. And reached. And reached. Where was he?

I covered the whole area but came up empty. Had he managed to escape? Good for him. But a frown came upon me despite the thought.

I hung up my dresses in the corner on a rope strung across the room and turned toward my next task of the day as if I didn't have a man on the loose and a woman searching for him. Tewy grabbed onto my hair as I headed for a couple buckets. Usually, I cleaned the house before I cleaned myself, but that hadn't happened. Time to change that, plus the work would keep my hands busy.

My trip to and from the river was uneventful, making me wonder if she was still around. Was she watching? The thought left a creepy-crawly sensation on my back. Ignoring it, I got to work cleaning everything from the stove to the table without slopping too much water on the floor. That was the hope anyway. The fresh scent of water filled the air as I worked.

When I finished scrubbing, I threw the water out back. Tewy never left my shoulder, clinging to me like he was afraid I might disappear any moment, his tail wrapped around my neck. I needed a friend like him. "You're a good monkey, Tewy."

He talked to me, keeping up a narrative all the way back to the house. I hesitated in the doorway, something not feeling right. A sniff didn't tell me anything. Neither did listening for a moment.

Tewy yanked on my hair as if telling me to turn around, but I couldn't leave my home. Plus, I'd left my staff inside. I wanted its protection, and I wanted it now.

I strode across the room to the corner where I left it, grabbed it, and whirled back toward the front of the house.

"Are you anxious about something?" the woman asked from near the door.

I jumped back. "You scared the life out of me."

"You didn't answer my question." Her voice was soft, but there was a note of sternness there.

"I sensed something in my home, probably you."

"You work hard. You could give that all up right now if you told me what you know. Help me bring in the man I'm hunting, and I'll see that you're rewarded with assistance out here."

The assistance I didn't need, but the company would be welcome. Despite what I'd told myself earlier, it was a tempting offer—one I was determined to turn down. "I'd let you know if there was anything to tell. I haven't felt or heard any hint of a person besides you all day." True.

"I'd love to keep things peaceful for you, but I can't do that if you don't give me any information on him. If I leave and he's around, who knows what damage he'll do to you."

I sighed, old fears bubbling up. If the animals hadn't reacted so poorly to her, I might have fallen for her act. "I wish I had something to give you."

She was silent, making me wonder what she was doing. What was she thinking? Did she believe me or had I somehow doomed myself? My pulse pounded in my ears, but I kept myself collected. Antonia had taught me about other people knowing what I was thinking and feeling by being able to see me. Told me I had to be careful. Don't know why she'd bothered, since she'd never taken me out of this place.

The woman said, "I have to go now. You're sure you haven't noticed anything different?"

"Nothing dangerous here." Tewy tugged on my hair, making my head jerk to the side. "Naughty monkey." Still, he didn't let go.

"Thank you for your cooperation," she said.

There was a soft crunch of footsteps as she left. I didn't dare search for Nikon even though it sounded like she was gone. She could have been nearby watching for all I knew. I had to continue through my day as if he'd never come along, which meant a trip to the riverbank to avoid chores.

I hummed a tune I made up as I sat on the wet sand, letting my feet dip in the water. The air held a hint of flowers. Tewy climbed on my lap, a sure sign that something was wrong. "Not visiting your lady friend today, Tewy?"

He nuzzled his head into my palm. I tried to take comfort in that, but it was hard with my mind buzzing about. Where was Nikon? Was he as dangerous as the woman implied? Was she still around? Had Nikon left because he knew she was here or had something else scared him off? How had he left anyway when I had tied him up? Was he only pretending he couldn't get out of the bonds?

Once again, there were too many questions and no answers.

CHAPTER SIX

I stayed on the riverbank until the air cooled and the monkeys and birds quieted. I'd contemplated leaving sooner, but worried about leading the woman to Nikon. Even though I didn't know where he was, I could do so inadvertently. And if I was honest, I didn't feel like doing any more chores.

I stood, wiping the sand off of me. Any moment, I expected to hear her voice, to have her say she was taking me with her to the city or to the Reding. If she did, she'd have a fight on her hands.

But with the monkeys calm, I expected she might have left already, hoped she had. I didn't want to spend my life cowering with worry.

The house was cold. I didn't feel like making a fire. There was no light inside me. Nikon had disappeared like he had never been here to begin with. I was back to being alone. It might not have been a long time that I'd been around him, but it'd been nice.

"What do you want for dinner?" I asked Tewy.

"Anything you have at this point would be good." Nikon's voice came from where I'd originally thought I'd left him.

I jumped back, putting a hand to my chest. "What are you doing in here? I thought you were gone."

"Never left. When I heard you talking to someone this morning, I rolled under the bed hoping she wouldn't notice me here."

"I can't believe that worked. You must be famished."

"Thirsty, more so."

"Let me get you some water." I ran and grabbed the bucket out of the outhouse. "You can use this if you need. I'll be back."

"Thank you," he said.

I grabbed a clean bucket and went to the river, taking my time in case he needed it. When I returned, I took care of the waste, washed up, and knelt beside him. "I'm so glad you're here. I thought something had happened to you." Or that he'd left me for good.

"Nope. Only hiding."

I reached up, brushing my hand along his jaw that had soft hairs growing on it. There was a strange flutter in my stomach as I moved down until I found his lips. "I'm going to help you drink now."

When he didn't respond, I assumed that meant he was good. I took the ladle and brought it up to his lips. Being more careful than the last few days not to spill it on him, I tilted it toward him. We went through several ladles like that. "You were serious about being thirsty."

He smacked his lips together. "Much better now though, thank you."

I paused. "The woman said you were dangerous."

"I am."

"That doesn't make me feel better."

"Perhaps not, but it's the truth. The thing is, I would never use my skills to hurt you."

"Why not?" I asked.

"That's a good question. You're innocent in all this. I've got you mixed up in things deeper than you know."

"You swear you mean me no harm?"

"I promise."

41

The two words settled comfortingly inside me. "And what are those things that you're mixed up in?"

He didn't respond.

"I'll get you dinner," I said with a sigh. I left the bucket and ladle next to him, trying not to think about what had happened today. It was near impossible though. My thoughts continuously prodded at me, nudging me to pay attention to them and address what needed to be taken care of. I stopped in the middle of cooking another fish fillet. "I think I should let you go."

He didn't respond.

"It feels like you were right. There's trouble for you here. I've liked having someone to speak with, but it's not the same if you're here against your will." I scowled at my own thought.

His reply was soft. "If you release me, I'll have to leave."

"I know." Even if the mere thought of him leaving made my eyes sting with tears.

"I want you to come with me."

"I can't."

"Why ever not?"

How did I explain the twisted feeling inside me? The worry and strangeness of it all? "My house needs me."

"It's true things will fall apart without you here to take care of them." His words were cautious. "I also think it's true you'll not only be safer if you come with me, but you'll be happier."

"That still doesn't explain why you care." I waited in silence for an answer.

"I don't know exactly. Something pulls me to you. I've gotten to know you over the past couple of days, and I know you don't deserve what those coming for me will do to you."

How would I change if I left? Did I want to change? I checked the fish, prodding the flaky meat with a finger, the succulent aroma filling the air.

"I want to keep you safe from the people tracking me. You may have tied me up but have otherwise been kind to me. You seem like the type of person to care. I want to repay that kindness."

"What about becoming a slave for the Reding and Vading? I don't want that."

"I'll protect you from them. Besides, you can't let fear stop you from living a life."

"No, but it can help me make wise decisions."

"If it's keeping you from the world, is it wise?"

I plated up the fish, trying not to think too hard on his words. If I did, I might not be able to stay. I knelt on the floor, set the plate to my side, and reached for him. "I'm going to untie you now. You can eat dinner and be on your way."

He sighed, but when I reached out to help him, he already had his hands outstretched toward me. I worked at the knot until it came undone.

"I can untie my feet." His words were close enough to brush up against me.

Could he have untied his own feet before this? I pushed the thought aside, only to have guilt at having tied him up in the first place rear its head. "I'm sorry about this whole thing. I wasn't sure why you were here." Still wasn't if I was honest, but at least I could trust my gut that said he wouldn't harm me. "I was afraid you wanted to hurt Tewy or me or steal from us. I shouldn't have tied you up, and I should never have hit you with my cane."

There was a faint sound I couldn't recognize, him untying his bonds maybe. "You did good. Having a stranger turn up at your house is another reason to go with me. What if someone else comes who isn't as nice as me? What if that woman comes back and isn't as patient with you? She will kill you given half a chance."

"How do you know this?"

"Trust me."

"It's hard to do that for someone I don't really know."

Skin brushed against my hand until fingers threaded through my own. "I promise I only have the best of intentions, Cassandra."

The contact was strange but nice. I liked it, but wasn't used to being touched. It made me feel like I belonged somewhere. That I was wanted. Needed, even. Ever since my caretaker left me, I'd been empty inside. But I wouldn't let a maelstrom of emotions sway me.

I pulled my hands away, forcing him to let go. "Eat your fish."

"Yes, ma'am." Sadness touched his tone.

There was a shuffle of movement. Good, he must be listening. I got up and cooked some fish for myself. As the grains of salt I grabbed with my fingertips fell, hopefully landing on my meat, I wanted to say more. To demand more answers from him or force him to stay.

I didn't want to be alone again.

But I wouldn't be. I had Tewy. That was enough, even if it didn't feel like it.

"Why did you come here?" The words pummeled from me.

"I can't say."

I let the fish slide out of my pan onto a plate I had waiting and slammed the pan back down. "You can't even tell me what city you're going to?"

"I shouldn't." But there was hesitancy in his tone.

"Another reason to not go with you. I can't trust you if you don't talk to me."

I crossed my arms in front of my chest. I wasn't hungry anymore.

"Tewy, let's go get some chores done," I said.

"You've been doing chores all day," Nikon said. "Give it a break."

"Unlike some people, I'm not willing to give up on this place." Where was my monkey? "Tewy?"

"He's on my shoulder."

Traitor. "Fine."

I stormed from the building, though I didn't really have any work to do. Who cared if Tewy didn't want to join me? Who cared if Nikon was leaving me? Who cared if Tewy ended up joining him, and I was left all alone?

I marched toward the river, tripping over something hard. I cursed under my breath. Dratted stone. I lost track of my way in my anger. If I was going to be mad at anyone, I should be mad at my parents.

But they were dead.

I sniffed. The coolness of night was creeping in. I wanted to go to sleep and wake up to find Nikon had never come here.

"I'm sorry I upset you." Nikon's voice came from behind me.

I started. Antonia had never been so quiet. "Why did you follow me out here?"

"You're distressed. I wanted to fix that."

"Then you shouldn't have come here in the first place. You've ruined everything."

"I'm sorry. I truly am. If I could have changed things, I would have, but I can't go back no matter how much I want, and even need, to."

I crinkled my eyebrows. "Why would you need to?"

"I can't tell you that either."

"There's a lot you can't say." Tewy jumped on my shoulder and patted my face. I swatted his hand away. I didn't want comfort at that moment. I wanted to be mad and stay mad.

Tewy whined. "Sorry, boy. I didn't mean to take my anger out on you." I reached up and he wrapped his little hand around my thumb. I was forgiven, even if I didn't deserve it. My monkey was too good to me.

"If you come with me, you could bring Tewy, of course," said Nikon.

"Why are you trying so hard to get me to go with you?"

"Because I don't want you to get hurt."

"Why would I get hurt if you weren't here? Wouldn't they leave me alone?"

"There's a slim possibility of that, but it's more likely that you will be taken in as an accomplice when they realize I was here."

"They didn't know before. Why would they later?"

"They're smart. They'll figure it out soon enough with the trail I left. And when they do… I just don't want something bad to happen to you."

I made my way to the river, certain he would follow. I didn't stop until my toes hit wet sand. Maybe the magic would help me make a decision. It would probably be the wrong one given my track record with the magic sand. "I don't know why you care so much. I hit you with my cane and tied you up."

"You were protecting yourself, I get that."

Glad someone did. "Can't I tell them you came and went after I told them someone was looking for you?"

"They're not the type to leave loose ends, especially with someone outside of society who isn't protected."

Fear clenched my chest. "What will they do to me?"

"It wouldn't be pleasant. They'd try to get information about me. If you tell them the truth, you'll be punished for what they perceive is lying. If you don't, you'll be tortured until you produce an answer they want. Either way, you'll end up a shell of your former self. That can't happen." He put a hand on my shoulder. His warmth was as comforting as his spicy scent. "I won't let it. Do you understand me, Cassandra? I'll do what's needed to make certain it doesn't happen."

"Even stay here with me?" Hope flared.

"I can't stay here where they could find me. Even if it means dragging you along with me if you don't want to go."

That wasn't what I expected. Did he really mean to take me kicking and screaming? Did I want to go that way? I wasn't sure I actually wanted to fight him.

A warm breeze picked up, swirling across my skin. The sand

squishing between my toes told me nothing. I shouldn't have expected it to. "And if I choose to go with you, how will you keep me from being taken to the Reding and Vading?"

"We'll be smart."

Was I really going to do this? It was crazy to believe I was considering it. "I don't know. It's been a long time since I was anywhere but here."

"That means now is your chance to explore a world beyond the one you know."

That sounded scary.

Tewy chatted animatedly, pulling at my ear like he did when he was excited. There wasn't much I knew about the outside world except that it could be dangerous for me. Despite that, there was something I needed to do that I couldn't do from here. Something I should have done long ago but was too frightened. I needed to find my caretaker. Whatever had happened to her to make her leave me? She might not have always been the nicest person, but she was the closest thing I had left to family.

"I think I'm willing to go." Because even if it meant going into the unknown, I knew I didn't want to be tortured or killed. Besides, I was ready for a change. And if it helped me find Antonia, all the better.

CHAPTER SEVEN

"We should go tonight. Actually, right now if possible. We don't know how long it's going to take her to come back." Nikon's words were strong and decisive.

"Why would she if she didn't find you here before?"

"Because of that sandblasted trail I left. She'll realize sooner or later that there was nowhere else for me to go."

I wanted to argue, to protest I hadn't really meant to say I'd go with him, but the problem was, I did mean it—I was just terrified of the results. "I can do that."

Footsteps hurried close by. "We need to gather your stuff together."

"Do you have a plan other than running?"

"I'm thinking on it."

That wasn't good, but it was enough for the moment.

Packing was harder than I thought it would be. There were items I wanted to take, but obviously couldn't with only the two of us; things like my pots, pans, even the entire stove would have been nice. My bed had to stay though I couldn't imagine life without it.

There was little we did pack. Food, as much as we could carry.

Water skins. Clothes, and my cane. The meager things made me want to stay home. How could I leave my life behind? Nikon said he'd found a long cloth to tie everything up in. We were good to go.

I hesitated in my doorway, Tewy on my shoulder. I placed a hand on the wood of the house.

"What is it?" Nikon asked from ahead of me. "Do you need shoes?"

"No, I don't own any." I tightened my hold on the top of my cane. "It's difficult to move."

Tewy patted my head, making me wonder if he understood the significance of the moment.

Nikon, brushing a hand across my shoulder, said, "I'm sorry I ever led them here."

"Why did you have to come? I really need an answer."

He huffed, frustration pouring from him in that single sound. "I stumbled across some information from the Reding that is sensitive enough that anyone who knows it could be killed."

"And that information led you to my house?"

"Sort of."

Did it have anything to do with Antonia or why she disappeared? "Did it have something to do with a person?"

"Not really."

Probably not my caretaker then. "What are you doing with the knowledge?"

"Nothing useful, apparently."

His vague answers were beyond frustrating. "Is that what brought you here? Or are you simply running because they know you know?"

"I'm not sure I should say. I want to keep you safe."

That didn't make me feel any better. It did make me feel like we needed to get out of there, though. If this sensitive information drew dangerous people even close to my house, I couldn't stay. Besides, Antonia wasn't coming back. I'd waited for her long enough. It was time to do something about finding her. "Fine. Let's go, but I want to know more."

I took my staff with me but didn't use it to feel around me. I'd need it, but not in familiar territory.

As we walked, me following the sound of Nikon's steps, he said, "I can't tell you more, it's too dangerous."

"Isn't it just as dangerous if I know that there's something?"

"No. It could cost more if you actually knew the truth. One day, I may share it with you, but not until it's safe."

At least he was trying to keep something bad from happening, even if I didn't understand what or why.

We fell into a silence as we traveled southwest along the riverbank. I didn't usually go south, but I'd done it enough times that I was familiar with the area. Still, I let the stick feel ahead of me, making sure I didn't bump into anything.

The air cooled, touching my skin with a chill. I wished I wouldn't have packed my shawl so tightly in my makeshift bag. It wasn't worth getting it out. It'd been a while since I'd been out this late at night, and I'd forgotten how cold it could be. The sand was dry and grainy beneath my feet, though I could hear the rush of the river. We were walking close to it without affecting the sand. The scent of water and leaves wafted to me.

I took a step and stopped.

"What's wrong?" Nikon asked.

I clenched my jaw. "I've never been farther than this before. Not since I came to this place."

A light brush skirted my elbow. "I can't imagine what that must be like."

"Terrifying. Thrilling." But I didn't keep going forward.

"Do you want to take my arm? I can help guide you if you'd like."

Did I? I'd been independent for so long, it was hard to give that up. But, having a guide might be nice when taking on something new. I didn't have to do things alone. Nikon and Tewy were here to help. "That'd be welcome. Thank you. Your elbow though, please."

That feeling of skin and warmth brushed against my hand again as Nikon slipped his elbow into my hand, an unfamiliar sensation of roughness and muscles. I liked it being there. With him helping and my staff swooping before me, I felt more confident. Like I could take this on. Great distances were nothing to me. I could conquer the unfamiliar.

Nikon stepped forward, and I went with him. Tewy gave a patting sound, a little squeak in my ear. I grinned. Why hadn't I done this sooner? I went forth with confidence, holding my head high—until I forgot to swoop my cane forward and tripped over something.

Nikon caught me before I fell. "I'm sorry. This way has lots of vegetation around it. Are you all right?"

"Fine. Just startled." And embarrassed I hadn't found whatever object that was. I'd be more careful to continue to use my cane in the future. It did bring something to mind though. "How are you going to keep that woman or anyone else from following us? Won't they know to come after us?"

He guided me forward a little quicker. "Once we stop, I'll go back and cover our tracks. That will help, but even then, they could still find us. They have good trackers. We'll be safer once we hit a city."

"So, we need to go fast?"

"Fast as we can without putting ourselves in danger or making a stupid decision, yes."

I was grateful for Tewy's comforting presence on my shoulder. He may be a trickster sometimes, but he was familiar and would help warn us if anything was going to happen. "Why didn't you cover the tracks as we went?"

"I wanted to get you safely away, and quickly. Plus, I can move faster without you."

"I'm sorry I'm slowing you down."

"Don't worry about it. I'm just glad you decided to come."

Hearing his voice so close to me made me want to lean into him. I didn't know what to do about it. I knew I couldn't, at least not while we were walking. Instead, I forced myself forward faster, hoping Nikon would keep a better eye out for something that might trip me up.

We went at a good pace, Tewy never making a sound of warning, though he did jump off me at some point. "Where did Tewy go?"

"He's on my shoulder," Nikon said.

I held in a groan. It was great that Tewy liked him, but I missed my monkey.

The night grew colder as we walked, my body wanting to take a rest. However, my mind was active, churning over everything that had happened in the last couple of days. It felt like a lifetime since I'd stumbled upon Nikon, but somehow at the same time, it seemed like just moments ago. There was so much I'd learned, and yet so much more I wanted to know about the outside world. So, I asked, "What are the cities like now?"

"Probably much the same as you left them. I lived in a bigger city and the hustle of it was always going on, even at night. They're working on building a new pyramid for the current Reding for after he dies."

"A pyramid? Isn't that only for the capitol building?" I'd seen it once when I was younger, the large stepped slabs leading into a sort of triangular building that extended far above our heads.

"Not according to him."

"Why not float him down the river?" That was what happened to most people when they died. Sometimes, a death boat would even get caught on its way down and someone would have to free it from the bank, sending it back on its way. We probably shouldn't be speaking of it, but this felt far enough away from mentioning death that it was probably all right.

"The new Reding believes his rule will be preserved, and he, with his wife, can live on in the afterlife, still ruling if they're kept that way. Sending him down the river would make them like anyone else."

"You sound as if you don't believe it."

His arm tensed beneath my hand. "You're very observant."

"I hear what others don't. I've had enough practice at it."

"Be careful what you say to others when we reach the city. We may be a blunt people, but there are some things that should not be said."

"How will I know what to avoid?"

His fingers brushed against mine. "I'll teach you as best I can, but if there's ever any doubt, you shouldn't say anything."

"I'll try." And I hoped I wouldn't fail. It sounded too serious to not excel at. "Do you have any suggestions now?"

"It's hard to pinpoint some, but avoid anything that discredits the rulers in any way or implies that others do. It's a dangerous line to play with."

"That makes sense, though I don't like skirting around issues."

He gave a low chuckle. "I've noticed that about you."

"So, you don't believe the Reding are preserved in the afterlife to rule over us?"

"Let's just say I'm skeptical. No, I think that life will keep going on as it always does, and the Reding's child will take their place as our next ruler—if he ever has one. It doesn't make sense to me that someone could rule us in Eppla from a life after this one."

It was true that it did sound difficult, if not downright impossible. But many people believed it was the case. "What about the rest of us? No doing anything after we die? That's a sad thought."

He didn't respond right away, his words coming out softly when he finally did speak. "I don't know what to think."

"There has to be more than this." I put conviction into my words. "I don't know what it is, but I have to believe that when we go on, there is more. Who knows? Perhaps when our bodies reach their destination downstream, life renews and we get to live on forever."

"A life without the Reding, since he doesn't want to go. I think I could get used to that idea."

There was something solid to my right. A boulder, perhaps? I skirted closer to him to avoid it. "You don't like the Reding much, do you?"

"That's what I'm talking about. Questions like that will find you in trouble."

"If I was with someone else, maybe, but it's you."

"You should start practicing for when we're back in civilization. If someone overheard you..."

I shrugged. It wasn't an issue at the moment, so I wasn't worried. "You're avoiding the question."

"It's probably time to stop for the night. There's a clearing by the riverbank up here. Are you ready?"

Definitely avoiding the question. "I'm tired enough, if you think it's safe."

"We should be fine. It will give me a chance to erase our trail and make a false one."

"You know how to do that?"

"I do."

"There's so much I don't know about you."

"You'll get a chance to figure it out soon enough. If we're going to stick together, you're bound to pick up more about me."

"Somehow, that doesn't make me feel any better."

He gently took my hand off his arm. "Let's get you settled."

My body was too weary to protest any further. "What can I do to help?"

"Are you hungry?"

"Yes."

"Why don't you make us something to eat?"

"All right." I sat on the ground with my pack and made us a quick snack of salted fish and seeds, making sure to set some seeds out for Tewy. He could probably find his own food, but since he took care of me, I liked to take care of him.

We ate quickly, and Nikon helped me find a clear spot on the sand. It didn't take long for exhaustion to win out. As I was falling asleep, Nikon said, "I'm going to go erase our trail. I'll be back soon."

That jolted me awake. "What if you don't return?"

"I will."

"What if something happens while you're gone? What if that woman finds me?"

"She'll still be looking at my trail, not over here. I won't be gone long."

I lay back down, trying to will myself to relax. I had to trust him; there was no other option at this point. Out here, I knew nothing. I'd tried to keep track of the world around me, but it was all so unfamiliar, and I'd made the mistake of letting myself get lost in our conversation. I supposed I could follow the river back to my home, but danger awaited me there if—or according to Nikon, when—that woman came back. I'd have to trust Nikon knew what he was about.

There was a faint whisper from Nikon. "Keep watch over her, Tewy."

Despite straining, I didn't hear him leave. Moments later, my little monkey came and curled himself up beside me. He was warm so I snuggled up tight against him.

I must have drifted off because I woke to Tewy shivering. He was sitting on my chest, his little body quaking. It wasn't cold out, or not any colder than it had been earlier. Could something be upsetting him?

I reached up to pet him, but before I got there, he grabbed my hand and pulled it to him. "What's wrong, Tewy?"

"He's afraid of me," a deep, female voice growled off to my right.

A voice was not Nikon.

CHAPTER EIGHT

"Who's there?" I tried to keep my voice from shaking as I turned toward the sound but failed. It wasn't the woman from before. The quality of the vocal tones held much different notes, deeper and almost magical somehow.

"If you want to know what is before you, my riddle you must correctly answer."

I leaned back in dismay. How had I drawn a sphinx to me? "No, thank you."

Her voice came, full of mystery. "I have a life, but none of my own. I bleed when torn. When I wake, I never die until the very last one. You take me away, and I'm left with none."

I hadn't a clue how to respond to that. If I answered incorrectly, she'd kill me, but if I didn't answer at all, I was just as dead. Legend said there were only four chances. I wracked my mind for a solution, hoping something would spring to mind. Even if I could see, I'd be no match for a sphinx. Despite making me feel better, the cane in my hand was next to useless next to a winged, clawed creature, with a human head.

"I'm waiting." The husky voice sounded not at all impatient despite her words.

"Get back, sphinx." Nikon's stern words sent a rush of relief cascading through me. I couldn't be more grateful he was here.

"The woman has yet to answer my riddle," she said.

"She's not going to, either."

"Ah, but she will if she wishes to keep her life."

My throat tightened, making me choke on my response.

A clink of metal scraping against metal snicked through the air. "She's under my protection."

"Big knife for a little man."

Nikon was anything but little from all my interactions with him. How huge did that make her?

"Perhaps, but I know how to use it."

Nikon had a weapon? How had I not noticed that before?

"If you say," the sphinx said. "But I'll be back to claim my answer or my prize. You have three more chances."

There wasn't a sound as I struggled to hear her leave. It was impossible to tell if she was moving or not. I wanted to be back in my house, tucked into my bed. This was all beyond me. What was I thinking, venturing out into the world? If Nikon hadn't returned when he did, I wouldn't have been able to give the correct answer, and the sphinx would have had me for breakfast.

A scratch of footsteps neared. "Are you all right?" Nikon's voice was close.

"Is she gone?"

"Yes."

I let out a relieved sigh. "I'm fine. A little shaken, but fine."

Skin touched my fingers as Nikon's hand encompassed my own. "There's no shame in being scared."

"There's no help in it either. Do you know what the answer to the riddle could be?" I didn't want to be caught unaware next time she found me, because there was certain to be a next time.

"No."

"Me neither."

"We'll figure it out."

"Did you finish what you needed to?" I asked, not wanting to think about a sphinx coming after me.

The grip left my own. "They won't follow us easily. We'll walk in the river tomorrow to help lose our tracks more, but for the moment, we should be safe." His voice moved farther away as he spoke. "I'm going to get some rest now. I'll wake if there's any problems."

"Like the sphinx returning?"

"She won't be coming back. At least not today."

Somehow that wasn't reassuring. "How do you know?"

"Sphinxes usually wait a while between questioning. Haven't you heard tales of them?" His reply was sleepy.

It didn't take long for a soft snore to come from Nikon. He wasn't far away, which was somewhat comforting, but still, those niggling thoughts of sphinx or other creatures bothered me. Or worse, what if whoever was chasing Nikon found us? Would we really be tortured and killed? I hated to think about it, but the truth was, it could happen.

I shifted, trying to get comfortable. Sleeping on the ground was harder when I was keyed up from the sphinx and other worries. If I could lull myself back to a place of semi-peace, things might be different. As it was, I spent the rest of the night shifting, Tewy yammering at me a couple times over it when I bumped into him.

After the third time of Tewy getting after me, Nikon said, "We might as well get up."

"Sorry."

"It's fine. I managed to get some hours in there anyway."

I stretched. "How do you know how long it was?"

"The movement of the stars, though I've gotten so accustomed to keeping track of time, it's like I have an internal clock."

I'd almost forgotten about the stars and their pinpricks of brightness shining down on me when there was nothing else to see.

"Should we eat on the road or now?" I asked.

"Now. It'll be easier navigating, especially if we're going to go through the river."

"Good point." I grabbed my pack from where I'd left it the night before and pulled some salted fish and berries out of a pouch. The fruit would spoil first. We'd have to get through it before anything else. We ate a quick breakfast, storing leftovers back in their pouches and in my pack.

Nikon helped me to my feet, and I tucked the back hem of my dress into the front of itself again before I settled my hand on his elbow. With my staff in my other hand, I was ready to go. "How deep into the river are we going?" It wasn't wide here, or at least it wasn't very wide by my house, but it could extend far down.

"Just deep enough to cover our tracks. It shouldn't be bad."

The water made me long for home the moment I touched it. I splashed through the river, Nikon not making a noise. "How are you so silent?"

"Practice."

"You really need to tell me more about yourself."

He grunted.

"Are you a fisherman?" I didn't think he was but wanted to see what his response would be.

"I fish sometimes."

"But it's not your profession. Hmm." What else could I guess without saying what I thought? "You have some type of weapon. What is it?"

A pause. "I have several different things."

Odd that I hadn't noticed them. "And you have armor. Do you make it?"

He whirled me around and grabbed my other hand so he was holding both of them. "You need to stop this line of questioning."

"I only wan—"

"No. It's not safe for you, Cassandra. I promised I wouldn't let the Reding or anyone else hurt you, but you can't continue down

this road. It's too dangerous. I have to protect you from yourself."
He was so close, I could feel the warmth of his words falling
on me.

"I don't understand how it will make a difference to me. If you
know, and it puts you in danger, aren't I already in that same
danger? Shouldn't I know so I understand how to better protect
myself?"

"I'll teach you to fight. That will help."

"You're getting off the subject. I need to know what you do."

"They'll torture it out of you. I can't have that, Cassandra. I've
got enough innocent blood on my hands."

That didn't sound good. "Why? How?"

"Just trust me."

"You haven't given me a reason to trust you." I flung myself out
of his grasp, stumbling a little before righting myself. I took
several careful steps away, the water pushing at me as the wet
sand and rocks hit my feet. It would be so much better if I could
storm away. I took several more steps when something caught my
foot. I went splashing down, landing face first in the water. I lost
my cane as my hands reached out to catch my fall.

The front of me stung. Drenched and wanting out, I struggled
to get my knees under me as my head was barely above water.

"Cassandra, are you hurt?" Nikon's voice was coming closer.

Of course, he had seen everything. As if the moment could get
any worse.

Tewy chittered away with an upset tone. Apparently, he didn't
like that I'd fallen in the water even if I wasn't the one whose
shoulder he wanted to ride on. I got my knees under me about the
time Nikon's hand wrapped around my upper arm.

"Let me help you." He pulled me up, yanking me to my feet,
causing me to fall on his chest.

"Great, now we're both wet." And it had done nothing to cool
my anger.

"I needed a bath anyway."

"You do stink," I said.

He chuckled, which made staying mad at him difficult. "I'll clean up once we stop for the night, but right now we need to keep going."

"All right." Still, I didn't move from where I was, feeling the armor over his chest. "You're a warrior."

He let go of me. "I'll get your cane."

He was a warrior, a soldier in the Reding's army. I knew it, even if he wouldn't say it.

There was splashing before something smooth nudged my hand. My staff. "Thank you."

"The wood might warp with all this wet."

I bristled. "I know."

"Just trying to help." His voice grew tentative. "Do you want my elbow again?"

No, but I needed it. "Give it to me, and let's go. I'm tired of fighting."

"It does put a damper on things." He linked my hand with his arm again while we got a move on.

"Do you think my fall in the river will be traced?" I asked.

"No. If there's any evidence, it will be washed away by the time they arrive."

That was a relief. I'd hate if I was the reason we were found. Despite all my arguing with Nikon, I was just frustrated. I despised these circumstances, and I disliked that I had come to be in them not knowing more. There was little I could do about it without turning back, but that wasn't an option. I had to put my trust in Nikon, which meant no more questions about his profession.

It would be nice if he'd confirm he was a warrior though. I'd be surprised if he wasn't one, even if he didn't want to talk about it. At least I'd learn skills from a warrior who knew what he was doing. If nothing else, it would keep me in good shape. I didn't know how I'd be able to defend myself against anyone. The only reason I'd been able to with Nikon was because he'd been hurt. Which reminded me. "How's your wound?"

"Healing nicely now that I'm remembering to put sand on it more often. Keeping it on the wound and changing it when it dries out."

"Good. I don't suppose you want to talk about how you got injured in the first place?"

"No."

"Didn't think so." Oh well. It had been worth a try.

We walked some distance that was larger than the whole area I had lived in for the last ten-odd years. It was strange traversing over so much land. Even more so, each step into darkness, into the unknown, left me wanting to hold on to Nikon tighter.

Despite it all, my legs never tired. I supposed I kept busy enough doing chores and exercising that I'd become stronger. And, I managed to keep a firm but modest grip on Nikon.

Tewy hopped on my shoulder, making me feel better. I petted him. "Thanks, little friend."

"He just put a bug in your hair," Nikon said.

"Ugh." I shook my head. "At least it wasn't something worse. Did I get it out?"

"I'll grab it."

We stopped, and there was a tug on my hair.

"That was one big bug," he said.

"Now you tell me."

"I didn't want you to go crazy."

"I'm glad you have such faith in me."

"Hey, it's not only you. I was having a hard time not screaming when I grabbed that thing."

I growled. "Tewy, you rude little monkey. I swear, someday I'm going to crochet you into a shawl."

My monkey gave a laughing sort of hoot.

"Yeah, laugh it up all you want now, but I'm warning you."

Nikon pulled me forward, and I went with him, going much

slower than I'd have liked. Which made me wonder, "Where are we going? Kenti?" That was the closest city, so it made sense to at least restock our supplies there. I'd lived there at one time and had friends there. I missed them. Did they ever think of me?

"No, we're going to bypass Kenti completely. They'll figure we'd stop there, especially with two of us eating on your stores. I can find us food, but it'll be hard. No, we're going to Itpy."

We had a long walk ahead of us. I hoped that someone or something didn't catch up to us because I was slowing us down.

CHAPTER NINE

"You smell better," I told Nikon after he came back from washing.

"Easy to say when you only have a monkey to compare me with."

Tewy grunted several times.

I bit back a laugh. "I don't think he liked that comparison."

"Too bad. He's going to have to deal with it or not get any food tonight. Are you hungry?"

"Famished."

There was a shuffle of things being hit together. "Salted fish and the last of the berries?"

"Sounds like a meal fit for a Reding."

Moments later, he grabbed my hand, putting my palm out flat. "Here you go."

Little round things were placed inside, probably the berries.

"I'll get you the fish when you finish."

"Fair enough." I popped a berry in my mouth, letting its sweet and tart juice coat my tongue. "So why are we going to a walled city? Won't that trap us inside?"

"Because it's what they won't expect. These people, they know me well. They'll plan on me going to an open and free city. They won't expect I'll choose a place harder to get in and out of. They'll never look for us there. Or if they do, not until we blend in and have cover."

"What type of cover are you thinking?"

"It'll have to be as brother and sister," he said.

"Will we pass as brother and sister?"

"We'll have to. Also, to fit in, you'll have to cut your hair, and I'll have to shave mine. I think that will be our best bet."

"Women have short hair now and men are bald?"

"Yes. Most women either shave their heads as well and wear a wig or cut their hair to about here." A warmth of skin moved along my jawline. His scent lingered in the air after it.

I shivered. "Does that mean I'll have to shave my head too?"

"No, your hair is dark enough that you'll fit in with it shortened. Unless you want to shave it and get a wig?" There was a tension in his tone I didn't understand.

"I don't need a wig."

"Good. We don't have the money for one. I'll have to find a job doing something useful. Until then, we might have to live outside the city."

"I understand." We wouldn't be able to pay for housing without a job, but I hated the thought of being stuck outside a city by myself all day while he found jobs to do. "I brought my crochet hook. If you can get me some yarn, I can make shawls to sell."

"How do you accomplish that without being able to see? And I'm not trying to be rude or flippant, I'm really curious."

I'd been making things for so long, I'd almost forgotten about my beginning. "I did handwork before I became blind. I've known how to do it for a long time now. When I lost my sight, my caretaker insisted I continue working on it until I could do it from touch alone. She'd bring me something and tell me what color it was, and then I'd get to work. I made a lot of things that way. I don't know what she did with most of what I made."

"You didn't keep it?"

"No, she took it." I shrugged. "It's not like I could look at it and enjoy it, and one shawl is as good as any other on a chilly night."

"Hmm. Do you want anything else to eat?"

I shook my head. "No, I'm good." I could eat more, but if we were going farther than I first thought, we'd need to ration our food. "I've been thinking, if we're going to cut my hair so that woman who came to my house won't recognize me, that's good, but she knows I'm blind. How are we going to hide that?"

The silence that descended grew heavy upon my shoulders. Or maybe that was just Tewy.

"You'll keep your head down when we're in public and follow my lead. Most of the time, you'll have to stay away from others."

I wanted to jerk to a stop, but knew we needed to keep going. The river sloshed as I stormed through. "You took me from my house, one where I could go outside anytime I wished, to make me stay in all the time? I don't think so. I'd go crazy."

"Do you have a better idea?"

No. I didn't. "That doesn't mean I have to like it."

"We'll figure this out."

I didn't want it figured out, I wanted the problem gone. "What do you think the Reding and Vading have against the blind?"

"I haven't a clue. Maybe he sees them as the weak to prey on, but obviously he hasn't seen you."

"Good save." Sarcasm laced my words.

"I mean it."

What difference did it make why royalty made prisoners of those that couldn't see? As long as he was doing it, I wouldn't be able to do much in the city. I'd be stuck away from people just like I'd been for years. The prospect wasn't heartening. At least I still had Tewy, and Nikon would be around. Unless he decided to abandon me too—there wasn't anything holding him to me other than his word. It had to be enough or I was doomed.

"How much longer are we going to be walking in the water?" I asked sometime later. It felt like we'd been there for a full day, but the heat was still pressing on me, unrelenting.

"Not much longer. We'll get on the riverbank for a while before we cross the chasm. Once we hit that, we'll have some difficulty navigating through but I'm sure we can do it. How did you manage it when you came through before?"

"Honestly, I don't remember a lot about that time. I was full on grieving for my sight. I blocked out a lot of memories. The few I have left, I remember my caretaker guiding me. We went around the chasm, I believe."

"She sounds like she means a lot to you."

Did she? I was still angry at her for being gone, yes, but she was the only person who had helped me after the incident with the magical sand and my parents' deaths. Death by hearts broken over what they did to me. She was the one to break the news to me. I might have been angry at my parents for causing my blindness, but their thoughts had been in the right place, and I loved them.

"You all right?" Nikon asked.

"You stirred up a lot of memories for me."

"Good ones, I hope."

I drummed my fingers on his arm. "A mix. My caretaker was a good woman. Complicated, but good."

"You speak about her in the past tense."

"For all I know, she's dead. Either way, she's no longer in my life." I needed to change that though. At the very least, I needed to discover what happened to her. Hopefully, once we were settled, I'd find a way to do so.

"I'm sorry." His words were empathetic, making me grateful I'd decided to go with him. He meant what he said. I was in good hands.

"What about you? Who did you leave behind?" I slipped over something hard, a rock maybe. He grabbed my hand, the rough texture of his callouses brushing against my own. With a lift of my arm, he helped me up. The feeling was natural, like we'd done this thousands of times before.

"No one. Not really. My parents gave up on me long ago since I never became an amant."

The amant who had fallen in love at first sight. They ruled society, or at least they had when I left. I didn't know if that held true. It sounded like it, with the Reding marrying and gaining a Vading. "I understand how hard that can be. My parents wanted that for me so desperately, they caused me to become blind."

"Tell me the story. I'm curious how magic and your parents came together to make that happen."

"It's difficult to talk about."

He gave my hand on his arm a squeeze. "If you can, I'd recommend trying. I bet it would be helpful for you."

I sighed. It wasn't something I'd ever talked about before. The story had stayed locked up inside me ever since it happened, though I'd given Nikon a few quick glimpses. "My parents were amant—of course, since only amant can have children. They were quiet people and kind. I really do believe they had the best of intentions for me." My voice broke.

Nikon stayed silent. I could do this. A slew of memories hit me. "When I was seventeen, they didn't tell me much, just that they wanted better things for me. That this would help. When they took me to a secluded spot of the river, they told me to close my eyes, so I did. The feel of wet sand being pressed on my eyelids made me fearful. Despite that, I still believed they knew what they were doing. Magic is temperamental, I know. They knew that."

I still remembered my last sight. My mother's face beaming at me, my father in the background, the sun shining down on us all. The thought jerked my heart, leaving me wanting to stop speaking of such things, but it needed to be said, so I continued.

"They left the sand on for a while. It needed time to work, they said. What they didn't plan for was that magic has a will of its own. That no one knows how it's really going to turn out. They talked with me about how this would change all of our lives. That things would be so much better after this. I trusted they were right, though I didn't fully understand. We had a good life. They were part of the upper merchant class. I suppose they simply wanted that for me too, or even to become part of the ruling amant class." I ignored the tears streaming down my face. "We were going to have wonderful things come to us. I'd be with them and live a happy life."

"But that didn't happen, did it?" Nikon's gentle voice prodded me on.

"No. When they washed off the sand, and I first opened my eyes, I thought I couldn't see because it was dark outside. That the moon had gone down or the night sky had become covered with clouds while I was waiting. But when I asked about it, my parents became alarmed. It didn't take long to realize I was blind." A hint of rage entered my words, but I didn't care. "They couldn't leave well enough alone. I was still so young. I had more time to fall in love. I just hadn't looked the right man in the eyes. It wasn't fair what they took from me. I stayed so angry even while I remained with them. They got me a caretaker and she helped out. Until a week later when my caretaker said they were dead from broken hearts. Then it was too late to forgive them."

The feelings pounding around in my chest gave way to a stampede. I didn't know what to say or think, or what Nikon must feel about me. None of it mattered. I hadn't understood they were trying to do what was best for me even though it failed. Miserably. They tried to apologize. But I wouldn't let them. I kept to myself, and was left with an emptiness that was never filled, not even by Antonia.

Nikon stopped. Fear shot through me. Was he going to abandon me too? Everyone else did, why would he be any different?

Instead of leaving, he grabbed the elbow of my free arm, pulling me closer to him until we embraced. It was a little awkward with my cane. I hoped I didn't hit him with it, but when he didn't complain, I let myself relax into him. To allow his warmth and strength to envelop me.

I would never have romantic love—destined to be one of many who never found the other half of themselves, never to have that someone to take care of me forever. But at least I had someone who saw me as a sister. The thought sat heavy on my mind, unsatisfied. I wouldn't let that stop me from receiving comfort in this moment.

I leaned my head against his shoulder, his armor strap hard, but the cloth to the side of it soft. He smelled spicy again, that scent that had grown familiar after only a few times of smelling it. I wanted to bottle it and enjoy it whenever I wanted. Instead, my journey to find Antonia might one day take me from him.

CHAPTER TEN

The journey forward was easier after that. I didn't worry about Nikon and his intentions for me. I trusted him not only to help me through the dark world, but to bring it to life for me. And he did exactly that.

Often, as we walked, he would tell me what he saw. Fish by our feet, plants at the riverbank, lush with the constant drink from the river, the shape of clouds as they went by. I, in turn, told him about what the world was like for me. The tweet of a melancholy bird. Heat blazing across my skin from the sun as the water caressed our legs. How wobbly I became when the sand grew rocky.

He stood by it all, listening to me talk and conversing with me. Antonia had never liked to chat much. Despite how long she had been gone, it was a welcome change to what I was accustomed to. I didn't want to arrive at the city and have things return to silence.

"We're going to train," Nikon said once we'd stopped for the night. "Tomorrow, we'll reach the chasm, and it won't be long after that until we start reaching cities. We should have started training you the first night, but I've been lazy and remiss. It's time."

We were only a few nights into our journey, but that was enough time to start training, I supposed. "My caretaker taught me a little bit. Enough to defend myself against someone untrained." At least, it'd helped me through. I'd never had any serious problems—people or animals—until Nikon came. Even that hadn't been bad because he'd been wounded. Which reminded me, "Are you healed enough to fight?"

"Almost as good as new. I'm being a lot more careful this time."

I got the sense he was speaking about more than just putting sand on his wounds, but before I could question it, he said, "Show me what you know."

Holding out my cane in front of me, I moved it using two hands, going from one to the other. When I was comfortable with that, I pushed it from one side to the other. I let my stick slow to a stop and pressed the end down in the ground while trying to hold back a smile.

"Is that all you can do?" Nikon asked.

My grin faltered as Tewy gave a dejected chirp on my behalf. "Thanks, Tewy. Yes, that's all. I try to hit things when they come at me, but I haven't had any real problems."

"It's good that you practice and move, but your cane isn't long enough to do any real damage. An opponent only has to stay out of your circle and silent. You'd never be able to find them before they did this." His voice had moved behind me so I was almost prepared when he wrapped his arm around my neck and tightened.

He gently released me, steadying me so I didn't fall. "Sorry. I didn't want to scare you, but I also wanted to prove a point. I'm worried about your safety."

"I thought you were going to keep me from getting into danger."

"But if it comes anyway, part of my job is to have you ready for it." He sighed. "I'll have to think on it. I'm sure there's some sort of solution to fighting without sight."

"Besides magically getting my sight back? I don't think so." I sat on the ground, having already tapped at it with my foot to make sure there were no sharp rocks.

"Speaking of that, have you tried putting sand on your eyelids again to see if it would counteract its own spell?" His voice was at my level. He must have sat down too, but he was so much quieter than Antonia ever had been. It was strange not to hear him move around. "Cassandra, did you hear my question?"

"Sorry. I was ignoring it." But I'd done enough of that for a lifetime already. I should focus on being better. "At first, I wanted nothing to do with sand, but it's hard to get away from with nothing but a river filled with it and a desert outside that. At least when you get away from the river, it's no longer wet. I did eventually try though, multiple times."

"It didn't work."

"Nope."

"And now you treat the sand like its magic is beneath you, but you still use it for everyday purposes like washing."

I bristled. How did he know? "It's not like other people don't do the same."

"Yes, but they do it because they want the magic imbued within their everyday lives. They want the blessings they think will come from using it often. You, on the other hand, seem to use it because it's there."

"You have no business deciding such things for me."

Something touched my shoulder. I jolted away until I realized it was Nikon. He trailed his hand down my arm and took my hand in his. "I'm sorry. I shouldn't have said that so rudely. I'm just trying to understand you."

"Don't think you need any assistance. You seem to have figured it out on your own. I use the sand to help with what I need, cleaning and the like. Plus, I couldn't stay away from the river. I have always loved the water, even as a small child. I wish I could still see it, stretched lazily before me in a wide array of tranquility."

"It won't be tranquil tomorrow."

"The chasm."

He gave my hand a squeeze before letting go. Tewy quickly took up a spot on my lap, curling into a ball as Nikon continued. "That's right. The water through there is rough and the drop-off on either side of the river goes on forever downward. The only way around it is to go through the mountains, but those possess dangers of their own, plus it will take more time."

"What are we going to do then?"

"I am going to lay a faint trail going toward the mountains and hope our pursuers follow it. Then, we'll keep together as we go through the water."

"That sounds dangerous." And not like a pleasant time at all.

"It would be good if we had a boat, but even then, it would be precarious. There's not time to build one. We'll have to manage the best we can. I'll tie us together, that will help."

"What about Tewy?" I stroked the creature in question. I couldn't imagine losing the only friend that had stuck by my side even when things had gone so terribly wrong.

"If we can get him to ride on my shoulder, I think we'll be fine."

"You think?" I'd feel much better if he knew.

"There are no promises with the chasm."

"That's wonderful."

"Sorry, Cass, it's just the way things are."

"No one has ever called me Cass before." Not even my parents. I'd almost forgotten what it was like to have both of those.

"Do you mind? I can call you by your full name."

"It's fine. I kind of like it."

"Good. I'll keep at it then." The soft material of a blanket landed in my lap, startling Tewy awake. "Get some sleep. We'll have a busy day ahead."

I woke to Tewy's screeching. "What is it, boy? What's wrong?"

The panicked sound turned to a laughing grunt.

"Tewy. Can you never let me sleep in?"

"It's just as well," Nikon said. "We'd best get a move on. The sun's rays are already touching the sky."

I groaned, so not ready to wake yet. Though I was accustomed to moving around, it had been more intense the last couple of days and my body was feeling it.

"Here's some food," Nikon said as a solid object bumped into my hand.

I took it and ate. "Yum. More fish."

"You're the one who did such a good job of keeping your fish stores up."

"That may be true, but if I hadn't, we'd both be starving right now."

"Or I'd find us something to eat. It's saving us a lot of time."

I finished getting ready for the day, before Nikon handed me my pack and staff. "How far are we from the chasm? The river is rushing by faster, but that doesn't tell me how close we are. If it's going to get worse."

"It gets worse, but we'll make it. Are you ready?"

"Where's Tewy?" After saying his name, my pet jumped on my shoulder with his usual weight. It was comforting to have him there even if I knew at some point, I'd have to let him go to Nikon's shoulder. I'd hate to have him lost or hurt.

We walked a ways, and Nikon was right. The closer we got to the chasm, the louder it became. A dull roar filled my ears, making me have to shout to be heard over it. "Is this it?"

"It's coming up soon. I'm going to create a false trail. It might take me some time. Are you all right? Do you need anything?"

"I've been alone for years, I think I can manage part of a day."

"I know you can, I just want to make sure you're taken care of."

The thought touched my heart, stirring it in ways I didn't understand. "Thank you, but I'll be well enough. Get moving so we can get past this noise."

"Yes, ma'am." He gave my shoulder a squeeze, and then there was nothing but me and the weight of Tewy.

For all I knew, Nikon could have stood there watching me, but I doubted he'd do that. I waited a short way from the wet sand.

As I stayed there, I listened for a sound that would give away another nearby. Between the woman chasing Nikon and the sphinx problem, I hated not knowing what was around me. I hoped Tewy would warn me like he had when the woman came, but I didn't know if I could count on that. To make matters worse, the roaring of the water was so great that I couldn't catch a sound of anything.

I'd heard stories of the chasm as a kid. A high priest had tried to control the magic instead of letting it speak how it wished. The result was an explosion where he'd been standing. They say two entire cities were swallowed up in the gorges on both sides of the river.

Some of the magic of the water and sand was lost as the river washed into some of those gaping holes. It was just as well with me. I wasn't concerned if there was less magic in the world—if the stories were even to be believed. What did I care if the magic rushed away into those holes? Other than the fact that if we fell in them, we might never stop falling.

"That's a comforting thought," I said aloud.

Tewy patted my hair. Or perhaps he was putting another bug in it. Who knew?

As time passed, the heat went from a soft caress to a searing punch. I dipped my hands in the water, scooping up handfuls and dumping them on myself. I didn't mind being wet as long as I didn't have to deal with it also being so hot.

"I'm almost to you," Nikon's voice came in faint across the water.

I turned toward it, grateful he'd alerted me so I wasn't startled when he grabbed my hand. Moments later, his scent mixed with sweat was faint in the air.

"I'm going to tie us together now." He proceeded to wrap something scratchy around my waist. The rope, I assumed.

"Did you get the trail laid all right?" We were yelling to be heard.

"Just fine."

"Do you think they'll fall for it?"

"Hopefully for long enough to give us more time to get away."

"You're worried about it."

Whatever he was doing yanked at the rope he wrapped and knotted around my waist. "I wish you weren't so observant all the time. Yes, if you must know, I'm worried. The people tracking me are skilled. They'd very much enjoy hurting people, and I don't want that person to be either of us."

"I can agree to that. Are we ready?"

Nikon replied, "Almost. I'm going to attempt to tie the rope around Tewy like a harness. I don't want to lose him. Will you hold him for me?"

"He doesn't like that, but I can try." I grabbed him from off of my shoulder, holding tight to him so he couldn't shift and get away. He wiggled as I hummed soothing things at him.

"I'll hurry," Nikon said.

Tewy let out an angry squawk.

"Or not. This is going to take some doing." Nikon was frustrated.

I didn't blame him. Tewy was often difficult to deal with. It was a wonder I enjoyed being with him as much as I did. He squirmed in my arms, almost jumping out, but I held him firm. "It's all right, boy. We're trying to keep you safe."

He returned a tirade of grunts and squeaks.

"I know, sorry." It would have been a good time to speak monkey.

"Almost done," Nikon said. "There. Hopefully, he won't get away from us. Are you ready?"

"As I'll ever be." I was grateful that I couldn't see—a rare occurrence. But I didn't want to look at the places I could fall and never stop.

His hand encompassed mine. "I'm going to do my best to keep hold of you, but if you slip through my fingers, remember we're still tied together."

There was that. "Which way do we go?"

He twirled me around and took me forward. "This way."

The water stayed sloshing around my ankles at first, but it didn't take long for it to splash against my knees.

"Tewy, hop onto my shoulder," Nikon said.

I expected more of a fight, but the weight lifted off of me. Nikon pulled me closer to him as the cold lapped my thighs. His hand left mine, and my chest tightened with panic until a weight pressed in against my waist. Without it, I would have fallen.

As it was, I wobbled, almost going down. The pounding of my heart roared like the water around us. How were we going to stay upright? One wrong move and we'd be dragged down to the chasm. I yelled so he could hear me, "What does it look like around us?"

"Trust me when I say you don't want to know," he hollered back.

My thoughts conjured up ideas of raging water flinging us over the edge of the gorge that was right next to us. The cold liquid pushed against me as if wanting to take me to my fears. Several steps forward, it only got worse, pushing and tugging. My foot slipped.

We were going down.

Nikon's grip loosened. His hand fumbled against me, but never found purchase. I went under, water ripping me away from him and my cane. I held my breath, struggling to get back to air. Without being able to see where the surface was, I didn't know which way to go. I jolted to a stop, the rope around my waist yanking.

The river still crashed around me. I flung myself around, trying to discover which way was up. My lungs ached for breath. I needed to get out of here and back to the air. The harder I tried, the more I floundered. People's voices flashed through my head. I'd join my parents if I didn't get out of this.

CHAPTER ELEVEN

My toes scuffed against something solid. I needed to get a better hold. The sand slipped beneath my skin, not letting me go anywhere. When I couldn't hold back any longer, I took a breath. Water rushed into my lungs, filling them with liquid. I tried to cough, but only more water invaded me.

There was a firm jerk on the rope, and I was yanked through the water, crashing and angry around me. The river didn't want to let me go. It wanted to take me to the depths of the chasm, but by the tugging in the opposite direction, Nikon was fighting for me.

No one had ever fought for me.

I'd have to help him if I was to survive this.

I struggled to find a safe place on the ground somewhere beneath me so I could assist him. Little by little, my foot touched more of the sand and rocks. I pushed hard against them, going the direction the rope was being pulled.

My head grew lighter. If I didn't find air soon to expel this water and get much-needed oxygen, I'd die. Just as I thought that, my head popped out of the water. I coughed and sputtered, liquid pouring out of me. I weakly grabbed on to the rope as if it was a lifeline to the air.

The air cleared my head, helping me gain a little footing. I needed more though. The current pushed me.

"On your feet, Cassandra," Nikon yelled. "We have a ways to go."

I groaned, but warmth encompassed my waist, and I was hauled upright. There was nothing left holding me beneath the surface. It didn't stop my fears from bubbling up in a mass of groaning. I shoved my foot down, making certain it had purchase with each new step.

Nikon's grip never left my waist, but the water snagged me, trying to pull me in. If I could go in so easily, my monkey would never make it on his own. "Tewy?"

"Still on my shoulder." Nikon not only seemed to know what I needed to hear, but his words made my heart calm.

My grip on the rope was so tight, my fingers ached. Didn't matter. I wasn't letting go no matter how much it hurt. I continued to slog forward a step at a time, the current pulling me one direction then another, never the way I wanted to go.

"Almost there." Nikon's words propelled me on.

We could do this. Just a little farther. The worst had to be over. Something brushed against my left side. I jerked away, trying not to think of what it could be. The river reached almost to my waist, making each step more difficult than the last. "I thought this was going to get easier."

"When I said almost there, I meant, almost halfway."

I grunted. He had to be joking.

The heavy thing, whatever it was, brushed against my leg again. This time, it didn't go away, but wrapped around my left leg. "Nikon, there's som—"

Something yanked me underwater. I'd no time to get a breath. My lungs compressed as I fought against the thing on my leg. I needed my cane to whack at it, but I'd lost it.

I kicked at it with my other foot as the rope tugged me against the current. With a quick thrust, I popped out of the water long enough to get a breath, only to get dragged back in. Hands scrambled across my body but didn't find purchase.

I splashed and struggled. It was shallower here, helping me to kick against the riverbed with my free leg.

Whatever was holding on to me didn't want to let me go. It tugged and tugged. What was that thing?

Kicking it didn't work, so I reached down and tried to pry it off with my fingers. The beast was thick and slimy. When yanking it off didn't work, I punched at it. The thing would not let go, and no matter how much my rope was pulled, the creature moved me farther from where Nikon must be trying to take me.

Hands grasped me from behind, under my arms, and yanked me up. The air hit with a shock, but I welcomed it into my lungs.

"What are you stuck on?" Nikon attempted to jerk me away from the beast.

"Animal," I coughed out. "Left leg."

He swore and pulled harder.

I gritted my teeth against the pain. If they kept this up, I'd be ripped in two. I gave a hard kick to the thing on my leg. It finally loosened enough that Nikon and I went flying backward. I landed with a splash back in the river.

Nikon! Tewy! Where were they?

There was no tugging on my rope. Nothing to let me know they were all right. I bobbed to the surface, gasping for breath. I pushed my legs the opposite direction, finding several rocks between my feet. Sand would have been better to let me sink into a bit.

I found the rope at my waist that was attempting to jerk me back into the water. It tried to shove me back down. Nikon was on the end of that rope with much power behind him. No matter what, I couldn't move from this spot. We'd never make it if I fell.

The weight around my midsection grew. I pulled on the rope with what little might I had, shoving myself backward. There was splashing and sputtering. Nikon? It wasn't small enough to be Tewy.

Some of the strain on my waist eased, but not my heart. "Nikon?"

A cough responded.

"Where's Tewy?"

There was no reply.

The cold swirled around me, trying to bring me down with it for far too long, but I stood my ground. After an indeterminable amount of time, Nikon said, "I've got him. We're going to the closest land."

Relief crashed through me, but there wasn't time to enjoy it. We were still in danger.

There was a pressure at my waist, and I followed it, trudging through the water. I carefully placed each step, taking the time to make certain I was as grounded as I could be before moving on to the next. I didn't want to go down again. Didn't want to take Nikon or Tewy with me. I wanted to get away from whatever that creature was that had wrapped around me. More than that, I wanted out of the river.

The water receded, going to my thigh, then my knee and shins before finally landing on my ankle. I couldn't go a step farther. Nikon must have agreed because there was no more tugging at my waist, the rope not straining even though we were close to each other.

"Tewy?" The word came out cracked.

"Give me a second." Nikon's words were breathless.

I clenched my fists, trying not to wave my arms about. What was happening with them? I had to know. I couldn't stand by and do nothing, though I didn't want to make things worse either. Better to act than to stand there.

Feeling for the rope, I found it and followed it a short ways until I ran into a warm mass. "How can I help?"

"Get some sand." Nikon's reply was curt.

Not good. I bent to grab a handful of the gunk between the rocks even as my mind spun. If Tewy needed magic, it must be serious. Especially when my little monkey wasn't making a noise. But would magic save him? It hadn't for me.

I held out the handful of sand. Nikon took it from me. Not knowing what else to do, I scooped up another batch and held it out. I strained for any inkling of a sound that would indicate Tewy was alive and well. I couldn't handle life without him. He was my best friend. My chest tightened just thinking about it, making me wonder what I could do to speed up the healing process.

The more time that went by, the more strangled my breaths came out. I couldn't lose him. Not in this moment. Not like this.

"His heart is beating now," Nikon said.

"Now?"

He didn't respond except to take more sand from me.

I got more, hoping Tewy would be all right, that he would survive this. There was a strange cough followed by a feeble but angry hoot. "Tewy."

Sinking to my knees in relief, all I could think of was that Nikon had saved us both. I was forever indebted to him. I didn't know how to pay him back, but it would happen. I'd make certain of it.

"He's weak, but alive, obviously. The magic of the sand brought him back." Nikon's voice was at my level, easier to hear even though there was still a faint roar of water. "Do you want to hold him?"

"Please." I held my arms out and a wet monkey was placed in them, though he hung outside my arms, bigger than I could carry in his weakened state. It wasn't as nice as soft fur, but at this moment, he felt like silk, though he did smell like wet animal. I bent my head over him, and a little monkey hand touched my cheek. His hand left almost as soon as it came, but the reassurance was what I needed.

Tewy gave a sluggish whoop. I said, "I've never been so grateful to hear you make noise before. Don't you ever scare me like that again."

"Speaking of scaring people," Nikon said, "you did a good job yourself. What happened?"

"The first time, I slipped, and the second time I was pulled under by some creature. I don't know what." I plopped back onto my behind, not caring that I was still in the river. I was soaked anyway; a little more water wouldn't make much of a difference. "I don't know that I'll be able to continue on right away."

"We'll give it at least until tomorrow. We should be safer now that we're on this side of the chasm."

"I am never going through it again."

"That I'd agree with."

CHAPTER TWELVE

I t took us two days to recover, during which time we all did little except sleep. By the second afternoon, I heard branches snapping constantly. "Are the people chasing you or the sphinx around? Or animals?"

"Animals. Some type of lizard, snakes, ferrets. There's a lot going on out here."

"Why so many when there's so few on the other side of the chasm?"

"Good question. I don't know exactly. Maybe it's because they've never figured a way across the depths and river."

"It would explain why they never bothered me at my house." Though I had fought off what I thought was a beaver once. How had the monkeys gotten to my side? Perhaps they were there from before the chasm?

"Are you ready? There's a scorpion nearby."

I squeaked. "Where?"

"It's some distance off. We should be fine. Plus, I don't think we're being chased by those people any longer but in case they find our trail, I don't want to linger too long."

I was all too glad to get out of there. After putting everything back in my pack that I'd thankfully held onto despite what we'd been through, I stood and said, "Lead the way."

"It's going to be harder without your cane. I'm sorry we lost it."

"I'll manage." Though I wish I still had it. Not having it was strange after it had accompanied me most of my blind life.

He gave my hand a squeeze, keeping a tight hold. "I'll figure something out for you. Maybe even something you can fight with."

"Thank you." I gave him a squeeze back.

I reached forward, grabbing his elbow, the position I was getting used to. "I'll keep a better eye out for things than I did before."

"I'd appreciate that." There was a smile in my words, but I didn't let it out full-fledged. "Tewy, shoulder." I waited, and nothing happened. "Tewy, shoulder."

"He jumped on mine." Nikon's voice was small.

I sniffed. "At least he's not so weak."

"That's true. If it makes you feel better, he keeps pulling my hair."

I chuckled. "Sounds like he's back to his usual self."

Nikon went forward, and I followed, taking extra care to pay attention to how he was moving. "He flung bugs at me this morning while I was trying to sleep."

Glad I'd been spared, but not wanting to tell Nikon, I said, "Sorry. That's never fun."

"Does he do things like that often?"

"Too much, I'm afraid." The sand zipped heat through my feet, making me wish we were still walking in the water. My clothes were stiff, if not the ones I'd fallen in the river in. Nikon couldn't say the same thing. He had nothing to change into.

Our food had mostly been ruined. I growled at myself for thinking of that. We'd tried to salvage what we could, but only so much could be saved. It was a concern, one I didn't want to dwell on. We could always get fish from the river, and Nikon said he knew how to gather food. I'd have to trust that when we ran all the way out.

Despite the nearness of the cities compared to where we'd left my home, we still had some distance to travel. "When do you think we'll arrive in Itpy?"

"Since we have to skirt around Kenti first, it will take longer. I'm trying to decide if we should continue on through the river or go around into the desert."

"What's wrong with staying in the river?" That was the way I thought he was going to go.

"Too many people, I fear. They'll remember us walking through, not doing chores or relaxing like the others."

"And that's bad because if anyone asks, like the people chasing us, they'll tell them what they've seen, and they'll know where we're going."

"Exactly," he said. "How do you feel about going through the desert?"

That was a good question. "I've always heard how threatening it is. More dangerous than dealing with crocodiles in the river? Probably."

"But less dangerous than dealing with those chasing us."

It felt as if we were getting nowhere. "There are too many things you're still keeping from me for me to help make a good decision."

"There's a big boulder in our path. I'm going to help you over it because it's too large to go around it." He did just that, helping me step up onto a hard surface, different than having my feet slip in the sand. "I want you to extend a little more trust in me, and go with me around the city, through the desert."

"What if the sphinx follows us?"

"That could happen, though I think we safely left her on the other side of the chasm."

I continued as if he hadn't said anything, trying to ignore the fact that sphinxes could fly. "What if there are snakes or jackals or lions? There are so many things out there that could be deadly, do you really think being chased is worse?"

"I do."

I sighed. The journey would take much longer if we had to go around. I didn't want to go through such a nasty area unable to protect myself, but what other option did we have? "You'll be separated from your magical sand."

"Which is another thing they won't be expecting. She'll believe I won't leave it. We'll have more time to hide if we do this."

I knew he liked using the magic for his wound, but I didn't know he was so attached to it. What was more, the fact the mystery woman knew meant the two were more familiar with each other than I thought. "Let's go for it then. I don't know how it's going to turn out, but we might as well go full-fledged." And I hoped neither of us lived to regret that choice.

"Good. I'll make it happen. We're going to walk toward the sunrise and to the north. We'll have to skirt wide around the Kenti, but it will be worth it."

East toward the sunrise and north, definitely toward the desert heading away from the river. I could perhaps figure out where the sun was coming from in the mornings and evenings, and make my way myself if I had to, but it'd be tricky, unreliable going, and I wouldn't know when to turn back toward the river. I hoped it didn't come to that.

When I stayed silent, Nikon said, "I've been keeping an eye out for wood we can use for your fighting staff and cane. There's a lot of branches around these parts, but they're all too short or wobbly for helping you find your way."

That meant going longer without a cane. I'd have to bear it. "Thank you for looking."

"I wish it was enough."

As we made our way forward, it came to me how much I wanted to know more about Nikon, who he was, and what he did. He was an enigma. He wouldn't tell me what job he had, that much was clear, but perhaps I could learn about him in another way? "What's your favorite thing to do in your spare time?"

"I don't have a lot of free time."

"Well, what would you do if you did? Or what do you do with the little that you have?"

"Work, eat, and sleep—that's me. But if I did have a lot of time to myself, I'd like chariot racing."

Not what I was expecting. Then again, I didn't know what to expect. "Have you ever been?"

"A few times." There was a wistful note to his voice.

"What do you enjoy about it?"

"It's fast. The wind blows across you, tearing at you to try and take you apart, but it can't. The thrill of being first. The disappointment of being last."

"Wait, you even like the disappointment?"

"It makes me feel like I can do better next time. That I can work harder and make good things happen."

"I like that. How many times have you been?"

"Not nearly enough but a couple dozen or so. Enough to get a taste for it but not enough for me to excel."

I was certain he did better than he thought.

"What about you? What do you like to do?"

My muscles tensed. "I'm afraid I have too much free time. Or did. I spent a lot of it out on the river avoiding chores." I paused. This wasn't a thought I ever admitted, even to myself, but something pushed me to share. "When I still had my sight, I loved to read. I miss reading. My caretaker would tell me stories, but it wasn't the same as reading of those falling in love the moment they saw each other. Or of heroes rescuing their love. Adventures and fighting. It was almost magical, but without the dangers that come with it."

"You think there's danger in falling in love?"

"Don't you?"

"Why would there be? It happens the moment you see someone, unlike obscure stories of old where people had to fight for another's affections. Still don't know if I believe those rumors, but it sounds a lot riskier. What if the other person never loves you back? Now, we know that every person in love is loved back. There's a harmony. A unity."

"You sound as though you wish you were an amant." Tewy let out a round of laughter, squawking all the way through it. "Be quiet, monkey."

Nikon released a sigh loud enough to wake the entire country. "He's all right. If I'm telling the truth, yes, I think it would be nice. I saw how my parents were together. How they loved one another continually, were there for each other through everything. The older I've gotten without that, the more I've wanted to search for just the right woman. To look her in the eyes and lose myself."

My heart twisted. I wanted that, but I didn't have a chance. Not without my sight. "Have you ever gone to a kofle?" I'd gone to many parties meant specifically for odiosom, those who had not fallen in love. The lines of girls and boys switching around until everyone had looked everyone in the eye had gotten old quickly, especially when they became less and less attended from people either falling in love or giving up.

"I went when I was younger. No one wants to see an old man at a kofle."

I nudged him playfully with my free hand. "You're not an old man."

"Perhaps not to you, but for a kofle, I'm ancient. Things have changed in the last ten years. Where before, occasionally older people would attend a party, now, no one does after the age of sixteen. Yes, people still fall in love after that, but the odiosom are being shunned more and more after that age."

What a sad topic of conversation we'd fallen upon. "Where do they go? What do they do?"

"The odiosom are still the lowest working class. They stick together in their areas of town, working for the amant as much as possible. They're earning less and less wages though. It's tough to be out there and not be loved."

"What happens when one of them does become an amant?"

"They take care of their own, picking up to where they can start a new, better life, leaving everything behind. Most are only too happy to have that happen to them and join the upper class or the elite."

"And you?" I asked. "How do you feel about it?"

His fingers brushed against mine. "You don't want to hear my thoughts on it."

"Why not?"

"Because I'm like a teenager still waiting to fall in love."

I gave his elbow a squeeze. "I think we all want that."

"Look at me," he scoffed. "Moaning and complaining."

Cold soaked into my heart. "You do still have a chance, and I hope you find it."

"I'm sorry."

"Don't be. I've accepted the way my life is." Mostly.

"If I could help you get your sight back, I would. It must be so frustrating."

It was, but that didn't mean I wanted to talk about it. "What's this area like? The sand feels looser beneath the soles of my feet." And there was a sound I should have known but couldn't place. A soft, almost scratching sound. Maybe it was the grains of sand moving against each other as we walked.

"The sand is dry. We're getting far enough from the river that the water can't be seen. There's less and less foliage, and what's here is more barren. We're coming to the desert."

What waited for us there? "Are you sure you don't want to go through the river?"

"Almost positive."

"That's such a comforting answer."

He spoke with more confidence in his voice. "We'll be fine."

But it was difficult to believe as a massive growl rent the air.

CHAPTER THIRTEEN

"What was that?" My words came out calm and rational, though I felt anything but.

"I don't know. I don't see anything around us." He sounded just as rational, making me wonder if he truly felt that way or was trying to keep calm for my benefit.

He moved us around in a circle, I assumed so he could look at everything that surrounded us. It was frustrating not knowing what was going on for certain. I wanted to ask him what we were doing but didn't want to help whatever it was that had growled find us any sooner.

A soft snick of metal reached me. I whispered, "What's that noise?"

"Just drawing my sword. I still don't see anything."

"Are you left-handed?"

"Random time to ask, but yes."

Made sense, since he always put me on his right. He was always prepared to draw his weapon if need be. The muscles of his arm tightened beneath my grip. He was tensing up for a fight for which I could only be in the way. I started to pull my hand away, but before I could do so, he said, "Don't."

I froze, hand halfway on, halfway off his elbow. There was a stillness to the air, a quiet that had me wondering what was going on.

All my senses felt wiped except for the softness of Nikon's skin. Everything else was blocked. Of course, my sight was gone, but I heard nothing. There wasn't a scent on the air or a taste of anything. Whatever was coming held a sense of wondering fear.

Nikon turned us around in a circle again, this time more slowly. I sank into the sand, getting grains between my toes as the sand made that scratching sound.

Just as Nikon stopped moving and tensed all the way up, Tewy screeched, filling the air with fear.

I couldn't wait to ask any longer. "What is it?"

"The sphinx." His tone was even.

"Same one as last time?"

"I believe so."

How did it get here? We'd gone through the river, and I couldn't see a mighty sphinx lowering itself to do what we had. It must have flown over the chasm to find us. "How far away is it?"

"Not so far away that I can't hear you speaking about me," the deep, female's voice said.

That was definitely her. I wouldn't forget what she sounded like, not ever.

"Get away from here," Nikon said as he moved away.

I let him go. He'd need full control of his entire body and not to be slowed down by me if it came down to a fight.

"Cassandra has yet to answer my question," the sphinx said.

I opened my mouth to say I didn't know, when Nikon shouted, "Don't reply. She'll kill you if you answer wrong."

"Only too true," she said. "But she'll have to answer sooner or later. Today, it sounds like later." There was a rush of air then hot breath on the back of my neck with a stench of rotten meat. The sphinx whispered, "The man will not always be here to protect you. Two chances left."

94

A snick of metal sounded. Nikon hollered, but the hot breath was gone.

He grabbed my arm. "Did she hurt you?"

"No. I'm fine." But she knew my name. It was hard enough that she had found me, but worse that she acted as if she was acquainted with me.

After he let go, there was a soft rasp of sand grains moving against each other as he paced around me. "I don't know how she followed us here. We should be safe when we get to Itpy."

"But we can't enter the city when it's walled, without alerting the soldiers—which you seem reluctant to do."

"It does change my plans. I can't leave you alone like I intended while I make arrangements for us. We'll figure something out." He gave me his elbow. "Let's walk while we decide. We've got a ways to go yet, and we shouldn't stay here where she found us. Not that it seems to matter."

She did find us easily enough. As we continued our journey, I asked, "Do you think the woman chasing us will find us as easily as the sphinx?"

"No. She's good, but not that good. We'll be safe."

"Are you worried about leaving tracks in the sand?"

"There'll be a storm soon enough. I just hope we're not out in it."

As did I. Sandstorms were legendary, sometimes even hitting the cities, though not as bad as they said it was in the desert.

We continued on some distance when the heat finally started to wane. It wasn't long after that when Nikon stopped. "We should be fine here for the night."

Unless the sphinx returned. I sat straight in the sand, it wasn't like there was anywhere else to sit, and I pulled off my pack. I rummaged around for something to eat before remembering most of our stores had been ruined when we fell in the river. Instead, I pulled out a blanket.

"There's not much to eat out here," Nikon said. "At least we have water. Are you going to be all right?"

"Yes."

Something brushed against my hand, soft but solid. I took hold of the water skin and drank, though not too much. He might be confident that we had enough to drink, but I wasn't. Once finished, I held it out and the water skin left my hands. I spread the thin blanket, but before I could lie down, he said, "Not yet. We need to strengthen you up so you'll have more of a chance in a fight."

I held in a groan. "Can't we start that once we're in the city?"

"Nope. Do you know how to do push-ups?"

"Of course, I do."

"Then get to it."

"What? Here in the sand?"

"There's no other place. If it makes you feel better, I'll be doing them with you."

That didn't make me feel better. I turned over to my stomach anyway, and pushed myself up, letting myself down and back up again. Over and over again. It didn't take long for something to jump on my back. "Tewy?"

He hooted back at me.

I grunted and kept going, feeling the burn in my muscles.

"You're doing great," Nikon huffed out between breaths.

I didn't bother responding. My arms ached and there was no air to spare for an answer. By the time I finished working a good sweat up, the air had grown cool. The temperature was a welcome relief from the heat of the day. I rolled over, Tewy jumping off me with the action, and found my blanket to lie down on.

"You're in good shape. Better than I thought you would be."

"I exercise. There's little else to do except chores when you live alone."

"Chores, exercise, and lounging about enjoying nature. Sounds like my kind of living."

I missed it already. But, "I'm excited for a new adventure. It's hard doing the same thing over and over again every day with no interaction except for a monkey."

"I can't fathom what that must have been like."

Lonely.

I rolled over, putting my back to his voice. Morning felt like it had already come as I shut my eyes. I groaned. I hated when that happened. Receiving dreams was much better, leaving me feeling like I'd gotten some rest. Instead, there was no respite.

My arms and legs were sore, and probably would be for some time if we kept going like this. At least it felt good to move and stretch in a new way.

Despite being still chilly out, I folded up my blanket and went on a search for my pack. It was right where I left it beside my head. I put the blanket in and wished for food. My stomach was growling loud enough, and I was surprised it hadn't woken Nikon yet. Then I realized, I hadn't heard him or Tewy breathing either.

I sat still, listening for anything, but no sound came. Did I dare call out? Had the sphinx come back and eaten them in the night? It didn't seem likely since she was questioning me, but it couldn't be ruled out. If marauders had found us, they would have attacked me as well. Where did they go then?

What if I was trapped here all alone? I'd never survive. If I tried to strike out on my own, I'd likely end up going deeper into the desert. Wait. Nikon had told me how to get to the city, so I might make it there once the sun rose. There was a chance anyway.

That didn't stop the rapid pounding of my heart. I wouldn't let my fears hold me back though. Not if I could counteract them.

After pulling my skirt to my knees, I crawled around in the sand. There was nothing there but more and more grains. No sign of anything. I could be going in the wrong direction for all I knew. I'd have to chance calling out. "Nikon? Tewy?"

A familiar chirp responded back. I sat down in relief.

"Sorry." Nikon's voice was some distance away but growing closer. "I didn't think you'd wake yet. It's still early. Tewy and I were on the hunt for food. You were still within sight."

I couldn't be mad at that, even if I wanted to. They'd scared the life out of me. "Did you find anything?"

"Nope."

I let my shoulders sag, gratitude rushing through me. "Let's get going then, so we can reach the city sooner." The quicker we got to the city and established ourselves, the better able I would be to put feelers out for what had happened to Antonia. I climbed to my feet, taking my pack with me and putting it on. Tewy jumped on my shoulder, bopping my nose. "Good morning to you too."

Nikon grabbed my hand and put it on his ever-more-familiar elbow. "You know we won't be able to buy food until I can find work."

"But you should be able to find something to eat when we're closer to the river and things are growing, yes?" We walked, hurrying along as fast as I dared go.

"It's true, but not as easy or plentiful as buying it."

I laughed. "You forget you're speaking with a girl who has been on her own for years. I can barely remember what it was like to get food at the market."

"True, but easily accessible items aren't as plentiful since there are lots of people in the city who are constantly trying to find food."

Good point. But it'd be better than what we found here.

It took us two more full days of walking, exercising, and being hungry other than eating a few bits Nikon found here and there. Finally, Nikon said, "The city is in the distance."

"That's a relief. I think my stomach is trying to eat itself."

"We wouldn't want that." The muscle in his arm contracted several times.

"What's wrong?"

"How do you know anything is wrong?"

"You're tensing up."

He gently pulled my hand off of him. "It's hard to hide anything when you read me so well."

"Then don't hide anything. Besides, most people would be able to read your expressions and body language. I can't do that, so I have to rely on what I can do."

"I suppose it's only fair," he said. "I'm debating whether I should leave you here or take you with me when I go for food. I hate to abandon you when the sphinx or anyone else could come by."

"Not to mention marauders." I shivered.

"Yes, them too. There are lots of dangers really. But taking you with me may be just as hazardous. We don't know how people are going to react to the fact you're blind. I don't want anything bad to happen to you because I kept you at my side. Someone could simply be mean or they may turn you in to the warriors."

"It is a problem." One I'd tried not to consider.

"Why don't you decide? It's your life. You're a grown woman. You should make the choice."

"You just want to blame me when it goes wrong."

My monkey started laughing from nearby.

"Shut up, Tewy," Nikon and I said at the same time.

Nikon said, "I don't, I want you to have a say."

I grumbled. This wasn't something I wanted a say in. Whatever choice I made would be the wrong one. Neither were good options, but I couldn't think of anything better. "You should leave me here. You'll go faster without me."

"And be wanting to hurry back to make sure you're not in danger. I'd give you a dagger, but I'm afraid someone could take it from you and do more damage than if you didn't have a weapon."

"I agree with that."

"Let's find you some shade so you can be out of the heat if nothing else." He took my fingers, and I slipped them where they belonged, between his.

We didn't have to go much farther before the air cooled. We must have come under some shade. Being out of the heat of the desert and back by the river was a welcome relief. Nikon led me farther in before stopping and saying, "There are several trees around here. I've taken you to the bottom of the biggest one. Any questions?"

Thankful he asked, I said, "No. I'll sleep under the trees while you do all the work."

"And I'll be jealous of every moment." He gave my hand a squeeze before letting it drop to my side. "You can wait there or sit and be fine. Try not to go too far so I can find you again."

"I don't think you have to worry about me wandering off."

"I suppose not. Tewy, stay here."

My monkey jumped on my shoulder.

"I'll be back soon." His footfalls receded until I couldn't hear them any longer.

I wanted to change my mind, to hurry and go with him, but it was just as well I didn't. I would slow him down like I said and give him more to worry about. This was for the best.

Once I sat, Tewy jumped in my lap. I tried to ignore the feeling of not knowing anything around me. It stuck out more than it ever had before. It was like when Nikon had left me alone the first night and the sphinx came. Except then, I was exhausted. I wished I was now, instead of fighting the unknown. I should have asked him more questions about the area before he left. He'd given me plenty of time.

Which led me to another thought. If he managed to find work, I would be stuck out here all alone until he'd earned enough to find us a place to stay. What would I do with my time until I could get some yarn? I couldn't sit around all day. Not only would I be bored out of my mind, but I wouldn't stay in as good shape. Plus, I'd be vulnerable to the sphinx and those chasing Nikon. It wasn't ideal.

The more I thought about it, the more worries swirled

through me. I petted Tewy, trying to think of a way around it, but nothing came to mind. "What am I going to do?"

He responded with his normal chittering.

"Do you think I'll be able to find Antonia? I don't even know where to start." I sighed, running my fingers through the coarse grains of sand next to me. "We'll figure something out."

Tewy gave a hoot.

"Thank you for always being here. I wish you could talk though. It'd make things so much easier."

I stayed there, petting Tewy, until we curled up and fell asleep.

I woke to someone prodding my thigh. I rolled my shoulders, letting the kinks out of it. "You're back."

"Only for you." That was not Nikon's voice.

CHAPTER FOURTEEN

"Who are you? What are you doing here?" Panic clawed its way up my throat, but I tried to keep it out of my words.

"Too dark for you to see our lovely faces?" another male voice said with nasal tones. "We can change that soon enough. Come on, get up. We're going."

"Going where?" I didn't budge from my spot, though the menace in his tone made my hands shake around Tewy. He was still breathing deeply, probably asleep.

"Doesn't matter," the first man said, his words harsh. "Get up."

I didn't know what weapons they had. Didn't know how capable they were. It wasn't a good idea for me to ignore them. Neither was it good for me to go with them.

Something connected with my back so hard, I cried out. Tewy screeched, flying from my lap.

"Look at this," Nasal Man said. "She's got a monkey."

"Don't care. She's coming with us. The monkey stays."

"Tewy, get Nikon." It was all I could think of that might possibly save me.

"Who's Tewy and Nikon?" the second man said.

"Doesn't matter." To them it didn't. But to me, it could be the only thing to save my life—or save me from whatever they were taking me to. The only hope I had.

I should have gone with Nikon.

A hand gripped around my upper arm, yanking me to my feet. I stumbled, almost going down again, but the man holding on to me didn't let me fall. It would have been preferable.

"What's wrong with you?" Harsh Man said. "Get moving."

"I'll yell for help if you don't let me go." Anything to get away from them.

All I got was a laugh in response.

Apparently, either no one was out here who cared or there was no one else in hearing distance. Maybe I could stall. "What do you plan to do with me?"

He shoved me forward, keeping his hand clenched around my arm instead of answering. I tried to go the direction he went, but only going by subtle feels left me steering off track and tripping.

"What's your problem? We've got to get out of here. Move it."

They were in a hurry to go. That was good information. If I could slow them down, perhaps I'd have a chance. There was no sign of a weapon yet. I could do this.

I flung myself backward into the man who seemed to be in charge. His grip on me loosened for a second, enough for me to lurch forward. He mumbled a curse and fingers clawed at my back and shoulders. I'd fallen on my hands and knees and tried to crawl away. Before I got far, my pack yanked me back.

"I don't think so, girly," Harsh Man said.

"She's feisty," Nasal Man replied.

"I can see that. Get down here and help me." Ooh, he sounded mad.

Hands gripped me from both sides, pulling me back toward my enemies. I screamed. Another hand clamped around my mouth, and he hauled me up. His rough skin smelled of rotten fish.

"No more fighting or this goes in your belly." The first man must have been holding a weapon up, but of course, I couldn't tell.

Despite that, though, the threat scared me enough to make me comply. I didn't know what plans they had for me, and though I didn't want to find out, it was either that or be gutted.

We trudged on, me trying carefully to follow where they were going. It should be night, with the air so cool. How long had Nikon been gone? Was he going to be back soon? Was there any chance of him rescuing me?

As much as I wanted it to be so, the more steps we took, the more fear stabbed with each beat of my heart. This wasn't going to end well.

As we went, the unfamiliar world was like walking out into the vast unknown where at any moment, the ground could drop from under me or something could loom in my path. It hadn't bothered me much when Nikon led me, but with these people, it was entirely different.

A faint noise of people talking shimmered through the air, though I couldn't make out what they were saying and it was muffled as if blocked by something. Would calling for help make a difference? Or would those people turn me in to the Reding as soon as they realized I was blind? Perhaps that was what these men would do once they found out I couldn't see, but until then, it seemed like I might have more of a chance with them than the Reding.

Whatever they planned for me couldn't be good, though. Maybe I was better off taking my chances. I opened my mouth to call for help. The hand clamped back over my lips.

"Don't go doing that," the first man said. "You let anyone know we have you at knifepoint and we'll gut you. You don't want to go and cost us money like that, do you?"

A sharp line of cold metal bit into the side of my face. A knife or dagger, maybe.

I closed my eyes tight, wishing I had gone with Nikon and

never let myself get into this mess. Too late for that, I pressed forward at the hand's insistence, leaning away from the metal. Wherever we were going, it was closer to the voices. More sounds were coming to me. Creaking. Carts being pushed, maybe, the cacophony of sounds that only a bustling city can produce.

Were people getting ready to go to work? It must have been early morning, before customers were out, but the workers were getting ready for them. That was my guess anyway.

There wasn't more time to think about it because the men took their hands off me and shoved me. The first man said, "Climb."

Climb what? I reached my hand out in front of me but didn't feel anything. No wooden ladder like I had expected.

"What's your problem? Get up there before I show you how good I am with this knife."

Nice to know what type of weapon he had. Though if he killed me he'd lose out on money from selling me, and maybe he'd be reluctant to use it. I couldn't count on it though.

I took a tentative step, arm still outstretched, searching for what I was supposed to climb.

The man behind me growled. A hand shoved me. I rushed forward against my will until I smacked against thin pieces going up and down the length of my body. I grabbed hold of it, feeling the hard wood beneath my skin. It was my ladder.

Trying not to waste time, but not wanting to fall either, I felt my way around the ladder and took a rung. Two steps up, I was doing all right but wondering what I was going to find at the top when there was a gagging noise.

The rung dug into the middle of my foot as I hung there. Metal clanged against metal. What was going on? Whatever it was, it didn't sound like something I wanted to be near. Then again, I didn't want to keep climbing a ladder that led to who knew where. Unable to go forward or backward, I held tight.

The sounds grew closer along with gasps for air. Someone was fighting—with my abductors, hopefully. I didn't want to go back with them. Maybe it was Nikon? I didn't dare call out and distract him if he was the one fighting.

They came closer and closer. A jolt hit the ladder. Luckily, I was holding tight enough that I stayed on. Unluckily, it leaned to the side. I tried to throw my body weight to the other side to bring it back where it was, but the ladder crashed to the ground, taking me with it.

Sand crept in everywhere as the right side of my body ached. I disentangled myself from the ladder and jumped to my feet despite the pain. I couldn't be in a vulnerable position when whatever was happening finished.

From there, I felt around until I found the wall. I put my back to it, the noise of the fight continuing. The stone was cool, digging into me as I pressed into it. If this wasn't Nikon, I should try to get away. If it was, I should stay put. What would be the best thing to do?

Before I could decide, there was a thunk and Nikon said, "Are you hurt?"

"No." I slumped in relief but stayed near the wall since I didn't know what was going on. "How did you find me?"

"Tewy. We shouldn't linger."

I reached out to find his familiar elbow. "Where does the ladder lead?"

"Over the city wall."

"Maybe we should climb the ladder and get into the city. It'd be a way around the warriors at the front gate."

"I don't think we want to go to that part of town."

He had a point. If that was where those men were taking me, it probably wasn't anywhere good. And he must know the city better than I expected. "How about the ladder? Can we take it for later?"

"Too big." He guided me away from the wall.

I let him take me some distance before asking, "What

happened? Did you find something to eat? How did Tewy show you where I was?"

"We're going to where I left the food right now. It was where you were. When I couldn't find you and Tewy tried to take me away, I dropped it and followed him. I don't know how he knew where you were, but he led me right to those men. I followed you for a little ways before you came to the wall. Once you were safe climbing, I attacked."

"What happened to them?" Not that I wanted anything good for them, but I didn't want them dead either.

"They'll come around, which is why we're not going to linger over our packs. I discovered another place where you can wait for the day if you want to stay outside the city, or we can chance you coming in with me."

I still wasn't certain of either option. Neither sounded viable.

We stopped, and before I could ask, Nikon said, "Just grabbing the stuff. Hold on." He let go and rustling met my ears. "I'm going to put what wouldn't fit into my pack in yours. Can you wait a while longer to eat?"

"If it means staying safe."

My pack shifted around as he must have been putting things in. Moments later, my hand was back on his arm, and we hustled away.

We went some distance, much longer than I'd traveled with those marauders. The day grew hot, burning at my skin. When it cooled a little, and we stopped, I asked, "Are we here?"

"Just about. There's some dense foliage. I don't think anyone will be looking for us here."

I'd thought that about the last place we'd found, and look what had happened.

"Duck your head or you'll hit a limb."

I did as Nikon asked.

"Good. A few more steps and you can relax."

It didn't take much longer for me to be sitting next to him, munching on plums. "You found quite the bounty of goods."

"Enough for a little while at least, but no protein. I need to get fishing, but there's still the problem of cooking it. We'll be better set up in a few weeks."

"We'll manage until then."

"Have you decided what you want to do? Come with me or stay here?" He asked what I wasn't ready to talk about yet.

"You need to head back already? Didn't you work all night?"

"I did outside the city, but there's a lot that needs done, and not enough food to forage around the city. I need to find a job in town. Would you like to come or not?"

"I don't know. I see disadvantages to both. After those men took me though, I'm inclined to go with you. But then again, if there's any problems, we won't know what we're getting into and the warriors might end up taking me to the Reding."

"It's a difficult decision. I'll stand by whatever you choose."

"Thank you." Antonia had never been like that. She'd always bossed me around. If I'd made a choice on my own, it usually left her peeved with me. It was because she was trying to take care of me, I knew that. But it didn't change the fact it was nice to have my decisions respected. I was a grown adult, even if I'd been isolated for most of those adult years.

After we'd finished eating our fill of plums, Nikon said, "I need to go into Itpy now and see if there is any work I can do. Have you made your decision?" When I didn't respond, he added, "You can always stay here and then come with me next time. Or go with me this time and stay next. It doesn't have to be permanent."

That was a valid point, but I still didn't know what to do.

"Your eyes are such a beautiful shade of brown. I always thought that someone who was blind would have their eyes look different."

I shrugged at the abrupt change of conversation. "I don't know much about my eyes or others, only that I can't use them to see any longer."

"It makes it harder to tell you're blind."

"Which is a good thing. Maybe we can use that to our advantage. It would be best if we could stick together."

He took my hand in his. "Let's go to the city."

I hoped I'd made the right choice.

CHAPTER FIFTEEN

"Remember to keep your head down and act shy," Nikon said.

"You've told me fifty times already," I countered. "I got it."

"Sorry. I'm nervous."

"Me too."

He patted the hand that was on his elbow, and we continued forward. I hoped it didn't look too odd to others that he was leading me. Next to going back to the ladder with the marauders, there was no other way into the city except by one of their checkpoints with breaks in the walls. Most cities didn't have these, but Itpy did. Defenses from long ago when the cities had been at war, people said. Whether or not that was the case, warriors still kept an eye on those coming and going.

The thud and patter of other footsteps grew more numerous. Someone bumped my right. I pulled myself in closer to Nikon.

"You're going too slow," a man from behind yelled. "Get a move on. We've got things to do."

Perfect. I was restricting Nikon, and the citizens didn't want anything to do with it. Nikon increased our pace and I put all my trust in him as we walked rapidly. It would be so easy to trip and fall at this speed, or run into someone. I didn't want to give myself away, but it was better to go the same speed as the others. I had to trust him, which I did, I thought. It was simply hard to do so in a different setting.

The people pressed in closer, cramming me against Nikon. I clung to him as I kept my head down.

"What's her problem?" a high-pitched female voice asked.

We came to a stop. Nikon said, "My sister's shy."

Even though the plan all along was to have me be his sister, I worked hard not to bristle under the comment. It wasn't clear which part I liked the least, but neither made me very happy.

"What are you in town for?"

Questions. This couldn't be good. My palms grew sweaty.

"Heard there were some odiosom jobs open this way." Nikon sounded nonchalant, as if he did this every day.

It was good I wasn't in charge of talking. I would have muddled everything up.

"Go to the northwest district. You'll find something there."

Not what I expected at all.

"Tell your sister she'd better hurry up and stop slowing everyone down," the woman said. "Get going."

That was more of what I'd expected.

"Yes, ma'am."

Nikon led me on and the crush of bodies stopped flowing around me. The footfalls continued, people talking and carrying on, but they seemed to be less crowded, as if they were going in different directions or the street had opened up.

I'd never been to Itpy before. Nikon said he had, and he tried to explain to me what the city would be like, but I'd had a difficult time following along when I was so concerned about getting past the guards.

The path was hard beneath my feet, with round bumps. A cobblestone street, I thought. It took a while to move through the city, the sound ebbing of people moving and talking and flowing like a river. The smell of people crammed together made me realize I'd lose out on nature in the route I was taking. I'd miss it if we had to stay here long. But at least we'd be going outside of the wall after we did what was needed today.

When the noise grew quiet, though not altogether gone, and the street turned to hard-packed dirt, I asked Nikon, "Where are we?"

"We're almost to the northwest area of the city where she said I could find a job."

That was good. But what was I supposed to do while he looked for work? I hadn't thought this through very well. I would have been better prepared to stay outside and hope against hope that no one found me. I almost asked about my caretaker but held back. It wasn't the time. "Is there some place I could stay that's out of the way?"

The muscles in his arm tightened, but his voice remained calm. "I don't know. I wish I'd spent more time in Itpy. It would have come in useful about now. Let's see what it looks like up ahead. We're about to turn a corner, and I believe there's going to be someone who knows about what's available. I hope."

We turned a corner as promised, and the street was hard beneath my feet. The light breeze carried no nearby words or steps with it, though some could still be heard in the distance. It sounded deserted. I wanted to ask Nikon if it was but didn't dare. If there were people around, they'd be able to tell something was off by me asking.

We changed to a purposeful stride, making me wonder if he had some destination in mind. I kept my head down like he asked. I would have been looking at the stones we walked on if I had sight. Tewy was silent, but kept playing with my hair, twirling it around.

"What are you doing in this part of town?" A man's voice was curt. Angry.

Tewy squawked back just as mad from Nikon's shoulder.

"Looking for something," Nikon responded.

"Why, do you and your wife need something?"

"This is my sister." He grabbed my hand and pulled it up, moving our hands around before letting them relax again. "We're looking to support ourselves. Find a place to live up here. That sort of thing."

There was a shuffle and the slap of sandals on stone coming toward us.

"My mistake." The man's voice was soft now. An amiable tone. "Thought you were amant for a moment there. I couldn't see if you had markings."

That's right. Amant gained a black, raised band of skin at the base of their pointer fingers when they fell in love. It rose up and colored the moment a couple's gazes met. That was what Nikon must have been showing this person, that my finger wasn't marked.

The man continued, "Looking for work and a place to stay, you say?"

"Yes, sir."

"Don't *sir* me. My name's Leo. I help the odiosom around these parts. Where I can, anyway."

"Nikon, and my sister is Cassandra. She's shy. The monkey here keeps her company."

I tried not to let my hackles rise. After being alone so long, I couldn't imagine not speaking with others, but I couldn't say anything and have his attention on me. That could cause him to find out I was blind and have him lead the warriors right to me. No, that wouldn't do at all.

"We have some odds and ends jobs to complete for the amant that we could have you do, Nikon," Leo said. "Do you have any skills, Cassandra?"

I opened my mouth to speak, but Nikon beat me to it. "She's good at crocheting, but I'd like to find somewhere safe for her to be. Alone if possible. She's skittish around others."

I wanted to conk him over the head. It was the best and safest course of action though. Just hard to remember that when all I wanted to do was get back into the world.

"Hmm. Well there is a house that's vacated at the moment. You may need to share it with others in the future though. It's big enough for everyone, mind you, but I know some folks don't like sharing."

"What do you think, Cassandra?" Nikon asked—finally.

"It's fine." I tried to keep my response demure. It was much better than fine, more than I could have hoped for.

"It's settled then," Leo said. "Let's get Cassandra there while we discuss further what needs to be done."

Nikon moved to the side and I followed his lead. He set a faster pace than I would have liked, but he was probably following Leo, leaving little choice. I attempted to keep my steps steady, following Nikon as he moved and shifted. My toe caught on a stone that jutted out, but after a little stumble, I righted myself.

It smelled different here, a scent I couldn't recognize. The city itself, maybe? And a hint of sewer. The streets stayed quiet. I probably shouldn't have said anything, but couldn't help myself. "Where is everyone?"

Nikon didn't elbow me. That was a good sign.

"Work. There's rarely anyone around during the day," Leo said.

"Why are you out then?" Nikon asked.

"Because I'm old and gruff and no one likes me."

I chuckled. He seemed the opposite of all those things, though I supposed he could be old.

"I like your sister, Nikon. She seems like a good sort."

I grinned harder but kept my words to myself.

We didn't go much farther before we stopped, and something, a door or box, creaked open.

Leo said, "Welcome to your new home."

A door then.

Nikon guided me up the single step through the entrance. A

musty scent met my nose, making me sneeze as I pretended to look around. He stood behind me as we went down what I thought was a hallway by the way the air pressed on me and the sounds of our footsteps stayed close. Nikon's hands were on my shoulders, directing me forward, but I reached out as I went until I hit a wall on both sides of me. I was right. A hallway.

"Back there to your left," Leo said, the sound of his voice filling a bigger space than the hall, "was the front living area. This is the kitchen. There's an outhouse out back and everyone here gets water from the river. The amant don't allow it to be pumped in for us odiosom."

The air seemed to move more, and Nikon came up beside me, making me think of a bigger room.

Leo continued. "There's four bedrooms on the second floor. The roof isn't much but has some nice air in the mornings. It's small."

"It's perfect." I'd have this place smelling fresher in no time with some cleaning and cooking.

"Are you blind?" Leo's words suddenly sliced into my happiness with sharp finality.

What had given me away? How long had he suspected? Had one of my actions alerted him? What had I been thinking? I didn't know, but I was ready to run.

CHAPTER SIXTEEN

"What makes you say that?" Nikon asked, stepping closer to me as I lowered my head.

"I'm not stupid." The hard edge was back in Leo's words. "I won't turn Cassandra in if she is, but I have to be familiar with these things to know how best to assist you."

I pushed Nikon aside, surprised he let me. "How would you do that?"

"There's not much I can do, but I can try to keep the warriors away from you." His tone calmed somewhat. "It's a little thing that I can't promise, but if you're honest with me, I'll try."

"I am blind." I kept the words soft but firm.

"Thought so. Sorry you have to deal with others looking for you. I won't risk myself, but I'll do what I can to keep the warriors away. You'd be best staying inside though."

I sighed. "I was planning on it. Why do they have such a force coming after the blind?"

"Why do the amant do anything they do? I can find you some company you can trust, if you like."

"That would be most kind of you." I already dreamed of having someone else to speak with. Would they be more curt like Antonia or more patient like Nikon? Well, patient most of the time. They'd probably fall somewhere in the middle. I wasn't the easiest person to be around. I understood that.

"I'll leave you to settle in then," Leo said. "Nikon, go ahead and take the rest of the afternoon off. There's not much time anyway once we get there. Come where you found me earlier tomorrow morning, and I'll get you to work. Most arrive about dawn."

At least I wouldn't have to get up that early. I hadn't been sleeping in much lately anyway, though. "Is there somewhere close, maybe an odiosom that sells yarn?" I wanted to get on making things to sell if I could.

"I'll show Nikon where he can purchase some for you tomorrow. We'll also discuss rent."

"Thank you, Leo. For everything." And I hoped payment would be something we could handle, or else we'd be back out roaming the streets, looking for a place to live.

"Yes," Nikon said. "Thank you."

"It's what we do. Must stick together, us unloved."

There was a creak, a soft plunk of footsteps, and then a door shutting. We were alone. In our new house.

"I can't believe our good luck," I said.

"Me either. Want to explore the kitchen or upstairs first?" Nikon asked.

"The kitchen since we're here. I can find my own way though, thank you. Just let me know if I'm going to run into anything that will hurt."

"Everything here looks fine."

I gave his arm a squeeze of appreciation and stepped away from him. I missed my cane, but things would be all right without it. Reaching out and taking cautious steps on the hard-packed dirt, I found the room was smaller than I expected. There was a counter space off to one side with cupboards above it, a washbasin on one end, and a stove-top oven fireplace next to that. The other side of the room contained a table with four chairs. I mapped out the entire room, counting as I went, trying to remember all the numbers.

When I didn't run into Nikon, I asked, "Where are you?"

"I stepped into the hall. I didn't want to get in your way."

"Thank you. Should we go see what's upstairs?"

"Let's. Do you want me to guide you again, lead you with my voice, or are you going to feel your way around?"

"I'll feel. It helps me get a sense of the layout of the area better."

"All right. Here we go." His voice became muffled and farther away as he must have gone down the hall.

I followed him, the numbers in my head following my path. We went back by the front living area, which I would explore later, my hand continuing to pat the wall until it was gone. I moved over to find steps, bumping my toes against the first one. Leo had said there was an upstairs, but I hadn't thought much about it. It'd been a while since I'd been upstairs—since I'd lost my eyesight.

My throat tightened at the sudden thought. I wouldn't let it get to me; it wasn't the moment for it. I could deal with this later. Or better yet, not at all. I'd thought about it enough through the last several years, and didn't need to worry over it more.

I went up fourteen steps, the musty smell growing ever stronger. I almost expected to suddenly see, since the last time I'd done this, I'd had sight. Or maybe it was because I was thinking about it so much. Either way, I was disappointed.

"There are rooms off to your right," Nikon said. "Stairs going up on the left to the roof."

I turned to my right. A big empty space was something I could explore another time.

"Two rooms on your right. Two on your left. A window is letting in light but only a little, since the house next door is close, at the end of the hall."

"Which room do you want?" I asked, not making a move forward.

"Doesn't matter. They're all the same. I'd say maybe we should both take the rooms in the back. They face the back of another house behind us. The ones in the front face the street."

"Why do you think that would matter?"

"Because we'll be less visible to the warriors from our rooms. They'll be more of a refuge. Though I guess it doesn't matter if your curtains are open."

"Right," I said. I liked that he didn't skirt away from the fact I was blind like Antonia had sometimes. "You choose. It doesn't matter to me where I'm at."

"We should have rooms next to each other for safety reasons. If you don't have an opinion, we should put you closer to the stairs and me next to the window, both rooms in the back."

"Sounds good." I used my hands to guide me to the first room and mapped it out. There was a narrow bed, better than I had back home, and a small dresser. The only other things of note were the window Nikon had mentioned and the fact that the floor was wood instead of hardened dirt like on the ground floor.

"What do you think?" Nikon asked from somewhere around the door.

"It'll do." What I really wanted were some cleaning supplies. At least a bucket and rag. But I didn't dare ask for any, not when we didn't have any money. I could live like this until he got paid.

"Good. I'm going to round up something to eat. You're welcome to join me if you'd like."

"Do we have anything besides plums?"

"A few things."

"Then I'm all for it. I'll be down in a moment." As I took my pack off, his soft footfalls receded. It felt like he was making more noise just so I could hear him, and it meant a lot that he would do that for me.

He went down the stairs, and there was a *thump, thump, thump, creak*, and the familiar weight rested on my shoulder. I petted Tewy's chest, before thinking about what I wanted to do and what

I needed to do. I wanted to eat and sleep. What I needed to do was find a way to help Nikon make money to pay for this place and our food. Plus, taxes which were certain to come now we were back in Eppla officially.

I waded through my things, taking out my blanket, change of clothes, and my hook, making sure to put the last item carefully on the dresser. Grabbing my pack with the rest of the food in it, I was ready to cook. We'd get things done, and I'd grow more used to this place. Then, I'd be able to search for Antonia and discover if anyone knew what had happened to her.

CHAPTER SEVENTEEN

The next day dragged, though I had Tewy for company while Nikon was at work. As great as he was, I wanted more. After being alone so long, it'd been a treat to have someone to speak with again. Things would be different with us being in the city. No more conversing with only my pet monkey, but with real people like Nikon. A knock on the door downstairs had me jolting upright. Nikon wouldn't knock.

I edged toward the end of my room, wondering what my best options were. The front and back doors were out since they were down there. What else? The window at the end of the hall. Not likely.

"Hello?" a woman's voice called out. She must have opened the door. "Leo sent me to see you, Cassandra."

Some of the tension left me, but not all. She knew Leo and me, that was a good sign, but I wasn't sure I was ready to be with someone besides Nikon and Tewy. What was I thinking? Just moments ago, I'd been bored. This was the perfect option. "I'm coming down."

"Meet you in the kitchen."

I thought she'd want to gather in the living area I had checked out the night before, though we would have had to sit on the floor. The room was small and had no furniture to speak of. The entire house was larger than anything I'd expected though.

Tewy jumped on my shoulder and by the time I got to the kitchen, spices met my nose. Definitely garlic and cumin. Maybe some fennel.

"Oh, you're here. Wonderful. I'm making you lunch. I hope you don't mind. I'm Hettie, by the way."

"Cassandra, but you already know that." Did she also know I was blind? If she didn't, she was about to find out. "Thank you for making lunch, but you didn't have to."

"Oh, but I love to." Enthusiasm pumped through her words.

"It smells good."

"Have a seat. I'll get you eating soon enough."

Hoping I remembered the right number of steps, I made my way toward the table. I bumped into it, leaving my right thigh hurting. Wrong number of steps then. I mentally amended the count and waited for her to say something about the incident. She went on humming away as she was presumably cooking. I pulled out a chair and sat with a smile, the wood worn smooth beneath my touch.

"So, Leo sent you?" I asked.

"He sure did." Her voice was pleasant. Friendly and sweet, though it sounded as if she was facing a wall. "Thought the two of us might get along."

"I don't mean to be rude, but don't you have a job to get to?"

"Market's closed today which means a day off for me. I work at a stall selling my food."

With how it smelled in here, she must make a lot of money.

"You have a monkey." Her voice was ecstatic and clearer. She must have turned to look at me.

"I do. Tewy here's been with me for some time."

"He's so cute."

"He's a rascal, but I love him."

She rummaged around, her voice sounding muffled again. "Not many pets around here. He'll be a hit whether or not he's a rascal."

"That'll be good for his ego." Good for making it bigger.

"There," she said. "It's ready. I hope you like it, but it's still hot so don't burn yourself."

A shuffle sounded in front of me. I hadn't reached out to see what the food was yet, so it had a chance to cool. "This smells divine."

"It's my grandmother's recipe. She's too old to make it now. I'm glad I could learn from her before she got lost inside herself. My food is the only thing that brings her around anymore, and even that's not a guarantee."

"I'm sorry."

"Don't be. Naane lived a good life. It's true I miss her, but I learned a lot from her, and when she does rouse herself, she always has interesting stories to tell. And here's a treat for the monkey." Tewy jumped off my shoulder. There was a plunk next to me and a scraping. When Hettie spoke, it was from much closer. "What about you? What's your story?"

I fisted my hands but forced myself to relax them. I wasn't sure I was ready to tell my own tale. "My brother Nikon and I decided to come here for work. Leo's been most kind."

Despite my trying to change the subject, she said, "Is it because you're blind that you had to move? Were people giving you a hard time? Were the warriors trying to catch you so you could work for the Reding and Vading?"

The male and female rulers must have been evil to force the blind to work for them. Still, I wasn't certain how to answer her. I didn't want to go into the full details of my life, especially since Nikon and I were posing as brother and sister. My story would be harder to understand with that. Yet I didn't want to drive her away by being snooty and not answering, either.

"Sorry. I ask too many questions. My sisters are always telling me to slow down and think about what I'm going to say before I say it. Of course, I never do." Despite her words, there was a happiness in her tone.

"It's fine. I don't mind really. Tell me more about you. You like to cook, and you work at the market?" I almost asked if she was odiosom but didn't want to be rude. It was likely she was if she was working at the market, unless she was an amant merchant. I didn't know if I'd trust her if that was the case. Even if Leo did, an amant would likely turn me in at first chance. I sat straighter, willing my muscles to be ready to run.

"I live with my three sisters. My parents kicked us out when each of us turned twenty without turning into an amant."

She was an odiosom then. I let myself relax. Parents chose to let their children stay until different ages, but twenty was definitely on the older side. Her parents must have had hope for her that never panned out. "How did you come to live with your grandmother? Or do you not?"

"Unfortunately, I don't." Her voice took on a sad tone for the first time. "She lives with my parents. My mother is gracious enough to let us visit once in a while, but I don't see her as often as I'd like."

"That must be hard."

"It is, but it's the way of things." Her voice cheered up again.

"Doesn't make it right." No matter how upbeat she was about it, that didn't make it any less wrong.

"No, it doesn't."

"If you don't mind me asking, why didn't your naane go with the other older people after the Govlin Wars?" I probably shouldn't have asked, not only because it was personal but because it was close to speaking of death, but I was curious to know.

"That is an interesting story." There was a scraping sound, as if she pushed her chair back or moved something. "When the elderly were being rounded up, she hid with the help of others.

For a long time after that, she didn't go out much and when she did, she dressed and used makeup to appear younger. Everyone leaves her alone now, but from the way she talks, it was a scary time."

It still was.

"There's a lot out there I don't like, with how she was treated— and now how our generation is being treated. I wish my parents had never kicked us out, and we were still with my naane. But I knew it was coming and tried to make the best of it. My parents were upfront about having to leave if we didn't fall in love. What about your parents?"

"They were kind," I hedged, if not a little unrealistic. It wasn't fair what they'd done to me, but it was for a good reason. At least they were trying. It also wasn't fair that they'd died shortly after.

"You look upset," she said. "Anything you want to talk about?"

"Not really. I'd rather eat."

"That's fine, but if you change your mind, I'm here." The thought warmed me from the inside; though she was a complete stranger, it was nice to have the option that I hadn't had before Nikon came to my home. She continued, "There's a water bowl on your right."

I put my fingers in the water bowl that I found where she said and gave them a quick rinse. I stuck my hand out to find some type of fish, by the flaky feel of it. The spices still filled the air, but it wasn't as hot as I'd expected, probably cooled during all our talking. I picked a piece up and ate it, the flavors melding on my tongue. "This is really good, even better than it smells."

"Thank you. I'm glad you like it. There's some beans to the left of the fish too."

We ate in silence, but the company was good to have. Even better, the food was delicious, better than anything I'd eaten in a long while, if ever. I wanted to ask if there was some for Nikon but didn't want her to feel bad if she hadn't made enough for him.

As she moved around the kitchen cleaning up, I said, "I don't have any money, but perhaps I could pay you another way."

"You don't need to worry about paying me. This is what I had left over from yesterday except the fish, which I caught before coming over here. I'll have to make some soon for your brother. I only caught one fish this morning, which we shared."

"I'd like to pay you back anyway. Come with me." Tewy jumped on my shoulder, chattering like he was the center of attention. He probably was.

I went down the hall, up the stairs, and to my room, grateful when I didn't bump into anything again. Footsteps followed. At least Hettie was willing to listen. I'd be able to find some way to repay her after all.

"Though I don't have any yarn," I said, going to my dresser and picking up my hook. "But I love to crochet. If I can get my hands on some yarn, the first thing I'll make is a shawl for you."

"I've never seen a hook before. I've heard about them, but they're very rare. Where did you get it? And how did you learn to crochet if you're blind?"

"Crocheting was a task I did when I could still see. After, I had to learn to do it more by feel, but it wasn't anything I couldn't handle. I make sure someone else picks colors for me, when someone is around anyway, and sorts them in a way I can find them."

"That's amazing. I'm glad you've been able to do that. If I pick up some yarn, you'd be willing to make a shawl for me?"

"Certainly. It'd be great for nights when it gets cool."

"I'll grab some when I'm at the market tomorrow. I'll bring it by on my next day off."

"Perfect."

We wandered back downstairs, lingering in the hallway by the door. She said, "It's been lovely to visit with you. I wish I could stay longer, but I'm afraid I have some errands and chores that need tending to."

"That's fine." I was tempted to ask her for a bucket and rag but decided to hold off until we could buy one ourselves. I didn't want to put her out, and she seemed like the type to do something for another even if it was to her detriment. "I'm so glad you came over, though I admit you gave me a fright when I first heard a knock on the door."

"I should have had Leo come by while Nikon was still here to let you know I was coming."

"It's not a problem. I'll be expecting it next time. I didn't think anyone was going to visit, so it came as a surprise, but a very welcome one."

"I'm hap—"

The door slammed open. Leo said, "The warriors are searching this area for any troublemakers. We have to get Cassandra out of here."

My stomach clenched. If they found me, I'd be going to the Reding and Vading for certain.

CHAPTER EIGHTEEN

The only sound was Tewy. No, that wasn't true. Off in the distance, someone was yelling—someone who would probably have loved to take me away, that or a person trying to escape the attention of the warriors just as much as I was.

A man grabbed my hand—probably Leo, since it was the person closest to the door—and propelled me toward the back of the house.

"We'll have to hide you, Cassandra. I know a place, but it won't be comfortable. Hettie, get as far from here as you can."

"But—"

He stopped her. "No arguing. Go now."

Something bumped against me, footsteps clunking down the hall followed by the soft creak of the door closing. He had said he wasn't going to stick his neck out for us, but this was doing so. Why would he care? I wanted to ask but didn't want to make him change his mind in the process.

"Sorry this had to happen on your first full day here," Leo said to me as he guided me through to the kitchen.

Tewy made a sad little noise.

"Not your fault," I said.

We reached the back of the kitchen, and there was a squeak. We were out, and a breeze hit my face that stank since we were by the outhouse. Leo stopped for a moment. To close the door, maybe? And then we were off.

He didn't lead me too fast, but quicker than I was accustomed to. I tried my best to stay with him, to trust him like I trusted Nikon. But all I could think was, what if he was taking me to the warriors and not hiding me from them? The smell grew more bearable, but still not pleasant.

"Almost there," he said, huffing for breath.

I strained for sounds of the warriors being close by yet heard nothing but our own footsteps. We stopped; a small screech and wood knocking against wood came to me.

"Will your monkey be quiet or should I take him?" Leo asked.

I didn't want to be parted from Tewy. "He'll stay silent." I hoped.

"In you go then. There are some stairs leading down to the cellar. There are lots of vegetables in there that we'll hide you in."

Probably bugs too. As long as there weren't any scorpions, sphinxes, or warriors, I could deal with a few bugs.

He led me by the hand, down the steps and to a wall the opposite side from where we'd come in. He said, "Sit down, and I'll cover you. Quickly now. I don't know how much time we have."

I obeyed, ending up next to a giant pile of something that bumped up against me. "Do these raids happen often?"

"It varies."

What had Nikon and I got ourselves into? We hadn't even had a chance to change our hair or become part of the community to help us blend in. As cold, hard things about the size of my fist and smelling of dirt were stacked against me, I wondered if Nikon was safe where he was working.

"What are these?"

"Turnips. Quiet now."

I sat there with Tewy, who jumped in my lap. It took less time than I expected for Leo to cover us.

"I'll be back when it's safe."

There was a scuffling and the door screeched again, probably closed this time, then all became silent. The potent scent of dirt clogged my nose as the dry, hard turnips pressed against me.

Tewy shivered in my arms. I tried to hold him close without shuffling around too much. I didn't want to undo all the work Leo had done and have the warriors find me. It would be all right, I kept telling myself. Everything would be fine. I'd be back to the house soon enough and with Nikon, telling him of my grand adventure. Well, not so grand, but something of an adventure.

Time ticked by. How long would it take for the warriors to come through? Would they bother looking in a cellar? What were they looking for exactly? People like me, that was expected, but that couldn't be the only thing they were trying to search out.

Tewy chirped.

"Stay quiet, boy. We have to stay safe," I whispered.

I hoped he listened. With him, I never knew if he was going to or not. He often surprised me with what he did or didn't do. I hoped it wasn't going to be one of those times.

Thuds reached me, growing louder by the second. Soon, voices were calling out. I couldn't make out the words with the turnips and door between us, but they were loud. I didn't want to think what would happen if they found me.

My thoughts dwelt on it anyway. Being dragged away, forced into slavery. I clenched my jaw to keep it from trembling. I didn't want to cry. It would give away my location.

"Catch that runaway," a man yelled.

The sounds of a scuffle came to my hiding spot. I shivered as a woman screamed.

"Please, no," a woman cried. "I've done nothing wrong."

"You didn't follow the orders of an amant."

A thwack sounded and her frantic cries stopped. What had

they done to her? And why was that considered wrong enough? I knew that we were supposed to do what an amant asked, but to capture people and hurt them over it seemed wrong. I shivered, wishing there was a way to help, but I'd only get myself in the same situation as her.

"Check in the house and that cellar," the male voice called out.

"Yes, sir," a female replied.

Moments later, a screech came, followed by the slap of sandals. Someone was in here with me. The woman who had answered, probably.

Tewy shifted in my arms. I willed him to be silent, trying to breathe as shallowly as I could. She was going to find us, either by taking the piles of turnips apart, or Leo not covering me well enough. He'd worked so fast it was possible he'd missed something. A piece of my foot or my head might be sticking out. Everything felt covered, but that didn't mean it was, not when the job had been done with turnips. If the person searching down here was doing so with a light, it would mean even more trouble.

The slap, slap, slap of the sandals came closer and closer. The sound came so near, I held my breath, afraid if I didn't, she'd hear it. The footfalls stopped. The silence was filled with someone else's breathing. Was that her or Tewy? Let it be her, I silently pleaded.

Seconds ticked by. I couldn't handle sitting there doing nothing, knowing I could be taken at any moment. To keep my mind off what was going on, I mentally went through my new house, counting steps in my head. Making a sort of layout that I could use later to remember better where I needed to walk, so I wouldn't bump into the table again. I'd have to double-check it again when I got back. If I ever returned, that was.

Why wasn't she leaving? Why was the person just standing there? My senses gave nothing away. The earthy scent and a distant sound of chaos echoing in the background were my only clues. Nothing that helped me know what calamity might be coming.

Ever so slowly, the slap, slap of footsteps receded. The door gave its screech as it closed.

Tewy shifted in my arms, but otherwise didn't make a sound. He was doing so well with this. Truth was, the way I handled it took some guts. I hadn't cried out or otherwise given myself away. I continued to stay mostly calm. I could do this.

The noises outside continued for some time before eventually fading. How long would I have to stay here? I wanted to at least get myself out from under these turnips but didn't dare in case the warriors came back.

"It's all right, Tewy. We'll be fine. Leo will come back for us when he can."

He made a little squeak back but didn't say anything further.

"I'm going to have to reward you when we get back home." Only, home was far away by the waterfall. The place we lived now was different. Unfamiliar. Full of dangers I didn't understand.

We waited and waited. The time passed slowly with no way to measure it. The dragging of the hours went on and on. I stayed as still as possible, not making a move.

The now-familiar screech came, followed by heavy but faint footfalls. They didn't sound like Leo's at all. Another warrior searching. I clasped Tewy tight, his fur the only soft thing about this place, my heart pounding in my chest. I wouldn't make a sound. Wouldn't be caught by them. We made it through the first time, I could do it a second.

Tewy tried to jump from my lap, squawking like a wild thing. He couldn't go far because of the turnips, but it didn't matter. We were going to be discovered because of his lack of control. I tried to ignore the fear stabbing at me, but it was impossible.

"Cassandra?" Nikon's voice cut through the fear encapsulating my chest.

I sighed with relief. "I'm here."

"They didn't find you. I've been so worried ever since Leo told me there was a raid. He wouldn't say where you were until it was over."

I wiggled, trying to get the turnips off of me. Nikon must have come over and helped, because the pile grew lighter faster than I expected. It didn't take long for the vegetables to be moved, and a hand enveloped mine with the callouses I associated with Nikon.

I stood, my monkey jumping away from me. "Is Tewy on your shoulder?"

"Yes."

"He seems to really like you. What happened? Are you certain it's safe?"

"We're fine now." He pulled me closer to him, turnips rolling to the side next to my feet.

My whole body shook. I didn't realize I'd been so affected. His chest moved beneath my hands, and I worked to follow his steady breathing. "I thought they had found us."

"It's just me. You're all right."

I allowed myself a moment. "Do we need to leave the cellar?"

"At some point we should go to the house. Leo said he would stop by when he could to see if you were all right."

"Did they find anyone?"

"We'll have to ask Leo. I don't know yet. I almost left work early, but Leo found me and told me if I did, both you and I would be in jeopardy. We'll have to figure out a better way to deal with raids in the future, but we managed today."

Tewy chirped proudly like he had something to do with it.

Silly monkey. "I'm ready to go whenever."

"Let's return now, then. Watch your step, there are turnips everywhere."

"I hope no one wonders why it's such a mess."

"It'll be fine. Leo said the cellar is actually his."

"He's a turnip farmer?" I asked as Nikon led me through a

rolling path of turnips, making our path precarious, but not as much as what I'd just gone through.

"No, but he has a connection to one whom he connects with someone else to sell at the market. They use his cellar as storage and he gets a cut as the middle man."

Leo had risked his life to hide me here. If any of the warriors had found me amongst his turnips, that likely would have thrown suspicion onto Leo. The man had jeopardized much for me and didn't know us that well. It was a lot to ask and he had gone above and beyond. Why? Especially when he said he wouldn't.

Did he want something from us? Or was there the faintest possibility he was actually that kind?

I climbed the stairs, the door closing after me. Nikon led me back the way I'd come before, the bustle of people talking and strolling about meeting my ears, but muffled, like they were on the other side of a building or something else between us.

It took less time to reach our new house, or at least it felt that way. We went in the back door, and I collapsed in the nearest seat. Another chair scraped, and Tewy pattered over to me, sitting in my lap. I stroked his fur, grateful for the comfort.

"You found a job then?" I asked Nikon.

"I did some labor. Carrying things around for merchants who needed assistance getting ready for the market to open tomorrow. Helping with heavier items. Things like that. Temporary, but they liked my work. Said if I kept it up, they might find something permanent for me to do. Paid me for the day too, instead of waiting the week out. I was going to grab food on my way here, but well, things happened."

"Honestly, after all that, I'm not hungry." Despite having eaten, it felt like it'd been hours and hours since that happened. Maybe it had been.

"I'm not either, though I should be."

I told him about my day. "I had a friend come over today,

134

someone Leo knows, named Hettie. She made me lunch and talked with me."

"I'm glad you weren't alone the entire time."

Tewy squawked.

"Except for your company, of course," Nikon said.

A knock sounded, light but urgent.

"I'll get it." A shuffling sound drifted to my ears as Nikon must have moved out of his chair. Footsteps padded down the hall, and a slight creak announced the opening of the door. "Leo, come in."

Nikon told him I was in the kitchen, and the two of them headed back.

"Lovely to see you, Cassandra," Leo said.

I skipped the pleasantries. "Thank you for saving me today. I don't know what I would have done if you hadn't let me hide in your cellar."

"I don't want to hear any of that," he replied.

"But you don't even know us, and you assisted me." I couldn't restrain myself. I had to ask, "Why would you do that?"

"I don't know where you came from, but in this city, the odiosom usually stick together. We aid each other with whatever we can. You're one of us now. We'll do what we can and expect you to do the same in return."

"I will do what I can," I promised.

"And I will as well," Nikon said.

"Thank you both," Leo replied with a quaver in his voice. "I'm afraid it will be needed in the future, though one can never tell exactly what form that assistance will take."

"You look as though something is bothering you," Nikon said.

He sounded as if something was bothering him too; there was a strain in his words.

"I'm just worried about Cassandra. There's going to be more raids, whether soon or not is difficult to say, but they will happen. What's more, not everyone is going to be as understanding as me and Hettie—even the rest of the odiosom might be willing to turn her in."

I knew I should have stayed home, though it wasn't safe for me there either. The world didn't have a place for me. How would I ever find Antonia when I couldn't even manage to keep myself safe?

CHAPTER NINETEEN

After Leo left, Nikon's words were agitated. "We need a plan if something happens, whether I'm here or not."

"That would be a good idea, but what?" Sands knew I hadn't a clue what to do.

"I'll think of some scheme."

After spending the next two days by myself doing nothing but sitting around and worrying during the day, and sharing meals with Nikon in the evenings, he finally came to me in the kitchen on the second night and said, "I've got it planned out, but it's going to be dangerous without your sight—and unpleasant."

"Do I even want to know?"

"You have to know in case I'm not here."

I sighed. "Can't I just go to Leo's cellar?"

"What if you're upstairs and don't realize they've come? How are you going to get down there? And what if you do manage to make it to Leo's cellar? There won't be anyone there to cover you with turnips, if there's any turnips in there at the time."

At the word turnip, Tewy let out an angry screech.

I didn't blame him. I'd had about enough of them too. "Fine. You made your point. What am I supposed to do then?"

"I'm going to show you."

We moved from the kitchen to my room. "Why here?" I asked.

"Because otherwise you can go out the back door or if you have enough time, you can run up here."

"What do you expect me to do this high?" I asked, because there was nowhere else to hide up here unless the warriors didn't check under my bed.

"Actually, we're going higher."

"The only thing higher is the roof."

"Exactly."

Odd. Leo had said it was nice up there, but I hadn't gone up yet. I might be a little afraid of finding a ledge by accident and falling off without anyone close by to help. But this was different. Nikon would be with me. There would be no way he would let me stumble.

I didn't want to go, but I pulled myself together, and followed him to the stairs. Tewy sat heavy on my shoulder as I climbed them, adding the count to the endless list in my head. When I reached the top, he already had the door open, the cool night air swirling down around me. The result was pleasant, if a little chilly. The fresh air smelled sweet and invigorating.

"Take a couple steps out and close the door," Nikon said.

I did as he requested, finding the door on my right, closing it, and facing where I thought he was. The day had probably turned into night with the temperature. "I don't understand how this is going to help. Warriors could search up here just as easily as the rest of the house."

"I'll show you, but first, let me take you around so you know where you can go up here."

His hand took my own and placed it on his elbow. A tension I didn't know I'd been holding in eased. This was better. No way could I fall with his presence.

As he showed me the roof, I made a map in my head. There

was a small door on part of the building, taking up space, and the rest of the way was fairly clear and open.

"I wish you could see the stars," Nikon said, startling me with the comment.

"Why?"

"Because they're so beautiful. Do you remember them?"

Did I? Some objects stayed clear in my mind, but others faded over time. I searched my memories for stars and found one hiding in the back of my mind—but it was dim. "Vaguely. They twinkle overhead, like an inky pool filled with flecks of glowing sand."

"Exactly."

We didn't move. I didn't know exactly what he was doing, but I had a feeling his head was tilted up, searching the sky. I let myself breathe in the moment, taking in all the goodness I could, away from worrying and the constant stress of the days that had preceded the raid. The faint scent of the river came wafting in with the breeze. Water and sand, a smell so familiar, it felt like home. Being up here with Nikon was a nice moment. A peaceful one.

Until Nikon said, "Let's find a good spot to jump."

"Jump?" I squeaked out. "What do you mean, jump?"

"Exactly that. How else did you think you were going to hide from those searching for you?"

"Not by jumping off the roof, that much I can tell you with certainty."

When he spoke, his words were patient. "Unless you're jumping onto another roof."

"I can't go that far." Fear pinged through me.

"Yes, you can. On the sides, there's barely any room between houses. Just enough to have a person walk through. Two people couldn't even pass through them side by side. I wish I'd found you a long enough stick to let you feel how close they are. I'll get on that during my next day off, but this can't wait that long. You have to trust me."

"But how will I know how far to jump and what I'm going to land on? This seems like a really bad idea. I'd rather hide in the cellar with nothing on me."

"But a warrior searched in there, didn't you tell me that?"

Drat. I knew I shouldn't have told him that detail. "She did."

"If you stay in there with no protection, you'll be caught. This is the only way."

"But where does it lead?" Because I couldn't imagine it possibly going anywhere more useful than the cellar.

"Ah. Well, uh…"

"Spit it out already. What is it?"

His words came out in a rush. "Theamantsewer."

"Correct me if I'm wrong, but it sounded like you just said, *the amant sewer.*"

"That's right." His words became cautious.

"Gross."

"It's probably not as bad as you think."

I snapped back. "You're right, it's probably worse."

He didn't respond.

"Well?"

"It is going to be a tight fit. I couldn't get in there at all, but you're so much smaller, I know it will work."

I clucked my tongue trying to hold in my patience. "You don't even know if I'll fit."

"You will. It's only me that's too bulky."

"And what's Tewy supposed to do, because I know I can't convince him to go in a sewer." His weight seemed heavier than ever on my shoulder. I reached up to pet him, but he grabbed my finger and tried to stick it in my ear. "Naughty monkey."

"Tewy can stay here if he wants or wait for you outside the sewer. No one will be looking for a monkey."

My chest tightened. I didn't want to be parted from him during such a traumatic moment. What if he ran off and I never found him again? No, Tewy wouldn't do that to me. More likely he'd be waiting to throw something at me when I returned. I had to find another excuse. "I only have a few dresses. I can't ruin them by going in the sewer."

"I'll help you wash them."

"Wash them? They'll be ruined if I go in there." I suspected.

"Then I'll buy you a new one."

"We don't have money for that."

Exasperation coursed out of him in a growl. "If you want to be caught. Fine, stay here. But if you want a chance at life, you're going to have to come with me and try this out so you know how to do it if I'm not here."

"All right, I'll go," I eked out. "But know that I'm scared."

He put a hand over mine, voice calmer. "It's fine to be scared if you do the right things with the fear."

"What if I don't know what the right things are?"

"You'll figure it out."

"Did you?"

His silence was telling. I didn't expect him to answer, but he eventually said, "Not always, but I'm trying."

Maybe that was all one could ask. To try. "I'm ready."

"Good. Here is the edge. Do you want to reach forward and see if you can feel the other building? I'll keep a good hold of you."

There was a ledge I pressed against that went mid-shin. I wasn't keen to lean over it, but if Nikon said he had a hold of me, I believed him. "I'm willing to attempt it."

He moved away from my hand and the pressure increased on both sides of my waist. It was a pleasant feeling, one that left me a little breathless. "I've got you. Go ahead and see what you can find."

His grip on me might have been firm, but that didn't mean my nerves weren't jangling in my throat. I leaned over, hand outstretched, searching for anything past the ledge.

"You're almost there."

I reached farther, his hands gripping me tight but also moving me forward.

He said, "Yes, you're so close. I don't think you can reach though."

I stood, and he released me.

"Are you ready to jump?" he asked.

Definitely not. "Can't we put a plank here I can cross? We could throw it to the ground or something if I have to hide."

"People would be able to see it from the street. Plus, even if you threw it to the ground on your way out, the warriors would be able to jump across. It's really not a great distance."

I tried to think of another excuse. "Shouldn't we wait until we get me another walking stick?"

"What if the warriors come tomorrow? You'll need to be able to do this."

I grimaced. This was going to be awful.

"I'll hold your hand the entire time. You won't have to do it alone."

"Not this time anyway," I muttered. I cleared my throat. "Fine then, let's jump."

A hand enveloped my own. I'd much rather study the ridges of Nikon's hand than continue on, but apparently that wasn't an option. I let him help me up on the ledge, planting my feet as firmly as I could.

"You've got great balance."

"It must be easier when I can't see the fall below us." Especially when my balance was usually so terrible.

"That must be it. Are you ready?"

"Doesn't matter if I am or not, let's just get it done."

"We'll jump on three. One. Two. Three."

I pushed off with everything I had, clinging to Nikon as hard as I could. Wind whipped past my face, tearing at my hair. The air was all around me. My feet slammed into something hard, knees buckling. I didn't stop there but ran forward a few paces before stopping.

Nikon went with me, his footsteps heavy next to my own, though not as loud as I expected. It was probably a large step for him and not a jump.

I worked to catch my breath before asking, "Where's the ledge we just jumped over?"

"It's over here."

He led me back to where we'd come from, taking in more paces than I would have guessed. "That wasn't as bad as I expected."

"Good, because we have a lot more to go."

I groaned but followed him as we jumped further. Each time, we'd stop to explore the roof so I had a good idea of what was there. "Aren't people going to wonder what the thuds are above them?"

"Probably, but we're going fast enough that as long as they're not next to their stairs, we should be fine. Besides, not all houses have easy access to the roofs like ours does."

When we got to the last house, he said, "There's a ladder we have to climb down. It's just over here."

I didn't like the sound of that, but it couldn't be worse than jumping from rooftop to rooftop, could it?

"Do you have any questions?" he asked.

"I've got everything in my head up to this point. I'd like you to go down the ladder first though."

"Of course."

He led me over to where the ladder leaned up against the wall. After letting him go down a little ways, I followed after him. The wooden rungs were narrow, much smaller than the last ladder I climbed. I went slowly, taking my time to find each new step with my foot before climbing down again.

When my feet both hit the ground, I gave a sigh of relief—until

I remembered that Nikon wanted me to go into the sewer. Gross. "Where to now?"

"We're between two houses. If you reach over, you'll be able to feel the other one." I did as he said, finding the stone while he spoke. "We're almost to the amant part of town. Just a couple more houses and then we'll be there. Once that happens, we'll be at the sewers."

He took my hand again, leading me down the alleyway from in front. Even so, every so often I would bump into one wall or another. It was nice when there was a break in the houses next to us, but Nikon took us through those fast, probably so we wouldn't be seen by others.

The map in my head was large. I'd need a few more times of going over it to feel truly confident in taking this path, but if I had to jump through it tomorrow, I could.

Once we'd gone a ways, Nikon stopped. "Here we are."

"It does stink over here." And it was only going to get worse.

Tewy chattered as if in agreement.

"Sorry. I wish there was a better answer. There's a stone laid over the sewer, let's make certain you can move it."

He led me to it, showing me where it changed from dirt to stone roads, the entrance to the tunnel not much farther. The stone was warm beneath my feet from being heated all day, an odd contrast to the cool air.

I took the stone and moved it with ease. "No problem. But do I have to climb in it?"

"Not tonight. I think you've done enough, and I'm certain you'll fit. Just make sure you leave the stone where you can place it back over the sewer when you're inside."

"Yes, sir."

He took my hand, leading me away from the area. "Please don't call me that."

"What? Sir?"

144

"That's the one." His tone was light but there was a tension swirling just beneath the surface.

"Why don't you like being called sir?"

"You've done well. Do you remember your way back?"

Definitely avoiding the subject. Again. "Vaguely. I don't know if it's the right way though."

"Why don't you lead and if you get off course, I'll steer you back?"

"I'd feel better doing that if I had my walking stick."

"I'll work on getting you one then, and we can do this again."

If we kept this up, soon I would be an expert. I hoped I never needed to use it.

CHAPTER TWENTY

The door creaked open followed by Nikon's familiar footsteps, a soft heaviness that I suspected was just for me.

"Tewy, let's go see Nikon." My monkey jumped on my shoulder, and I raced down the stairs. I might have been a little too eager, but staying home alone all week was getting to me. I should have been accustomed to it, but knowing there were people around, I wanted to take advantage of that and not be stuck inside.

By the time I got downstairs, his footsteps had moved to the front living space, not where I expected him to go. We avoided that room if for no other reason than there wasn't any furniture.

"Evening, Cassandra," he said. "How was your day?"

Boring. But I didn't want to tell him that and make him feel bad for leaving me alone. "It was a day. What are you doing in here?"

"I've got something for you. A few somethings, actually." A smile graced his voice.

I bounced on the balls of my feet. "What are they?"

"Let's start here. Hold out your hands."

I did as he directed. Moments later, a familiar, soft bundle landed in them. "Yarn. You found me some."

"Yup. This is a pale blue. I figured it would give you something to do while I'm gone."

"And then I can sell it. Hettie wants me to make her a shawl, too, but her day off hasn't come yet to bring me the yarn. This will give me a project to accomplish in the meantime. Thank you." I hugged the yarn close to me before a yank tried to take it out of my hands.

"Tewy, leave Cassandra alone." Nikon's words were firm, and the tugging stopped.

"He's always liked soft things," I said. "This will be the best thing I can do with my time. Thank you, again."

"It is my pleasure. But that's not all. I caught some fish for dinner."

"That will be nice. I'm surprised you had time for it though, with work."

"They let me off early. Which brings me to the last surprise I have for us."

I couldn't believe he'd obtained so many things. "This is too much, Nikon. You didn't have to go through all this."

"Well, the fish is for me too, and besides, I don't want you to be too bored and regret coming here. Not to mention, if you make things we can sell, we'll actually be able to pay our rent to Leo."

No pressure. "I'll do my best to help."

"Sorry, I didn't mean to make it sound like it's all on you. Working lugging things around for shopkeepers or amant who buy goods is going well. I just know it's going to be hard to purchase all the things we need without more to help it along."

"Don't worry about it. I'm happy to be a part of the team." Though it did feel better to know it wasn't solely on me.

"The last thing I have for you is hopefully the best. Though it could fail completely, so don't get your hopes up."

"All right." What could it possibly be?

"Hold both of your hands out in front of you, palms up."

Strange, but I did as he requested. Tewy jumped off my shoulder, pattering away from me toward where Nikon was speaking.

Something smooth, hard, and long was placed in my hands. "A cane?"

"Not just any cane. And, we're not done with it either. There's something else I want to try, though I'm not certain it will work." He words shook a little as if he was nervous. "I'm going to set a bucket of sand at your feet. It's wet, so the magic should still be in it. I want you to rub it all over your stick."

"What will that do?"

"Honestly, there's no way of knowing. Why don't you test it and we'll see what happens?" A thump sounded next to me. "The bucket of sand is on your right."

It was worth a try, though I didn't know what it could accomplish—except perhaps to get this stick permanently stuck to my hands. "Maybe this isn't such a good idea."

"The truth is, I was hoping it would make your walking stick nicer. That it'd smooth out the rough edges."

"It doesn't feel rough."

"I meant of my craftsmanship."

I shrugged. "It feels fine to me."

"I wanted...will you please just try. For me?"

When he put it that way, how could I refuse? I bent down and searched for the bucket. When I found it, I reached inside, grabbed a handful of wet sand, and rubbed it down the wood. The sand had to be at least damp recently from the river or else it didn't work. No one knew why, but rewetting with river water never brought the magic back. It had to come straight from the river. "This is going to make a mess. Why didn't you do it yourself?"

"I'll clean it up. It'll be easy enough," he replied. "I didn't put the magic on for you because it works better when you apply it on the item yourself."

"So, if I would have put sand on my own eyes, I wouldn't have become blind?" A bite stung my words.

"I don't know about that, but I suppose it is possible the outcome could have been different."

I tried to keep my shoulders from slumping, instead focusing on the activity at hand. I let the grains rub against the wood. When I got about halfway, there was a strange catch, like the sand didn't want to move right away. "Is there something on this?"

"Kind of. We'll get to it."

Odd. I pushed past the notch and ran the sand across the rest of it. As I went, something strange brushed against my arm. The magic at work. What was it doing to me? Why had I let Nikon talk me into this? I didn't want something bad to happen to me. Not again.

I plopped the extra sand into the bucket.

"You didn't finish," he said. "You still have the tip on the left side to do."

"I'm done."

"But the rest of the walking stick is shiny now, all except that one spot."

I held the staff out toward him. "I don't want it. I should have never done it. Something strange is happening."

"I know. It looks like someone who knew what they were doing made it now, instead of my incompetence."

"There's more than that." How did I explain it? "The magic isn't just changing the wood, it's tingling up my arms and through my body. I can feel it working on me. To be honest, it's got me worried."

"All right." His voice was nearer though I hadn't heard him move. "I can take it from you. I'll make another one and we won't use magic on it."

"Are you certain? You must have put some time into this."

He hesitated. "I did, but if you're not comfortable with it, then we won't use it. Can you do one thing for me first? I want to see if you like what I did with it. If not, I'll make a normal cane for you. If so, I can duplicate this one without the magic, though it won't be as nice."

He had a point. The wood was sturdier in my hands somehow. Smoother. But it wasn't worth risking whatever change it made. "What did you do that's different with this stick?" I might not want to keep this specific one, but I wanted to know what change he made.

"Twist it. It should come apart straight in two. That's what the change you felt in the middle was."

"Why would I want it to break in half?" It sounded like a defect, not a feature.

"Stick fighting. A way to protect yourself."

"I don't think that would work without being able to see."

"Just take it apart and try. If it doesn't work, I won't bother trying it with the next one."

I twisted the stick in my hands and pulled. It came apart easier than I expected.

"Whoa." Nikon sounded much more excited than I felt. "The magic did a good number on it. I know you're not comfortable with it, but it was not that smooth when I made it."

"You don't give yourself enough credit."

"No, really. These look like they could do some damage."

It seemed a moot point. "But I can't see my opponent to do the damage to them."

"Let's give it a test try. You can hear well; maybe you'll be able to recognize an opponent coming that way. If so, I'll make the new one like this and teach you."

The sticks felt like clumsy extensions of me that had no feeling. "If that's what you want, but I don't think it's going to work."

"I'm going to come at you now," he said, clearly ignoring my misgivings.

A tingling spread through my body, through my arms and hands to the sticks. As Nikon's fist flashed forward, the wood flared to life in an unfamiliar sensation almost like another sense. I knocked it back with one of the sticks, and the sensation left.

"Ouch. What was that?"

Tewy laughed in his sort of way. Naughty monkey.

"Good question. Sorry, I didn't mean to hurt you." I lifted the sticks, waiting to feel the tingling, but nothing happened. "It's gone."

"My hand? No, it's still here, just smarting like it's going to fall off. Your senses must be working on overload to get me that good."

"It wasn't that. It was almost like…"

"Like what?" He was closer again, his voice floating across me.

"This is so strange, but it was like I perceived you coming. Not through hearing or feeling or anything like that. It was almost like I could sense you coming to attack me through the sticks, and they knew to protect me if I listened to them."

He didn't respond.

"Nikon?"

"Sorry, I'm just surprised. I never suspected that the magic would do something like this. I thought it would make it better, but not to the point of helping you sense attacks around you."

I shook my head. "I had to be imagining things. The magic couldn't have done something that helpful."

"Maybe it could. I'm going to pull out my dagger, but I'll be careful."

"I don't like the sound of this." Not. At. All.

Before I had time to protest any further, the feeling was back. The stick tingled, shooting a sensation up through me, making me know Nikon had a dagger coming toward me. I lifted my left stick to block it, clumsily pushing it aside. I doubted I could have done that if he hadn't let me. But then, there was nothing. The extra sense didn't stick around.

"That's amazing. I think we know what the sand did, and I don't think we should make new fighting sticks. The sand did wonders for these ones. I don't think a new staff would do nearly as well for you."

"I don't know. Keeping something that has magic like that, I'm not sure."

"It's up to you, but I think you should give it some thought. This might be exactly what you need."

I pushed the two sticks up against each other and they met better than I expected, so I twisted them together. "I promise to give it some thought, but I can't promise the outcome will be what you want."

"Fair enough."

CHAPTER TWENTY-ONE

I worked on making a shawl as quickly as I could without making a mistake. It was nice to finally have something to do. Despite it all, the fighting sticks Nikon had made me kept calling out to me. Not in a creepy, *I hear voices* sort of way, but more in an, *I want to see what they're capable of* sort of way. What *I* was capable of.

But they were tainted with the same magic that had left me blind, so I left them be.

A knock on the door downstairs had me bolting to my feet. Before I had much more time to worry, a voice called out, "It's me, Hettie."

I let the tension stream out of me. "I'm upstairs."

"I'll be up in a moment."

Some rummaging around went through the bottom floor before steps came up the stairs and into my room. "I brought some more food. What are you making? It's beautiful."

"Thank you. I'm making a shawl with some yarn Nikon purchased."

"It's a gorgeous color and design. You could probably sell it for more money to an amant, it's that elaborate."

Heat rose to my cheeks. "It's simple. Just a bunch of knots strung together."

"Strung together in a beautiful way. It makes me even more grateful I brought you some yarn to make me one, though after seeing your work, I think I need to pay you for it."

I set my work aside, hoping Tewy didn't play with it when he got home. He'd gone with Nikon to work today, leaving me lonelier than usual. It was fine though. I had things to do and Hettie to visit with. "There's not a chance of you paying me. You brought food and company, that's better than any payment."

"I don't mind paying in lunch if you're fine with it, but my company is only worth so much."

I gave a short chuckle. "You're a wonderful accompaniment to my day."

"You're too kind. What's that? Did you get a cane?" she asked.

She must have been referring to my new walking stick. It called to me from where I'd left it leaning against the wall at the head of the bed. It was almost if it wanted to be in my hands, a part of me. But that didn't make any sense. "Nikon made it. We treated it with magic last night, so I'm a little wary of it."

"Why would magic make you wary?"

I hesitated. It was one thing to have her over and knowing about my being blind, but quite another to tell my life story. Then again, Leo trusted her. Not only that, but if she wanted to turn me in, she could have already done so. Telling her my story wouldn't make a difference. I explained what had happened with my sight.

"That's awful. Why did your parents do that to you and not your brother?"

Sandblast it all. I forgot she didn't know Nikon and I weren't actually related.

"Sorry. That was a very personal question. I didn't mean to offend you." Hettie's voice broke.

"You didn't offend me. It's hard to explain."

"You don't have to explain it to me." Though her words said that, her voice hinted at being hurt.

What could I tell her? She was my only contact besides Nikon. Antonia had left me so long ago. Tewy teased me and was a monkey anyway. I wanted to befriend her, which I couldn't do if I didn't tell her the truth. But that was a dangerous thing.

"Can I tell you about the yarn I bought?" Her tone perked up.

Grateful for the subject change, I said, "Please. Can I feel it?"

"Hold out your hand."

I did as she requested and a soft ball was placed on it. There felt like enough yarn there to make a shawl. "This is good quality. What color is it?"

"It's white. It will look perfect against my skin. Plus, it'll match my dresses on formal occasions."

"That's lovely. I'll get started on it as soon as I finish this."

"No rush," she said, but the excitement in her voice made me want to.

"There's one thing I need done. If you can't help, it's fine, but if you can, it'd be wonderful."

"What's that?"

I expected there to be a note of caution in her tone, but it wasn't there. "I need my hair cut."

"Ooh, I would love to do that for you. I cut my sisters' hair all the time. Are we shaving it and getting you a wig or going short?"

"Short, please. About to my shoulders, maybe a little shorter. I think I'll fit in better with it like that if I end up going out at all."

She must have lifted a section of my hair because it became lighter with a slight tug. "It's true, you would fit in better, though you probably shouldn't be going outside anyway. The thing is, your hair is gorgeous. This black, shiny hair is perfection and looks so great on you. I wish I had the guts to grow my hair out like this, but mine is thick and frizzy. I keep it shorn and wear a wig."

"Will I be too out of style if I don't wear a wig?"

"No, your hair is so perfect. All the other women will be jealous if they ever see it. Let me run home and grab my scissors."

"I have my scissors for my yarn."

"Mine are extra sharp for hair. I'll be right back."

She left in a flurry, and I crocheted while she was gone. It didn't take her long to come back though, and holler at me to come downstairs where my hair wouldn't get all over my bedroom.

I didn't need my staff. Not really. But I grabbed it anyway. It was like an itch had been scratched. The call of it soothed as I carried it.

Once downstairs, it didn't take long for Hettie to arrange everything and cut my hair to my shoulders. She said, "I'm going to give you bangs too. They're so in style with the amant these days and everyone else is copying them. I wish I could afford a new wig to get some myself."

"I've never had bangs before."

"They'll be easy to take care of, and I'll keep them trimmed for you."

"All right. I'm willing to try them."

The scissors snipped, snipped, snipped, the hair tickling me as it tumbled down my face. Hettie said, "I'm going to ask a personal question, but don't feel like you have to answer it if you don't want to."

"What is it?" I asked, tone wary.

"Have you ever wondered what would happen if a man saw you and fell in love with you? I mean, you'd never be able to love him back."

I'd given this more thought than I cared to admit. "Do you think it works like that? After thinking about my youthful experiences and kofles I've been to, it seems that the couple in love has to see one another to fall in love. It's not a single-sided thing."

"I suppose that's true. I've never heard of anyone falling in love and the other person not seeing them. They must both have to catch the other's gaze to make the process happen."

"That's my guess."

A final snip. "All done. You look like you could fit in anywhere."

"Except for the fact I can't see."

"Pijo. You'd be welcome at our home any time at least."

Her exclamation that it didn't matter did little to make me feel better. I tried to ignore the fears inside me, but they crawled on top of one another, eager to let at least one out. "Until I'm caught and have to become a slave. And who knows what would happen to you or anyone else helping me. No, it's not a good idea."

"But you want to go out. Otherwise, why cut your hair?"

Why, indeed. "I do wish to, but this is more of a precaution than anything else."

"If you say so. But when the time comes that you're ready to get out of this house, I'll be happy to take you. We'll figure out something to do with your blindness so people don't notice."

"Thank you for the offer."

"That's what friends are for. Now, let me sweep this mess up, and you can help me make lunch."

As we worked, my mind kept straying back to her comment, wondering if someone could fall in love with me when I couldn't see them. It didn't seem possible, but so little in my life did.

"Whoa," Nikon said. "You look different."

The words perturbed me for a reason I couldn't ascertain, made me scowl in the direction his voice was coming from.

His footsteps came out of the hall and nearer to the kitchen where I sat waiting for him. I'd made dinner earlier, leaving it to simmer while I waited on him to make it home. I had to admit to myself this wasn't the reaction I wanted, though I wasn't certain why.

"In a good way," he said, but not fast enough for my liking. "Sorry. It's just strange to see you looking so, well, honestly, you look like an amant. You fit right in with them."

"Maybe if I had nicer clothes." Though it still seemed unlikely I'd ever fit in with the loved without my sight.

"Perhaps. It's good to have your appearance changed. That will help with those who were following us. Make it harder for them to find us if they think we stuck together. I'll shave my head tonight. Should have done it sooner, but I've been so consumed with other things, I forgot. I'm glad you remembered."

I wasn't certain I was. It might have been better to not have Hettie cut it because I wasn't used to factoring other people into things. But there was no changing it. "Let's eat."

"Thank you for making dinner. I'll dish up."

He clunked around for a moment before a tap of a plate indicated it was placed on the table before me. It smelled of garlic and cumin. Dinner. I said, "I hope it tastes good. It's difficult to cook in a different environment than I'm accustomed to."

A response came in the form of the sound of Nikon eating. "Mmm. It's good."

"I'm grateful you think so." I found my own spoon and dove in. It wasn't the best, but it tasted better than what we had been eating. "How is work going?"

"It's a job. I don't mind physical labor. It makes me feel like I'm getting something useful done and leaves my mind clear."

"Do you ever wish you could go back to being a warrior?" The words popped out before I could stop them. I regretted it as soon as they were out. Though he'd never confirmed he was a warrior, I felt certain he was, but he never wanted to talk about it.

"We should practice," he said.

Tewy responded amiably.

I wasn't so sure, but at least he hadn't gotten upset over my question. "Practice what?"

"Fighting. Let's go to the front room. Bring your cane." His footsteps fell toward the hallway.

I grabbed my staff from leaning against the wall where I'd left it. A hum of rightness vibrated through me. I didn't know how much fighting I'd really be able to do, but maybe with these sticks, it wouldn't be so bad. It may actually work.

As I followed after Nikon, I twisted the stick into two and braced myself to feel something. Nothing happened. Maybe the last time had been a mistake?

When I entered the room, he said, "Good, you're ready. Let's get this going. First, I want you to move with them. Let yourself feel what they are like to heft and turn about."

I did as he requested, feeling a little silly. After some time, they felt more natural in my hands, like the extension of me that they'd been before. "What should I do now?"

"We're going to start with one stick. You can put the other down." I went to put one of them down as he'd requested when Tewy's monkey talk scrambled over to me and it was taken from me. Nikon continued. "I want you to keep your stick moving throughout practice. We're going to start with drills. The more you get used to moving a certain way, the more naturally it will come to you when it's time to fight."

"I hope it never comes to that."

"I do as well," he said. "I need you to hold the stick a little differently. Lower. No, not that low. Here, let me show you."

Skin brushed against my own, moving my hand on the stick so that it had a little gap between me and the end.

"That should do it," he said, his touch leaving me. "This will make it almost like two weapons, a short one and a long one. Don't hold the stick so tight. You want a firm grip but not choking. That's it."

The wood didn't feel as familiar as I wanted, but it would get there. The more I moved around with it held like it was supposed to, the better it felt.

"Good. We're moving on to the drill now. I want you to do this every day while I'm gone, and we'll practice it more when I come home."

"I can do that." It'd break up my day from doing nothing but crocheting.

"What I want you to do is move diagonally from on the top of one side to the bottom of your other side. Got it?"

"I think so."

"Good. Then move horizontally one side to the other so you're back on the same side you started, but by your waist."

"All right."

"Finally, go with a vertical move that puts you back where you started to do it all over again."

I moved jerkily, trying to copy what he said. "I don't think I have the hang of it."

"Nope, apparently not. That's not surprising though. It takes time. Let me move through the motions with you so you know what it feels like."

There wasn't a sound or warning before he slipped behind me. I jumped. "Didn't expect you. Why are you so quiet?"

"Habit, sorry. Let's focus on this."

Because he was a warrior? What happened to him? I wanted to know his story, wanted to know what was going on with him, and what his past looked like. But I'd let it be—for the moment.

He pressed up against my back, running his arm along my own, and pulling it through the motions he had tried to explain. Feeling the warmth on my skin made me focus on every little touch. Each movement was deliberate but smooth. It wasn't long before his hands moved to my shoulders as I completed the action on my own.

"That's perfect," he said in my ear. "Practice that as much as you can. I want you to do drills with both sticks too. Tewy, stick."

He pattered over, and I felt that tingle go through me. Before I knew what was happening, I blocked Tewy from swinging at my legs and grabbed the other stick from his hand. "Naughty monkey. You're supposed to help me, not take a swing at me." Though it confirmed that the magic was still working on my stick.

Instead of backing down, he stayed close, laughing.

"He's pointing at you," Nikon said. "I believe he's a little crazy."

"More like full-on mad." Of course, I couldn't say that without a note of love in my voice, even if he was an imp.

He pattered away, and Nikon came from in back of me again to take hold of both of my hands. He showed me how to move both of the sticks at the same time, going through the motions in a smooth, unconscious way.

Nikon was built to do this. When he let go of my hands, I didn't think I was. The sticks became heavy in my grasp, my movements awkward.

"You're getting it," he said.

"Are you sure? It feels more like I'm a camel with knobby elbows instead of knees."

He laughed. "It'll take some getting used to, but you'll get there. Just keep practicing, and I'll guide you as much as I can."

I pulled the sticks down to my sides and faced him. "Are you ready to tell me why you're so good at this?"

"Nope."

"I don't see why it's so hard for you to talk about being a warrior."

"No one ever said I was one."

"Everything you say and do implies that you are." I turned around and moved through the drill he'd shown me with two sticks. Despite the awkward feeling, the tension drew out of my muscles. "It's fine if you don't want to talk about it, but when you're ready, know that I'm ready."

"You'll never be ready for what I am."

With that sinister thought, he marched off.

CHAPTER TWENTY-TWO

As time melded together, life took on a pattern. I would do drills upon waking up, crochet, do more drills, make dinner, and Nikon would come home. After we were both fed, he'd help me with more stick fighting. I slowly grew more confident in my abilities, and he moved toward fighting against me as practice.

It wasn't what I expected it to be, but quickly grew to become my favorite part of the day. I loved moving and feeling more while with him. The magic sand in my sticks helped more than I expected by giving me extra sense when fighting. I didn't ever want to stop. Nikon had to convince me to each night, and the loss of fighting turned back into not knowing the world around me.

Not that everything was perfect with the magic. I could only sense objects coming at me with ill intent. Nikon had tried approaching me but not hitting me, and I hadn't noticed anything. Because of this, I had to keep aware of my surroundings and be extra cautious in them.

We fought all over the house, trying to vary things as much as possible. The hallways were difficult, but not impossible. Mostly, I wanted to go out around the city, in the river, in the sand, in the desert, wherever I could to learn more about my surroundings. But I stayed inside, slowly festering with the desire to get out.

My favorite days were when Hettie came. She always had to leave mid-afternoon before Nikon got home, and didn't come again until mid-morning after she finished chores. It didn't matter though. Every moment with her became enjoyable. She was the friend I needed.

It was in the in-between moments that I was sad and alone, drawn toward the forbidden outside.

I knew why I couldn't go. I understood the reasoning behind it, even. But it didn't make it any easier to stay inside all the time. The forbidden called to me almost as much as my staff. I pushed it to the back of my mind whenever I could, but sometimes that didn't feel like enough.

It couldn't hurt to go out back and wander around. I went once in a while anyway to use the outhouse, so how would walking around just a little bit be any different?

The front door creaked open and closed. Whatever I wanted to do would have to wait another day because Nikon was home. His footsteps went down the hall to the kitchen before going up the stairs, stopping at my bedroom.

"How was your day?" I asked.

"Busy. I heard you sold several more shawls from our seller, so I picked you up some more yarn. What are you making there?"

"Another shawl. Why?"

"It's four different colors."

"What? I had them placed out where I wouldn't—Tewy," I yelled. "You are in so much trouble."

From nearby, the little imp laughed his monkey laugh.

"Is it fixable?" There was a hint of a chuckle in Nikon's words.

I ignored it. "Maybe, but it's a lot of time gone to waste. Does it look good?"

"I'm sorry." He sounded serious again.

The bed dipped. Nikon had come to sit by me. I put my work down, disgusted by it. Who knew how long it would take me to undo it and have to redo it all? What a waste.

"We could hang him out the window by his toes."

I let a small smile slip out. "As tempting as that is, I don't think he'd learn anything. Stupid monkey."

Tewy squawked in protest.

"You brought it on yourself," I replied.

He complained again, the faint thumping of his movements coming near.

"I don't want you right now either," Nikon said. "Sorry boy, but you messed up big this time."

The thumping moved toward me and the furry little thing jumped on my lap, putting a hand on my cheek. I said, "You know, for such a little troublemaker, you sure know how to get out of the wreckage you make."

He made a soft grunting sound.

"You're forgiven, but don't mess with my yarn again."

His reply was higher pitched this time. I pulled him close to me, enjoying his company even after his naughtiness.

"Are you always quick to forgive?" Nikon asked.

"I didn't used to be, but with Tewy around, it was either forgive or be alone."

"I see. I suppose I'll use that to my advantage."

"Have you done something that you need forgiving for?"

He didn't reply.

"Nikon, I understand you have secrets. I wish you didn't, but I know you must have a reason for keeping them. As much as I wish I knew them, I can be all right with it."

His familiar hand, calluses and all, enclosed mine. "That means a lot to me."

"Well, I do what I can."

We sat there in silence, me enjoying the feel of human connection. I wanted more of it, to lean into him. And I shouldn't do that; it seemed too personal, but maybe there was something I could do. "Tell me more about yourself. And before you get all edgy, I don't mean about what you're hiding. Tell me about your childhood or why you're so quiet. Tell me how you grew to be so caring and kind or how you're liking work."

"You ask more than you know."

"Sorry, I just want a connection to you that will carry me through everything."

"And you don't care what it's about?"

"Nope."

"Well, there was this one time when I was little, my family traveled to Sirya. My parents wanted to be at the capitol for one of the Reding's assemblies. This was before the Reding had fallen in love, but my parents still thought he was a great leader—one who would help build up the magic in Eppla."

I didn't say anything, but it didn't sound like Nikon agreed with them. What experience could he possibly have with the Reding? Maybe there was a law enacted while I'd lived in my house by the waterfall or some other similar situation.

"We journeyed with a large group where I often went to play with friends. My parents thought that was what I was doing when in reality, I scampered behind the end of the group. I was playing some imaginary game, one where I used a stick as a sword and leaped across the sand. I needed room to do that without one of the grown-ups getting angry with me, so I kept my distance from everyone. I was doing one such maneuver when a large sphinx jumped in my path."

I gasped.

"I had a similar reaction. I didn't know what the thing was at the time, but I knew it was dangerous. She looked ready to eat me, though I don't know if she actually would have or not."

I knotted my hands together. "What did you do?"

"I asked her what she wanted. She didn't toy with me like I

would expect now, but back then, I didn't have any idea what was going on. She simply stated a riddle for me."

"What was it?"

"You get these cute little lines between your eyebrows when you're thinking hard." His finger brushed that very spot, smoothing it out.

"What can I say, you've got me curious. I'm trying to imagine how a little boy handled the sphinx when I struggled."

"Everyone struggles."

"But you survived the sphinx, which says a lot."

"I believe it was because in my youth, I was more creative, but it's hard to say for certain. I don't remember the riddle anymore, but the answer has stuck with me throughout my life. It was the hatred of men."

"Deep for a little boy. What happened when you gave the correct answer?"

"Nothing much. She grinned and told me I was right, and not to forget what I'd said. Then she bounded away."

"I can't believe you survived a sphinx's riddle. So few do."

"Don't be sad now, we'll figure out the answer to your own riddle."

I shook the sadness away. I really should have worked on my own riddle. "You just amaze me. What did your parents say? Were they frantic looking for you?"

"Actually, they hadn't even realized I was gone. I've never told another soul about the sphinx until today."

"I'm glad you shared it with me." I understood how hard it could be to give a piece of yourself to another.

He said, "Sometimes I wonder, if you had your eyesight, would we have fallen in love at first sight?"

I skirted back, surprised at his line of thinking. "Don't say things like that."

"Why not?"

"Because it hurts, Nikon. Right here." I pounded on my chest.

"I can never fall in love because of what my parents did. At least you still have a chance."

I turned away from him, pain ratcheting through me. As if I needed another reminder I could never have someone who felt that way about me. Sure, Nikon and Tewy cared, but it wasn't the same as having someone who loved you romantically. Someone who would always be with you. The soul that matched mine. An opportunity to have children. I would never, ever have any of that, and it left my eyes stinging.

Nikon cleared his throat. "I'm going to go make dinner."

I should have made it before he came home, but I didn't apologize for losing track of time. Didn't think I could catch my voice.

The weight shifted off the bed, and I leaned away from him. Tewy, who'd been oddly silent during the entire thing, snuggled up to me as I listened to Nikon's footsteps going down to the kitchen. Once he was there, I cried, though I didn't know why.

CHAPTER TWENTY-THREE

Hearing Nikon's declaration stuck with me for days. Hettie even noticed something was going on, asking me what was wrong when she visited. I told her it was nothing. It might as well have been. I didn't understand it myself, let alone know how to explain it to someone else.

Tewy stuck close by my side and didn't tease me, though he laid it on thick with Nikon. My little monkey stole Nikon's sandals at night, hiding them in a kitchen cupboard, took Nikon's pillow onto the roof, and all sorts of other tricks. For some reason, it made me smile even though I knew I shouldn't encourage Tewy's antics.

My monkey was currently missing as I worked on another shawl. He was probably playing some other trick on Nikon, but I didn't say anything. I crocheted as quickly as I could without making a mistake. The shawls had been selling as fast as I could make them. Between my things and Nikon's work, we'd managed to pay Leo rent for the first several months we'd been here.

We were finally doing good on our word, and I wanted to keep it that way. No getting behind or taking advantage of Leo's goodness anymore by not paying him full rent right away. From what

Hettie said, this was a common theme in the odiosom crowd. Leo would take care of people and in turn, they took good care of him.

It must have been past time for Nikon to come home—or at least, it felt that way. It was difficult to know without having sight or being out in the sun, but it seemed like it'd been long enough. Where could he be?

I made furious loops, hoping that they were coming out right. They felt even on my fingertips when I checked, but I made them so quickly, I worried about it.

When the door finally opened, I dashed downstairs. "Are you all right?"

"I'm fine. Sorry I'm late," Nikon said.

At least I'd been right that he'd been late and hadn't made a fool of myself over nothing. "What happened?"

He let out a soft groan.

"Are you hurt?"

"Not at all, just worried."

"Has that woman found us?"

"No, no. Nothing like that." Still, his words did nothing to reassure me.

"What is it then?"

He took me by the elbow, the first time we'd touched since I'd held his hand the first month we were here, and said, "Let's go into the kitchen."

I hadn't cooked anything for dinner. I should have, but I'd been lost in my own thoughts again, which had turned to worry when I realized how late it'd become.

Despite knowing the way myself, I let him guide me down the hallway and to a chair. Once seated, I asked, "What's wrong?"

"It's nothing, really. People are just starting rumors about you."

Not what I expected. I put a hand to my chest. "About me?"

"Yes. It seems that they know you exist because of your shawls but have never seen you. Everyone has a different opinion on why."

"Oh." I slouched back in my chair. "That can't be too bad."

"But it draws attention to us. If the warriors hear of it, they'll come looking into it, asking questions and wondering what's wrong. That, or it will get back to Valeriana."

"Who's Valeriana?"

He muttered something under his breath. "Nothing. Forget it."

"Is she the woman chasing us?"

"You shouldn't be going there." It was difficult to tell if he was more exasperated or grudgingly respectful.

"It wasn't a hard deduction. It sounds, though, as if you know her personally."

"I might. But right now, we need to focus on the problem at hand."

It wasn't what I wanted to do, but I doubted I was going to get any more information about Valeriana. "What should we do about the rumors?"

"I don't know. It's trouble, no matter which way we handle it."

"What if we let people meet me?" Before he could protest, I hurried on. "Not everyone, but those you and Leo trust. Those who would keep my secret but would also spread the word that I'm shy, or whatever they want to say."

Tewy chattered in agreement.

"We could give it a try," Nikon said. "I'm a little wary of bringing people here though. What if they end up turning us in? I promised to protect you. I don't want to give someone a chance to break that."

"We can't live in fear, not when we have a chance to do more."

"You're right. Of course, you are. It's just..." His footsteps fell away. "I'm going to make dinner."

I wasn't hungry, not after that conversation. I was too busy being scared but didn't want to tell him that. "Sounds wonderful. Would you like some help?"

"Sure."

We worked together to make beans, garlic, and fish, though I

170

had a hard time concentrating on it all with the thoughts of meeting new people on my mind. Was it scary or exciting? Perhaps a little of both.

The next day, I practiced with my fighting sticks more than usual. Though I should have been crocheting to help earn us much-needed income, I was too busy being worried about who might be coming home with Nikon that night, and if they were someone I could trust to help me find Antonia. I should have done more about searching for her before, but wasn't certain where to start or who would assist me safely.

My movements came out fast and sure, more so than they would have when I first practiced. Though the change was nice, it didn't distract me from what was coming.

I was still practicing when the door creaked open and two sets of footsteps came in the house. I paused mid-drill and wished I would have been upstairs crocheting instead of down here and sweaty.

Did I introduce myself? Did I tell them from the start I was blind? Or did I stay here doing drills and let them figure it out for themselves?

"Looks like Cassandra is practicing with her fighting sticks."

Nikon's voice came from behind me. "She's improved a lot over the last several months. You should see her in action during a fight."

"Is there a reason she needs to be fighting?" a woman asked.

"Hopefully not," I said, turning my head to my shoulder so they could hear me better. "But one never knows." Pulling my arm back, I let my stick whip through the air. The second followed after it in a frenzy that would have been difficult to keep up with when I first started.

"Let us all hope," the woman replied.

The footsteps drew nearer.

Nikon said, "Cassandra, this is a friend from work. She also hauls things around for those who need it. Meet Chloe."

I turned around, ready to hear her harsh words at me being blind. "Hello, Chloe. It's a pleasure to meet you."

"And I you." Her voice was smooth, almost like silk.

Unsure what to do with a new person, I twirled one of my sticks. "Do you fight?"

"Yes, but with knives."

I lifted an eyebrow. "Sounds like a challenge."

"Sounds like a good way for one of us to get injured," she replied.

"We're careful when we train," Nikon said. "Though I've gotten more than a bruise or two."

Chloe laughed. "Sounds like a good way to break a bone. I need all those for my job."

"If you ever change your mind and want to practice with someone, let me know." I put my sticks together and twisted until they became one. It never ceased to amaze me how easily they did that.

"Is she...blind?" Chloe asked, clearly not to me.

"*She* is right here and isn't deaf," I snapped.

"Oh. Sorry. I thought—"

"You didn't think," Nikon interrupted. "If you did, you would treat Cassandra with respect and not make me regret bringing you here."

I stood taller.

"Forgive me, both of you. That was unkind," Chloe said. "I've heard the warriors searching for blind people among others, but I've never met one."

It was impossible to know if I should be put out or understanding. In the end, I was a little of both. "Keep it a secret and you're forgiven."

"Of course, I will." She sounded affronted. "I would never betray you to such a cruel people. The Reding and Vading should have never ordered such a thing. I won't pretend to know a lot about the blind, but I see no reason they should become slaves who are treated even more cruelly than the rest of us."

My faith in Chloe was restored the instant she said that. "Agreed. Would you like to join us for dinner?"

Over the next several weeks, scenes similar to that played over in our house again and again as I met different people Nikon brought home. Soon, there were people coming over all the time, and it felt as if the entire community of odiosom knew of my circumstances.

After a month of this, I asked Nikon, "Are there more rumors about me?"

"A few among the amant, but the rest of us are quick to dispel them. I don't think you'll have to worry about the warriors coming to look for you—at least not because of strange rumors."

"But it could be someone we've told gives in to them."

His tone came out sad. "It's possible."

"Well, then, we'll just have to continue to have them over and feed them. Show them how much like them I am and hope for the best."

"Your cooking has gotten even better than when I first met you, which is saying something."

I beamed. "Hettie has been teaching me."

"One of these days, I'll meet her and thank her for all she's done for us."

"You just need to stop working so much, and that would have already happened."

Tewy squawked his agreement.

"Nikon?" I asked.

"Yes?"

"I've been thinking. Since most of the odiosom know me, perhaps it would be all right if I went out of the house sometimes. We could be careful to stay in our part of Itpy so no one else would see."

He was quiet. "I don't know. It's a risk for those who haven't seen you and if the warriors happened to come into the area while you were out, it could be a catastrophe."

"But there'd be a lot of noise alerting us, and Tewy would let me know. I think we should at least consider it. The walls are making me insane. I need some space. Need to get out of here."

He sighed. "We'll try tomorrow, but only if I don't hear any hint that the warriors will be in our part of town."

I leapt over to where I thought he stood. When I bumped into him, I wrapped my arms around him. I said, "Thank you."

He tensed before relaxing into me like a sigh and gave a gruff, "You're welcome."

Tomorrow, I'd be able to enjoy something beyond this building, and I'd get to be there with Nikon.

CHAPTER TWENTY-FOUR

The excitement turned to nervousness sometime during the night. As much as I wanted to be happy, the pit of my stomach felt as if it was being devoured by a sphinx. That couldn't be good. When Nikon came home, I barely touched my dinner.

"What's wrong? Too excited about going out to be able to eat?" he asked as Tewy picked at my plate from my lap.

"Something like that."

"You do look a little pale."

I forced a smile to my face. No matter how this went, I wouldn't let a little fear stop me. "We should get a move on."

"Are you sure you're ready for this?" A squeeze on my hand sent a wave of comfort through me.

"The truth is, it's difficult when I don't know what's out there. But I'll manage."

His chair scraped against the hard dirt floor. "We don't have to do this. I'll understand. Otherwise, I'm ready to go when you are."

I urged Tewy onto my shoulder, grabbed my cane, and hurried to my feet. "Let's go before I do change my mind."

It only took a moment for me to find my place at his arm. I kept close to him as we went outside, following his moves. I remembered a little from coming in when we first arrived, but it didn't take long for us to move into an unfamiliar world, dark and cold except for Nikon at my side and Tewy on my other shoulder. The air was fresh compared to being in the house all the time, even though I'd cleaned. The area didn't smell of sewage tonight, probably from the breeze blowing it in the other direction.

Each step was a foray into the unknown. A chance to explore, certainly, but also a chance to fall or fail.

"Your grip is tight," Nikon said, voice smooth. "Are you certain you want to continue on?"

I forced my grip to be tamer. "Yes. I need to do this."

We went forward, and Tewy whooped in my ear. I said, "What's he so excited about?"

"Chloe's carrying a bushel of seeds and fruits. I think he wants dessert."

"No, Tewy. You just ate." Besides, we didn't have the money for it.

Tewy jumped off my shoulder. A woman's laughter followed.

"Just a moment," Nikon told me, and pulled away from me. "Tewy, get back here."

Alone in the unknown. Or at least, it felt that way. I clenched my teeth and held back the fear with nothing but grit and determination. Using my cane to survey my surroundings, I went toward the voices.

"Sorry," Nikon said. "He's a rascal."

"It's not a problem," Chloe said.

"We can pay for that."

Actually, things were pretty tight. I wasn't certain we could, but we had to try.

"Don't worry about it. He didn't take much."

Lucky us.

"Cassandra, it's good to see you," she said.

"It's nice to meet you out here."

"Oh. I'm sorry. I shouldn't have said *see you.*" Her tone was distraught. "I should have been more considerate of your...condition."

How she reacted after the fact was more annoying than her first statement. "Please, don't worry about it."

"All right."

If I had to guess, I'd say she was embarrassed.

"We're out for a stroll," Nikon said, coming back to my side, Tewy jumping on my shoulder. Probably had some little treat in his hand.

"Enjoy then." She sounded skeptical, but thankfully didn't push anything else.

We continued on our way, the path only slightly bumpy beneath my feet. The dust collecting on them was a welcome and familiar sensation, if not quite the same as it had been at home. I took a deep breath of fresh air, enjoying its qualities as we went along.

The longer we were out, the less my fears plagued me. This was where I was meant to be. I loved it outside at Nikon's elbow, Tewy on my shoulder, the breeze taking away the usual chill from this time of night.

"How much longer until the rainy season?" I asked.

"Oh, a ways off still, but getting closer," Nikon replied. "How are you doing?"

"Wonderful." It was the most honest answer I could think of. "Do you hear that?" A faint noise came from somewhere to our left. It sounded like a rhythmic stomping and chatter.

"I do. We should probably avoid it."

"Why? We're in the odiosom part of town, what could it hurt?"

"A lot of things."

I nudged him toward the sound. "You're worrying too much. I'd like to see what it's about."

"You're right, I'm probably over worrying, but do you really want to risk it?"

I deflated. "Not really."

"Tell you what, we'll peek at it and if there's any danger as we get closer, we'll back away."

I perked up. "You think that'd be all right?"

"I do. My other thoughts aren't based on facts. We'll be fine." His tone sounded like he really believed that.

"Then let's go."

He gave a soft chuckle and pulled me to the left. We headed toward the sound as I tried to figure out what it was. A *thud, thud, thud, thud* came and then all was silent. Then the *thud, thud, thud, thud* would come again. What could it possibly be?

There wasn't an ominous feel to it, but neither was it happy. I didn't know what to expect, only that whatever it was made a lot of noise in intervals.

The noise grew louder as we came closer. Nikon's steps slowed, and he whispered, "It's a kofle."

That didn't make any sense. "Where's the music?" The laughter and the talking were missing too. This was more like a gathering for marching and silence.

"Music? Oh, right, you haven't been around for a while. The kofles have changed."

Seemed like they'd changed a lot since I'd last been to one over ten years ago. They used to be full of happiness and anticipation. If there was any of that left, it was lost to me.

We went a ways more before stopping and listening to the *thud, thud, thud, thud.* Nikon's words brushed my ear. "They're lined up in two lines facing each other like they used to, but there's no fun about it. The joy has been taken out."

"Why is it in the odiosom part of town instead of amant?" The loved part of town was where it had been held when I was a youth.

"Because this is for those odiosom who have been kicked out of the amant part of town but still have hope of finding love."

I wished I had that sort of hope.

"What are they doing?" I asked when the thudding returned.

"The men and women take turns walking different directions so they have a chance to look over everyone. The noise is the walking."

Noisy walkers could take lessons from Nikon. The thought of him being among them had me pulling back, though. I didn't know what it was, but something about the idea of him among all those unattached odiosom had me wanting to get away. It wasn't like he didn't meet new people every day, but this was a purposeful way to see as many new people as possible.

I must not have wanted him to fall in love with a woman and have him taken away from me, because that was exactly what would happen. In an instant, he'd go from being an odiosom to an amant who would move to the upper-class part of town, even if he had to share a house with another couple until a place of their own opened up or was built. He wouldn't need to be with me anymore. He'd get married and have a wife, eventually some children. There would be no point in keeping with a blind woman he had no relation to.

"Are you ready to go?" Nikon's words were close.

"Why do you ask?"

"Because you're tugging on me."

"I guess I am."

"Good. Let's get out of here." As we walked away and the noise faded into the distance, relief hummed through me. Still, I couldn't stop myself from asking, "Don't you want a chance to go to the kofle and look at all the women hoping to find true love?"

"I'm not going to find her here."

"How do you know?"

He sighed. "I don't for certain."

"We could at least try."

"We have much more important things to take care of. I wouldn't want to bring a wife into our troubles."

I liked the way he said "we," but the word *wife* had me itching to move faster away from the kofle we could barely hear. "We do have a lot going on, but becoming an amant would change that."

"Being an amant would only make things more complicated."

Not the reply I'd been expecting. "How so?"

"Why don't we talk about something more uplifting on your first foray out in months?"

I expected him to sound exasperated, but instead, he sounded like he truly wanted me to have a good experience.

"What do you have in mind?"

"Why don't we get some plums? I've got a small amount of change we could use to purchase some from a nearby cluster of trees a friend from work owns."

"I do like plums."

"I thought so."

We went off to get the plums, enjoying their sweet juice once we purchased them from the man Nikon knew. After we finished, we walked a while more before heading home.

It had been a long night, but a good one. I yawned, ready to get to bed as the door creaked open. We entered the house and headed upstairs. Halfway up, I froze. Voices came from the bedrooms.

Someone was in our house.

CHAPTER TWENTY-FIVE

I pulled back, trying to get Nikon to go with me. Together, we took several steps down when Tewy let out a squawk.

I burst into a run down the stairs as the voices came nearer.

"Cassandra? Nikon? Is that you?" a woman called out.

I'd never heard her voice before, but with her familiarity with our names, I stopped. Hesitantly, I called back, "Yes."

"Oh, good." The voice had come closer, along with two sets of footsteps. "We'd love to meet you. We're your new housemates."

The shock of having someone in our home, someone who could have been dangerous, still coursed through me.

"Leo was supposed to tell you," a man said. "Did he not?"

"No." Nikon's word was firm.

"Sorry," the woman said. Her voice was scratchy, like she'd been yelling for a long time. "He was supposed to come this evening before we got here to let you know. We moved from Ruso. Leo said you'd be fine if we moved in, but we don't have to stay."

"That explains it," I said. "We went out this evening, so Leo probably didn't have a chance to find us. We're just a little surprised by you, that's all. If Leo welcomed you, then we'll welcome you." Though I had to wonder if they knew I was blind, and what they would say about it. Had Leo told them? And if so, how did he know they could be trusted if they'd just moved here?

"This is a little awkward talking on the stairs," the man said. "Why don't you come up or we'll come down, and we can introduce ourselves."

"We'll come up," I said. I wanted away from the narrow space in case it came to a fight. I didn't expect it to, and I had training in the small spaces, but I didn't want to push my luck.

I went up the stairs, Nikon's familiar footfalls coming after me. When we reached the top, I realized it was a bad move. Though there was a little landing, I was bumping into the wall and another person in the space. It wasn't meant for four people.

"I'm Zoe and this is Kaius," the woman said. "We're so excited to be here. We've heard a lot about you, Cassandra especially, and it's wonderful to finally meet you."

My nerves stood on edge. "How have you heard a lot about me?"

"Oh, only from Leo," Zoe replied. "When we arrived this morning, he told us all about you. How you can't see, but you're persevering in the face of it all. And you don't have to worry, Kaius and I will most definitely keep your secret. We wouldn't want anything to happen to our housemate."

"That's...thoughtful of you." I didn't know how to respond. I was too busy trying to adjust to the fact that they were here. We'd known getting roommates was a possibility, but it'd been long enough that I'd sort of forgotten about it.

"It's no trouble. We like to do what we can to help others after so many people have helped us."

Were they doing something illegal or anything that would otherwise get them in trouble? I didn't want to be rude and ask, but it seemed like they may have been in some danger that people had helped them get out of.

"Are you brother and sister?" Nikon asked.

"We are," they said in unison, a little too fast. Zoe continued alone with a little laugh, "We heard you are too. That would be great fun for us. We can trail around together when it's not work time."

"I don't leave the house often." No matter how much I wanted to.

"Oh, that's not a problem. We can have all sorts of fun here. Though both Kaius and I need to find jobs. That should come, though. Leo said there are lots of them open right now, especially for those willing to do manual labor, which we both are."

"If you didn't have a job, what did you come here for?" The question popped out of me before I could suppress it.

"We were looking for a change of pace, weren't we, Kaius?"

"It's true." His words were curt, but not completely unkind.

"And so, we came here. Sands knows we didn't want to stay put in our tiny little shack doing nothing but work. And here we are, in a lovely new home with new friends and soon-to-be new jobs. It's wonderful." She sounded a little overenthusiastic. Or perhaps I was projecting my worries onto her and making it feel like she was overcompensating.

"We're happy to have you." I put as much truth into those words as I could.

"Unfortunately, we already ate for the night, and there weren't any leftovers," Nikon said.

There never were, not when we were scraping by day-to-day. I'd never given it much thought before, but Nikon worked hard to bring food to the table. Sure, I helped by making shawls, but I wasn't bringing in as much as him. If they expected us to feed them, they'd be sorely disappointed.

"Oh, we already ate," Zoe said. "You don't have to wait around for us to do things, though it'd be nice to see you and have your company. We know you have your own lives to live."

The hall grew warm. And silent.

A knock echoed up the stairs.

"I'll answer it," Nikon said.

Lucky him, getting out of the uncomfortable situation while I remained stuck here. No one spoke as I listened for whoever was at the door. It creaked open.

"Hello, Leo. Think you forgot to tell us something."

"They're here then?"

"Upstairs."

A couple sets of footsteps came up the stairs, and moments later I was more squished than before. An elbow that must have been Nikon's bumped into my upper arm. My other arm kept brushing against someone else. Zoe maybe.

"I trust you are getting to know each other," Leo said.

In a manner of speaking.

"Well enough," Zoe replied.

"Good. We'll make this work. Take good care of each other." Leo enunciated each word carefully.

"Keep secrets from the warriors," Zoe said.

That put it blatantly. "That would be kind of you."

Nikon squeezed my shoulder.

Zoe said, "I don't want them around here any more than you do. Besides, I could use a good friend and that won't happen if I sic the warriors on you."

Not sure if it was a good or bad thing to have another, unfamiliar friend, I plastered a smile on my face. Life was about to get more interesting.

The days started off with me being wary of Zoe and Kaius. When they went to work about the same time as Nikon, I was oddly grateful. Even more so when Nikon returned, but they were still gone.

Though we bought our own food, we soon grew accustomed to cooking meals at the same time while Zoe would talk. Despite my hesitance, I found myself becoming relaxed in her company, and even looking forward to it when she came home. She grew to be as almost as good a friend as Hettie. Nikon's friendship continued to be wonderful, but it wasn't the same as having another woman I could talk or listen to.

Zoe had the day off while Kaius and Nikon were going into work. Nikon slipped his hand into mine and whispered in my ear, "Are you certain you're all right if I leave?"

"I'll be fine," I whispered back, knowing he worried about leaving me alone with Zoe. "If the worst comes to it, she doesn't know how good I've become with my fighting sticks." I wouldn't really use them on her because it wouldn't come to that, but the tease pushed out my lips anyway.

He gave a small chuckle. "You are becoming an expert."

"As much as I can without my sight."

"There is that." The tone of his voice grew sad, and I wondered if he was thinking of the time he said that we might have fallen in love if I wasn't blind.

My chest gave a sudden, painful tug away from him. I let his hand go, wanting to have that touch but knowing it was useless.

Tewy jumped up on my lap, grabbing my fingers. Sweet little buddy must have known I needed something—until he placed a small item on my palm.

"What's tha—" I jumped from my seat, throwing the crawling thing off of my hand.

"What in sandburst was that?" Nikon said, voice heated, though no longer next to me.

"Tewy dropped what I think was a bug on my hand." I shuddered. "Gross."

"I see it," Zoe said from somewhere across the kitchen. "It's just a beetle. I'll see it out."

Grateful it wasn't something worse, I said, "Thank you."

"No problem. I don't mind crawlies as long as they aren't poisonous."

The back door creaked open and closed.

"I'd better get going," Nikon said. "Are you sure about this?"

"I am. It will be good to get to know our new housemate better."

His hand was in mine again, Tewy chirping as soon as we touched. Nikon said, "Stay safe."

"I will if you will." Which was easy to say while he remained, but the moment he was gone, I wanted him back. I should have been used to him leaving, yet it never became any easier. He was my connection to the world, the one good thing I knew I could count on. I didn't want that to change. Not in that moment. Not ever.

But he did have to go to work, and I had Zoe to get to know better. "I'll see you later."

"I'll plan on it."

Once the front door opened and closed, the back did the same.

"He's gone then?" Zoe asked.

I nodded.

"Good. We can have girl time then. What do you want to do today?"

Truthfully? "Go to the river. It's been way too long since I've been around the water. I miss it."

"We could do that." The enthusiasm in her voice was only dampened by my reality.

"There's no way to get in and out of the city without going through the warriors, which was hard enough the first time. They'd be certain to catch me a second."

"True enough—if you go out one of the gates. I know another way out."

Did she? She couldn't...and yet, the marauders had tried to

take me in through a ladder and not the gates. "How do you know about that if you just got here?"

"There's always a way." Her tone held a hint of secrets that I wanted to know more about.

"What's your story? Why did you really move?"

"Because we wanted a change of pa—"

Not buying it. "No, I think there's more to it than that. You're always happy, but you seem even more so—" almost in a fake way "—when we talk about you moving here. There has to be more to it."

Silence rained down, which said more than her words.

"You already know my secret," I said. "You can tell me yours. I promise it'll be safe with me."

It was still quiet except for a thumping noise that must have been Tewy hopping around.

"I don't know what's going on, but I know there's something. For example, why did Leo trust you so quickly? I mean, don't get me wrong, he trusted us too, but that's because I'm blind and he knew we wouldn't sell him out for anything. How did he know he could trust you?"

"Leo knew us before we came to Itpy." Her voice came out smaller than I'd ever heard it.

I leaned toward her where her words came from. "How?"

"I shouldn't be telling you any of this. Let's go wander around town and get to know each other better. By that time, maybe I'll be up to telling you." Her chair scratched against the floor.

I wasn't going anywhere. "How?"

"You don't make this easy, do you?"

"Nope. I'm as stubborn as they come." Not really, but for this, I could be.

"Listen, I would like to tell you, I really would, but I can't. Not yet anyway. Maybe one day soon, but until then, I need you to trust me and trust the fact that I won't tell anyone you can't see. I may have connections you didn't know about, it's true. The thing is, I can't talk about them much, not yet anyway. I've already said far more than I should have. Do you understand?"

Not at all. "I can understand that you can't talk about it. I hope you will soon though."

"I'll do what I can. Now, how about we get you to the river?"

CHAPTER TWENTY-SIX

O n our way, a familiar voice called out to me. "Cassandra, it's good to see you out," Hettie said. "I was just coming to visit."

I turned toward her voice. "I didn't know you had the day off."

"It's that time again."

I must have lost track of the days. It wasn't the first time that had happened. "Why don't you join us? Hettie, this is Zoe, my new housemate." I lowered my voice. "We're going to the river."

"I'd love to come. And all the food I have doesn't needed heating today. Plus, there's enough for all three of us."

"Wonderful," Zoe said. "Let's go."

We hurried through the odiosom part of the city until Hettie said we'd come to a wall. She also gave me details as Zoe pulled a ladder out from behind some crates and put it up.

"Let's go," Zoe said.

"You can't expect me to climb a ladder," I said to her.

"It's easy, just put one foot up and then another, along with your hands. I'll help."

"Climbing isn't the problem. I can do that fine. No, last time I went up a ladder by the outer wall, it was because marauders made me. Going out this way makes me feel like they're going to be waiting on the other side."

"Ooh, you met marauders. How frightening. You'll have to tell me all about it, but not until we're on the other side of the wall. We need to hurry."

"Do the warriors patrol it?" I asked.

"No, but I don't want others to see us."

Tewy gave his agreement from above my head. I had an inkling he'd already climbed the ladder and I didn't like the sound of that. "Maybe we should go back to the house."

"Don't give up on me now. You wanted to be with the river again; we can make that happen. A quick climb up and down ladders and then it's a short walk to the river. We'll find a nice, quiet place where there's no one else and we can enjoy the water."

"I'll go first if you'd like," Hettie said. "Marauders are frightening, but we'll be fine."

It sounded so nice. I wanted it, desperately so, but fears continued to cloud everything. "What if we're caught?"

"We won't be as long as we move quickly." Her words came out rapidly, but then she slowed them down. "Look, I know it's hard moving past something scary that happened to you, but you need to do it for your own peace of mind. Especially if it's going to give you something you want."

She was right. Of course, she was. Having fears wouldn't change, but I could change my reaction to them. I stuck my hand out. "Where's the ladder? Hettie, you can follow after me if you want. I'm going to do this."

"I'm good with that," Hettie said.

"That's right. You go get them." Zoe placed my hand on a wooden rung. It only took a few moments to climb to the top, even with balancing my cane in one hand. The harder part was when it came time for switching over to the other side in my skirt. I managed it and went down the ladder on the other side. Tewy jumped on my shoulder, giving me a scolding of monkey chatter, probably because I'd taken so long to climb up the wall.

Not long after, there was a creak of wood followed by a whoosh of sand. And then another.

Zoe said, "Let's get to the river."

I grinned as she let me put my hand on her arm. I would have preferred Nikon, but he likely would have been furious if he knew I'd escaped the city. The rush of the river was easier to hear out here. As we came closer to it, I wanted to run to it, but stopped myself.

On the way, Hettie told me about her week. It was much like any others. She kept busy and took care of her sisters, but otherwise kept mostly to herself. It surprised me, given she was so bubbly and welcoming around me.

We drew closer to the sounds of the river. I'd forgotten how much I loved the water. How much I'd missed it when it wasn't a part of my daily life. The magical sand I couldn't care less about, but the river, it held my love like nothing else. I wanted to bask in it the rest of the day. No, the rest of the week.

When I said as much to the others, they laughed. Zoe said, "We'll have to go back before work ends for the day, but the river will always be here waiting for us."

"True. How much farther?" The rush had grown louder.

Tewy answered with a whoop.

"Only a few more steps and you'll be in."

I released her arm and held out my staff. "Will you put this somewhere safe, please? I don't want it to get ruined in the water." Once probably wouldn't hurt it, but I wanted to take good care of it.

The wood left my hand, and the familiar tug of wanting to pick it back up came to me, but not as strong as the call of the water.

"I'll put it by some trees that are nearby," she said.

"Thank you."

I didn't wait any longer. I rushed forward, eager to return to the liquid I'd spent so much time in and around when Antonia had taken me to our lonely home. Thoughts of her drifted to me. Did I trust those I was with enough to tell them of my self-imposed task to find her? Maybe, but not today. This was a moment for fun, not worry and strife.

My feet touched the water, the coolness bringing a rush of memories. Sitting on a lazy day with Tewy on my lap, legs dangling in the river. Washing dishes. Being splashed by Tewy. Hiding away after Antonia lectured me.

The last one brought a damper to the moment. I brushed it aside and walked deeper into the river.

Though the liquid was cooler than the air, it wasn't as bad as it'd been by my old house. Compared to that, it was almost warm.

"You look so happy," Zoe said from somewhere to my right.

From my left, Hettie said, "I've never seen someone look so thrilled to be in the water."

"I feel happy. It's incredible how the walls of that house started to eat away at me." I wasn't meant to be an indoor person. Not like I'd had to become.

Tewy jumped off my shoulder as I went deeper into the river, not caring if my dress got wet.

"Your monkey looks like he's going to take a nap in a tree," she said.

I laughed. "Sounds about right."

We spent a good long time at the river, enjoying the break from the heat of the day. All I wanted was to savor the day, to let the familiar river soothe me. Though, there wasn't much time left before we needed to leave.

I lay down in the river, hearing a couple splashes of water nearby. Hettie said, "I wish I had more time like this."

"You do work too hard." They all did.

"It would be worth it if one day I found my true love." Hettie's words were an almost whisper.

Zoe asked, "Why do you say that? Does having some magic tell you to love another make that big a difference? It may be the only way nowadays, but I don't like it. People may fall in love, but they aren't always happy with the path they choose."

"That may be, but the amant get treated better than the odiosom," I said. "It would be an easier life I would think. Hettie? What do you think?"

"The truth is, I always wanted to be a mother. Yes, falling in love would be nice, but more than that, I want to have children."

That never happened outside an amant coupling. "I wish I could help."

Hettie gave a sad laugh. "There's nothing anyone can do. I stopped going to kofles a couple years ago. It doesn't seem likely I'll ever find the one. It leaves my heart aching."

Too bad she couldn't work caring for the amant's children. Though, maybe she didn't wish to. Maybe she didn't want to grow attached to children who would never be hers.

I let the water envelop me, going down until I touched the bottom with my fingers before popping back up. "Should have brought the laundry so Nikon wouldn't have to do it on his day off."

"Next time," Zoe said.

A thrill arced through me at the thought of a next time.

"This time," Zoe said, "must come to an end though. We've got to get back before it grows too late and we're more likely to be caught."

She was probably thinking of the guards, but the person that came to my mind was Nikon. He wouldn't stand for me risking myself like this.

It wasn't like he was my Reding or Vading though—not that I listened to them either. I didn't have to obey him. Guilt pierced me. He tried to keep me safe, and how did I repay that? By going off to the river without telling him. Though, he was the one to put me in danger to begin with. Still, when we all arrived back at the house, I would let him know what we did, and deal with the consequences. I didn't want to keep things from him.

And maybe if he knew how important getting out, especially to the river, was to me, he'd accompany me himself on his next day off.

I slogged out of the water, the magical sand squishing between my toes. Somehow, I'd even missed that. So much for my claims not to care about magic. Though, it wasn't the magic I missed, but the wet grains. Too bad that being in this water with the grains was what made the magic work. Did the High Priest or royalty know how it worked? If they did, they kept a tight lid on it.

"Do we have time to lie out and dry?" I asked.

"We've already stayed longer than we should have," Zoe replied. "Here's your cane."

The familiar tingle raced through me as I came in contact with the enhanced wood. I had a mad urge to untwist it and move through drills, but it wasn't the time. I forced myself to take a hold of Zoe's arm and use my staff with my free hand.

"Tewy, time to go," I said.

Hettie gave a soft laugh. "He's pretending to sleep in the tree."

"How do you know he's pretending?"

"He keeps opening one of his eyes to look at us."

"Dratted monkey. Tewy, you come now or you're going to be stuck out here by yourself."

"That got his attention," Zoe said.

Sand shifted, creating the scratching noise I knew, and then Tewy jumped on my arm and walked up to my shoulder. I reached up and petted him.

"How close are we?" I asked after we had gone some distance. It felt like it was taking longer to get back than it had to get to the river.

"We're about halfway."

"But you won't make it," a familiar female voice said.

We froze. The sphinx had found me.

CHAPTER TWENTY-SEVEN

I turned to face where the sphinx's voice had come from, cane in both hands ready to be untwisted and whipped into our protection. "What do you want?"

"It's simple. Answer my riddle. I have a life, but none of my own. I bleed when torn. When I wake, I never die until the very last one. You take me away, and I'm left with none."

My mouth went dry. I hadn't any idea what she could mean. How had Nikon known the answer right away when he'd been just a child? I should have spent more time thinking of it.

"Well?" Her breath fell on me with the word, sending a shiver of fear through me.

I opened my mouth to respond with something like I didn't know, but before I could get a sound out, Zoe or Hettie elbowed me in the stomach. Right. I couldn't say a word or that could be construed as an answer, and a wrong reply would get me killed.

Instead of replying, I made my staff into two and brandished my weapons.

"Leave us alone." Zoe's words shook.

"Fine, little ones." A space of silence filled the air until the sphinx spoke again from directly beside my ear. "My patience grows thin. You can't avoid answering forever. One chance left."

I swung toward the voice but met with air.

The sphinx laughed as her voice grew more distant.

After the sound was gone, Zoe ripped her arm from mine and growled. "You didn't tell me you had a sphinx after you."

"I didn't think to mention it. I'm sorry. Why is that such a big deal?"

"Because they rarely come into cities, but they'll always find you on the outside. We should have never come and now we're going to be late getting back. You're lucky you're still alive to return to the house, though I don't know if your brother is going to feel the same way."

"Is that true?" I'd never heard such a thing.

"It's true." Hettie's voice shook despite only saying two words.

I was stuck inside the city forever? It couldn't be. I had to figure out the answer to the sphinx's riddle so I could live again. Today had been too wonderful to not make it happen again.

My monkey trembled on my shoulder. "Tewy, are you well?"

He gibbered back to me.

Clearly, he didn't like the sphinx any more than I did. "It's all right. She's gone now."

"And we've got to be too," Zoe said. "It's going to be harder getting back in with everyone off of work." She grabbed my hand and guided it back onto her arm.

I twisted my cane back together and let it return to being a guide instead of a weapon. "I'm sorry."

"Forget it. Though I am glad I got to see the neat trick you can do with your staff. That's sandlious."

"Nikon made it for me."

As we walked, she said, "That was clever of him. Can you use it?"

I didn't know whether to tell her about treating it with magic or not, so I said, "Of sorts."

"It appeared to work. The sphinx left after you brought it out. Well, after coming so close I thought she was going to eat us both."

I shivered at the thought of her breath on me as she said her words of warning. I was as much of a mess as Tewy, who remained on my shoulder still shaking.

We hurried back as quickly as I could go. It felt like forever as the heat waned. If Nikon wasn't already home, he would be soon. He would be furious. I was in for it.

By the time we reached the wall of Itpy where the ladder stayed leaning against the wall, it had grown downright cold. I needed one of my shawls.

"Let me go up first," Zoe said. "I'll make certain there's no one on the other side before giving you the all clear."

"All right," was what I said, though I really wanted to tell her to hurry. I could already hear in my head Nikon's footsteps pacing the hard dirt floor angrily.

A soft scraping of Zoe climbing the ladder came to me. I bit my lip and petted Tewy, who had finally stopped shaking. I wanted to take his place, what with all the nerves going through me. I didn't know how much more I could handle. Jitters filled my body.

"It's clear, hurry up."

"You go first," I told Hettie.

"All right."

After waiting to hear signs of her passing, I reached out until my fingers brushed against a rung. Balancing my cane, I went up, Tewy jumping off my shoulder and bouncing up the ladder ahead of me. When I navigated the top to move to the next ladder, it was easier than the first time but still tricky.

Once I was at the bottom, Zoe shifted the ladder somewhere else while Tewy jumped back on my shoulder, and then she let me grab on to her arm. Hettie shuffled somewhere near my left. We hurried through the streets, the chatter and footsteps sounding.

They must be the people coming off of their work. Hopefully, we'd beat Nikon home. And Kaius, though I wasn't as worried about him.

"Here's where I part from you," Hettie said. "Thank you for the wonderful day, even if it ended poorly."

"Thank you for coming with us. I'm sorry about not letting you both know."

"Don't worry over it. We'll see each other again soon."

The slap of her footsteps receded as we turned the other way.

"Almost there," Zoe whispered to me.

The turns were familiar. She was right. We were almost there. I happily stepped up to the door, opened it without assistance, and went inside, my shoulders slumping with relief when Nikon didn't jump on us the moment we got back.

The door creaked closed, and Zoe bumped into me. I stepped forward so she'd have some room and said, "I think we beat them home."

"Think again." Nikon's words came out slow and barely above a whisper. They were the most ominous things I'd ever heard from him.

"Nikon, hello. It's wonderful to hear you." My voice was bright, full of fake life.

"I'd like to say the same about seeing the both of you, but I'm not sure I can bring myself to at this present moment."

After a moment of nothing, footsteps rushed to me, and I was gathered up in Nikon's familiar arms. His spicy scent held me close. I'd leave more often if this was how Nikon would treat me. I didn't want to let go. The comfort of his arms held me in. I sighed and leaned into him.

He tightened his grip before letting me go. He said in a gruff tone, "I can't believe you did that. You are in so much trouble, Cassandra."

From his tone, he was beyond furious, trying to keep it simmering inside.

"I…uh…better run upstairs," Zoe said. "I have some things I need to attend to."

Her steps went up two stairs before Nikon said, "Kaius will hear about this when he gets home. And Zoe, I never, ever want to hear about you taking Cassandra with you somewhere dangerous again."

"Of course." Her voice shook, and she headed up the stairs.

"It wasn't her fault," I almost yelled. "I'm the one that wanted to go—" I just stopped myself from saying where we went. Then I realized, he'd said we'd been somewhere dangerous. "How do you know we weren't doing something safe?"

"I scoured the city for you after coming home early for the day. Thought I would surprise you and take you out into Itpy, but it seems you took matters into your own hands."

The fight went out of me. He came home early—to take me out of this stupid house. I could have gone out with him today anyway. Instead, I left the city and went running into the sphinx. It was worth it though. The river had been a happy release that I'd needed for far too long. "I'm sorry. I didn't mean to go out into danger. I wanted—"

"Doesn't matter." Nikon's voice was hard. "I have to go tell Leo you're home. He's had people out looking for you too. He probably knows you are home, but I am going to be responsible."

I didn't know whether to grit my teeth or sigh. The fact was, I had been irresponsible, but I was a grown adult. I didn't need him lecturing me on anything. "You're not my parent," jumped out of me.

"No. Apparently I'm not anything to you."

The sting continued to hurt long after he'd banged the door closed.

CHAPTER TWENTY-EIGHT

When the door slammed closed later that night, I knew Nikon remained furious at me. I crocheted faster, yarn whipping between my fingers as I was huddled up on my bed with Tewy in my lap. I didn't want to know what Leo had said. Probably nothing good.

The stairs creaked but I couldn't hear Nikon's footfalls; he must have been angry to be so silent. Moments later, he said, "Leo's been informed."

"That's good." I didn't know what else to say. Everything was uncomfortable, leaving my insides twisting.

He sighed, closer than before. "Look. I'm sorry I said the things I did. It's been tense around here, and when you turned up missing, I was worried. When we couldn't find you anywhere in the city, I figured the worst had happened. I thought I'd failed at my job to keep you safe.

"If truth be told, I've thought about leaving you here. You seemed safe enough, and I don't know when the people after me are going to find me. I didn't want them to discover you too. I thought if I left you here, things would be better for us all. I didn't count on growing attached to you. Once I realized you were gone, probably to become a slave, I was more devastated than I had counted on."

The bed sank beside me. He continued, "I don't pretend to understand the connection between us, but there's something here. Something that makes me not want to lose you. Please, if you're going to do a dangerous activity, at least take me with you."

Not what I was expecting. He felt the connection too? I turned toward where his voice was coming from, and admitted, "I appreciate you being willing to go with me, but I probably shouldn't go out again."

"Why not? Don't get me wrong, I'm glad you want to stay in the city, but I don't understand why you wouldn't want to go out again. You seemed so eager to in the first place."

I didn't want to tell him, but I had to. He needed to know what was going on. "The sphinx found me again."

"Sandblastitall." The weight lifted from the bed and his footsteps paced the floor. "What happened? Tell me everything."

I went over what had happened with the sphinx. It wasn't my favorite thing to recall, but he needed to know the truth. "So, you can understand why I need to stay in the city."

"Yes, but what we really need to do is figure out the answer to the riddle. The correct answer, that is. You'll never be fully left alone if you don't figure it out."

"I was afraid of that."

The bed shifted again, and Nikon wrapped an arm around me. I leaned into him, taking in the comfort he offered. I needed it more than I would have guessed.

The embrace lingered, leaving me feeling as if there was something there. What was that?

"I know you don't want to hear it, but I still wonder what would have happened between the two of us if you had your sight."

I stiffened. This wasn't a line of thinking I wanted to go down. I ached for something more between me and him, but it could never, ever be. "When you fall in love with someone else, you'll know we could have never been." Because there was only one true matched partner for everyone. No one had found more than one person, even if their spouse died.

He said, "The longer it takes, the less likely it is to find that one person. Besides, I think I found that person in you. There's a connection between us, can't you feel it?"

Despite wanting to get closer, I shifted away from him. "There's something there, but it's probably the fact that you rescued me from where I was alone and I clung to that. You, on the other hand, feel responsible for me. That's the connection we have. Nothing more, nothing less." No matter how different I wanted it to be.

His arm left my shoulders. "I understand that you feel that way, but I will always wonder."

I would too.

"Besides, we're friends, aren't we?"

"That's true." We had more than the connection then, but it didn't feel like enough.

"Did you get dinner?" he asked.

"I'm not hungry, but th—"

A crash came from outside. "What was that?"

The thump of his footfalls hurried over to the other side of the hall where he knocked on Zoe's door. It opened with a squeak, and Zoe said, "The warriors are in the streets."

"We've got to go. Cover for us?" Nikon said.

"Of course."

Tewy gave a short squawk.

I agreed. I jumped to my feet. "We can't leave Zoe here alone to deal with who knows what. We have to either take her with us or you stay here with her."

"There's no time to argue," Nikon said at the same time as Zoe's voice came.

"I'll be fine," she said.

Nikon's calloused hand grabbed on to mine as I reached for my cane. I wasn't going without her, not if I could help it. "But Zoe."

"They're coming toward the house," she said. "Please just go. I'll take care of it."

I hated each step I took away from her, but Nikon pulled me up the stairs, out the door, and to the edge of the roof. He said, "Remember the way?"

"Of course. Does that mean you're staying with Zoe?"

"No. It means from here on out, we're going to be silent."

"But you won't fit in the sewer. Where are you going to hide from them?"

"Don't worry about me. Just go." He gave a gentle tug to my free hand and together, we jumped across to the other building.

It was strange going over air when I didn't feel the gaping hole under me. I knew it would be bad to fall or to mess up, but I didn't notice the difference. I hurried with Nikon through the rooftops, my chest tightening more and more the farther we went.

Breathing grew difficult. I didn't want to admit defeat, but this felt like it.

Nikon must have noticed me flagging because he slowed, though he didn't stop and still remained quiet.

Shouts came from below. Frantic voices called after them. The soldiers took people away, that much I could tell. There were protests and cries of dismay followed by shouts and the smack of skin hitting skin.

We jumped past it all. A warrior could look up and we'd be caught. Any moment, I could ruin both our lives. The thought of causing him to be captured along with me ripped at my soul. I couldn't let that happen to him. I had to get to the sewer before we were caught. That was the only way to save him, the only way to help.

Nikon would never let me go otherwise. He'd insist on staying with me until it was safe. Besides, I didn't dare speak without knowing what was happening in my surroundings. The voices and shouting were becoming less frequent, but that didn't mean a warrior wasn't lying in wait below.

We made the final jump, sailing through the air as it whipped across my dress. Despite the chill out, I burned with an internal heat. Anger and unfairness ripped through me.

Nikon guided my hands to the ladder. I could have found it myself eventually, but he made it much easier. Assuming he'd tell me if I couldn't go because someone was down in the alleyway, I made my descent.

I'd gone partway down when the ladder shifted as if someone else was on it above me. Nikon must have followed at a quick pace. I hurried down the last few rungs and stepped out of the way, grateful for Tewy's silence throughout the affair.

I gave him a scratch on the head, wishing I had a treat for him. Knowing he couldn't go with me in the sewer made this all the harder. I could handle being without other humans, but it was much easier with help.

The cries grew faint as we crossed over to the amant part of the city, hand in hand. Any second a warrior could come by and claim I was blind and take me away.

As the thoughts swirled within me, I knew I had to be braver than allowing them to drag me down. I clenched my hand around my staff, the only thing I'd be able to take with me besides the clothes I wore. It was unthinkable I was about to be among refuse, but it was better than being taken away to the Vading and Reding.

We walked through what Nikon had told me was a back alley and stopped when we reached the sewer. He gave my hand a squeeze and whispered in my ear, "I'll come get you as soon as it's safe again."

My throat tightened, making speaking impossible, so I nodded.

A heavy sound of a rock moving against another came, and it

was time to get in the sewer. The smell made me cringe from where I stood next to the entrance.

With Nikon's help, I gave Tewy a pat on the head and lowered myself in. Tewy jumped off my shoulder, probably as disgusted as me about where I was going. I wanted to say goodbye, but voices came from off in the distance.

We weren't alone out here.

I hurried in, trying to ignore the smell and failing with a gag. Nikon had been right. The place was tiny. I sat down and wedged myself in. I could scoot forward a little at a time, but it would be difficult to go far. Moments later, the scraping came again, and the air grew heavier, the stench not eased by the fresh air. I gagged, knowing I'd never get used to the stink.

The stone covered me, and I was jammed in place. If a warrior searched for me here, I was done for.

The voices I'd heard before climbing in grew closer. My nose burned with the stench. I gripped my staff to my chest, hoping it wasn't being covered in horrid filth like I was. This might have been the worst place I'd ever been in.

"What are you doing out here so late at night?" a stern female voice came.

"Going for a walk," Nikon replied, his response farther away from me than the first voice. As good as that was so he didn't give away my hiding place, I wished him closer.

"Get out of here and go home," she said. "If I see you loitering about during a raid again, I'll have you sent to the dungeons for a week."

"Yes, ma'am."

Was he as reluctant to go as I was for him to leave?

Didn't matter what I felt. He needed to take Tewy and get out of here. I strained to hear the sound of retreating footsteps. They were there but faint. And only one set. What were the people I assumed were warriors doing?

"Odd that he should be wandering the streets at night like that, and during a raid too," a man's voice came.

The stern woman replied, "He may have been up to something. Scout the area."

"If you think that, why didn't you hold him over?"

"Maybe he was doing as he said and is innocent, though I've yet to see an innocent odiosom."

She must be an amant. Anyone could be a warrior, and many odiosom chose the path for the food and housing.

"I take offense to that," the man said.

"Tell me I'm wrong."

There was a pause before he replied with, "It is suspicious. I'll check over there." The man's voice grew farther away, but when the woman spoke again, her voice was closer. "I'll search through here."

If they thought to look in the sewer, there was nothing I could do. I tried to follow the flow of water and yuck without making a sound. I shifted my weight to one side then the other, trying to pull myself along feetfirst, but it was slow going.

Footsteps echoed on the ground above me. I couldn't risk Nikon getting in trouble because of me, and I certainly didn't want to become a slave. Despite that, I couldn't gain much distance. I squeezed myself away from the entrance I'd used to come in but created a splash.

"Did you hear that?" the woman asked.

I was done for.

CHAPTER TWENTY-NINE

I took a shallow breath, both because of the stink and the fear of being heard. My hands gripped my cane so hard they hurt, but I didn't care. It was better a little pain bothered me than I cried out in fright, which was what my lungs wanted to do. That, and get fresh air.

"There's something over here," the woman said. Her voice was so close.

Had she found the entrance to the sewer? Did she know it was here and that a person could fit inside it? A small person, but I fit nevertheless.

"What is it?" the man asked.

"Don't know yet."

How could she not know? The sewer couldn't be that well-hidden, not if Nikon had found it.

"I think it's a—" The woman cried out. "Sandblasted monkey threw a rock at me."

"I'll get him."

Tewy. It had to be. He was making a pest of himself on my behalf. I squeezed my eyes shut tight and silently pled he didn't get caught. Who knew what these warriors would do with him?

"Ouch, he just bit me," the man cried out.

I wanted to cheer my little monkey on but didn't dare make a sound.

"Get him," the woman yelled.

A scuffle thundered overhead. What were they doing?

"You stupid monkey, get back here," the woman said.

Only I got to call Tewy a stupid monkey. At least it sounded like he was safe, if not being well behaved. For the first time ever, I was grateful for that. I hoped he got away though, and without any problems. The way the man and woman were hollering above me, they were having far more difficulty than he.

"Just let him go," the woman said. "We've got to report to the maveor."

The ruler of the city. Was he the reason for the raids? It made sense. Whether or not he was, it made my job of staying hidden easier. They couldn't look for me if they headed back to the maveor.

Their footsteps faded past my hearing. I didn't have anything to do except wait and try not to think about what I was lying in. It was a vain hope as I took shallow breaths. Time passed slowly, taking its odorous path. I didn't know how long I could handle it, though the longer I remained there, the less it bothered me.

I dozed a few times before the high scraping sound of the rock moving came from above me.

"Cassandra, you can come out now." Nikon sounded tired.

I wiggled back up and out, trying not to think too much about the filth covering me. "How am I going to wash? I can't go back in the house like this."

"I brought a change of clothes for you," Zoe said. "We'll have to chance you going to the baths in the amant part of town. No one should be there this time of night."

That explained the dozing.

"Do we have money for that? And won't the workers be suspicious we're there so late and I smell of sewage?"

"I know a back way in. No one will bother us. Besides, workers aren't here this time of night. Come on."

Grateful she was there, I followed the footsteps. Nikon tried to wrap my hand around his arm, but I pulled away. "You don't want to get any of this on you."

"If you could stand to stay hidden there for almost a full night, I can handle getting a little on me. Come on, I'll clean up while we're there too."

Reluctantly, I took hold of him, letting him guide me to wherever Zoe decided to take us. We wove through the streets until finally stopping. After several long minutes, Zoe said, "Got it. We can go in. But we have to hurry. It's getting close to dawn, and the workers will be here before too long."

Hurrying and getting this gunk off of me didn't seem to mesh, but there wasn't another choice.

Nikon took me past the cool air, and we stepped up into a building. The stone beneath my feet was surprisingly warm. It smelled damp in here, but not mildewy. While we navigated the hall, I asked, "Where's Tewy?"

A pause.

"I locked him up so he wouldn't come with and be noisy. He created quite the fuss when I left you in the sewer," Nikon said. "He left and didn't return home for some time. I was worried he might repeat the incident."

"He came to where I was and distracted the warriors who shooed you off," I replied. Good little monkey.

"Here we are," Zoe said. "Nikon, you go that way. Cassandra, come with me."

I followed the sound of her voice until she put my hand on her elbow. We went past the cool steps and into a hot room where the splash of water sounded constantly.

"If you don't mind, I think we'll burn your clothes," Zoe said. "I brought you a change from your room."

"It's not that I mind, it's that I'm not sure we can afford another set."

"We'll make something work. Those things aren't good for anything but burning."

"I'd hate to be around the smell of that fire." I stripped down and went into the pouring water. It made me shiver with its coldness, but I basked in it, cleaning both myself and my staff with a chunk of soap Zoe gave me.

I scrubbed as quick as I could, but I couldn't get the feeling and stench of grime off of me. After scouring as much as possible, Zoe helped me to the baths. When I stepped in, I was grateful they were warm at least. I wanted to stay in there and soak for a good long time, but Zoe said, "They'll be coming in the next hour. We need to get moving."

With a sigh, I soaped up one final time and rinsed off. It felt so good to be clean and slip on a fresh change of clothes. I just hoped my cane wouldn't be adversely affected by all the disgusting mess and water it'd been exposed to.

We met Nikon in the hall where we'd left him and he took over guiding me from Zoe. Once we stepped out of the building housing the baths, the cool air swirled across me, making me shiver. My hair dripped onto my shoulders. There hadn't been time to dry it. We could take care of all that at home.

As we hurried through the streets, I kept expecting a warrior to stop us, but no one ever came. Stepping into my house made me almost fall with relief. It felt safe here, even if it truly wasn't. Better than that, it didn't smell like waste.

I wanted to climb into bed and sleep for the rest of the day, and possibly night, but there were other things that needed taken care of first. "What happened while I was gone? Why did it take so long?"

"They ransacked the house," Zoe said. "The warriors were certain we were hiding something, though they never figured out what, but made quite the mess looking for it."

"I'm afraid your room is a disaster," Nikon said.

I sighed. "At least I can stay home and clean it up."

Footsteps came from down the stairs. I tightened my grasp on my cane.

"You made it," Kaius said, the relief clear in his voice.

I relaxed my grip. I'd almost forgotten Zoe's brother was around. He worked more than even Nikon, being gone most hours of the day. I didn't usually hear much emotion from him. This was the most I'd ever heard. He cared for me? Perhaps, but the concern was more likely for his sister.

"We did," Nikon replied. "No problems. Got past all the warriors and they were none the wiser."

"I think it's time then," Kaius said. "You should invite them, Zoe."

I asked, "Invite us to what?"

"Are you sure?" Zoe said, clearly not to me.

"They've earned the right to know. I think Leo would agree with me."

Leo? That left me more confused than ever.

"Tell us," Nikon said.

"You have to promise to keep this a secret," Zoe said solemnly. "Lives are on the line if you don't."

"If it protects innocents, I can do that," I said.

"Only the innocents," Nikon added. "I'm not making any promises that will protect those who don't need it."

"Fair enough," Zoe said. "We, Kaius, Leo, and I, would like to invite you to the odiosom rebellion."

"What?" Nikon and I said at the same time.

"You heard me, and I hope it's something you'd both be interested in."

"This is the secret you wanted to tell me but couldn't," I said. "I didn't realize it would be anything of this magnitude."

"I'm sorry I didn't tell you," Zoe replied, voice soft. "I wanted to, so much I wanted to, but Leo told Kaius and me to keep quiet until we were positive that you could both be trusted."

I tried not to be hurt, but the sting still affected my chest. "I'm blind. Just that fact alone could make me a slave for the Vading and Reding, and you couldn't trust me?"

"We had to be sure."

"How much more certain could you be?" I snapped back.

A footfall came closer to me. When Kaius spoke, his words were soft but voice stern. "That's why Leo took you in. You don't think he really picks everyone off the street and gives them a house to live in, do you?"

Stupid me, I thought he did.

"He should have known then we could be trusted," Nikon said, words sharp.

"If he risked it and you betrayed us all? Too big of a risk," Kaius said. "Besides, Cassandra he trusted right away—she'll never become an amant. It's you we had to be sure of, Nikon."

"Nikon would never tell." He wouldn't. Not when it would affect my safety, and the safety of those we'd come to know. But how well did I know him really? I still didn't know why he ran or what he was before he did so.

"I wouldn't." Nikon's words were vehement. "If it risks Cassandra, I wouldn't dare. Besides, I have no love for the Reding and Vading."

"We know that now, but we had to be sure," Kaius said.

"You've both proven yourselves. We have a meeting tomorrow night you're welcome to come to if you would like. But know this: we will not tolerate even a hint of betrayal." Zoe's tone left no doubt she meant every word.

I could understand that. "Why are you rebelling? I have ideas, but I'd like to hear yours."

"The raids, coming after innocents like you or those of us trying to do something against them. They've taken slaves not just of the few blind they find, but anyone who disagrees with them—

or who they perceive disagrees with them. Not letting us rise in status simply because of something we can't control. They treat us like we're worth nothing. It's intolerable."

That was beyond true.

"We'll keep your secret, but we're not going to the meeting," Nikon said.

I whipped toward where his voice came from. "What do you mean we're not going?"

"It's too risky."

"We'll leave you to settle this," Zoe said. "If you decide to come, meet us here tomorrow after work."

"Thank you, Zoe and Kaius, for everything," I said.

A slim hand grabbed my own. "You're welcome."

Zoe let go of me and two sets of footsteps went upstairs.

Once they were gone, Nikon grabbed my arm and helped me to the kitchen. He spoke, keeping his voice low. "You can't go with them. It's too risky."

"Perhaps, but it's better than sitting by doing nothing."

His touch left my arm, making it cold. I rubbed it, trying to bring the warmth back in, but it wasn't the same. When he spoke, his words came out shaken. "Sometimes, doing nothing is best."

Where was this coming from? I doubted he would tell me, but then, it wouldn't hurt to try. "Do you say that because you did something? Something that Valeriana knows?"

"It'd have been better if I had instead of stumbling onto what I did, but that's saying too much. Look, I think that what they're doing is probably a good thing. Despite that, it's going to be dangerous. I can't protect you if you go there. Anytime there's a rebellion, the Reding has his maveor and warriors find them and smash them. Anyone caught with them is considered guilty whether or not they actually are."

"Is that what happened? You were a warrior, a soldier who followed orders and had to capture people who didn't deserve it?"

That wouldn't explain why he was being chased though, yet, it felt as if there was some truth to it.

He didn't respond.

I'd probably hit a spot I shouldn't have, at least not aloud and not in this moment. "Look, we need to focus on the fact I'm going whether or not you want me to stay. I can't do much, but I need to do what I can. I don't believe the rulers should be able to get away with what they do. It's not fair that the amant lord over us just because they've been the few who have found love. We need to do something about it."

He gripped me by the shoulders. "Are you certain this is what you want? Even if it means being caught and becoming a prisoner? Because if you do this, I'm not sure I can protect you from that fate."

I licked my lips. It sounded scarier when he put it that way. It was not that I wanted to give in to my fears, but neither did I ever want to become a slave. Didn't matter. There were some things that were worth the risk regardless of the cost. "I'm going. No matter what happens, I need to show the amant can't win no matter how hard they try."

"If you're positive, I'll go with you, but if we're both caught—"

"I won't blame you."

"But I'll blame myself." With those final words, he stormed off.

He made me doubt the choice I'd made and felt was right in my heart, but I wasn't turning back.

CHAPTER THIRTY

I t was time. We all gathered in the hall by the front door, and I waited for Zoe or Kaius to tell us what was going on.

"Where we have the meeting changes, for safety reasons," Kaius said.

"The meeting should have already started. They tell those trusted where the next meeting is. We should be all right to leave now." Zoe's words trailed toward the door.

I followed on Nikon's arm. "How will you know where to go next time?"

From behind me, Kaius replied, "They know we're bringing guests so they'll let us know sometime before the next meeting. And if you're both proven worthy, eventually you'll be added to the beginning of the meeting."

"The meeting is split in two?" Nikon asked.

"It is. Those who've earned more trust are included for the whole thing. Hopefully you'll get there someday soon."

I didn't know if I hoped for that or not.

Once we were out on the street, Nikon guided me through the roads behind two sets of footsteps. Tewy had been instructed to stay home, left in my room with treats. I'd cleaned it enough from the warriors making a mess of it for him to have a place to stay. I didn't know if having him with us would be good for anyone, not when we were supposed to remain silent and hidden from any warriors. I wanted to ask what would happen if there was a raid during the meeting but didn't want to alert anyone who might be walking by to what we were doing. They probably had a plan for it.

We walked some distance, turning enough times that it became hard to keep track of. A door creaked open, and we stepped toward it. After we were in and the door closed, we headed down some stairs. They were narrow, making it difficult, so I went down after Nikon, one hand on his shoulder, the other on my cane.

Voices drifted to me. I didn't know what they were saying yet, but a lot of them floated to me. They stopped before we got to the bottom, probably Zoe or Kaius letting them know we were here. I didn't know what to expect and nerves grabbed ahold of my gut. What if I did something wrong? What if they didn't like me? What if we were trapped in this basement when the warriors came?

I brushed my thumb along the top of my staff. I could do this, I needed to remind myself of that.

"Zaykai, Nikon and Cassandra," Leo's soft voice pierced the silence with his greeting. "We're glad you could join us. Please, make yourselves comfortable. Kaius, Zoe, thank you for bringing them."

"It's our pleasure," Zoe said.

Nikon led me not much farther before he whispered, "There's a seat right in front of you."

I reached out, found the back of a chair, and made myself comfortable on it—or as comfortable as I could. With all the shuffling of other people and my nerves on edge, it wasn't easy. Someone sat next to me, their leg brushing against my left one. Nikon whispered, "I'm on your left, Zoe is on your right with

Kaius next to her. There's about fifty people maybe, in the basement of this warehouse. Leo's standing at the front."

Fifty? That wasn't anything. Not compared to the warriors. Yet, it was more than I expected.

"Now that we're here, let's get to the important things," Leo said. "We have a common purpose, and it is that the amant are too oppressive to others not like them. We want—no, *need*—to change this. We can't do it without your support. It can't come to violence though, not without everyone here consenting. We want as peaceful of a process as we can make. We don't want a repeat of the Govlin Wars."

The wars had been ghastly, at least the little I knew of them. My parents hadn't wanted to speak of them. It was said everything was different before them, but I didn't understand exactly how. I knew the government was newly formed and that was why the Reding was able to rule without being an amant, but slowly the amant took over as the ruling class. They must have been grateful when he found his love and became one of them.

All that happened while I was gone though. I couldn't imagine how much that'd changed Eppla. It seemed it'd only made the people more divided and those ruling even stricter.

"We want a camaraderie the amant can't destroy. An understanding of each other and the way we do things. We need to help each other. Bring a sense of belonging to our world and spread it across Eppla. Itpy isn't the only city with rebellions."

A collective gasp came from the crowd. I had to control one of my own. This was a bigger operation than I'd thought.

"That's right," Leo continued. "Kaius and Zoe have moved from the city of Ruso and have come to tell us more of what's going on there. Kaius?"

Footsteps moved from the side of me to the front of the room. Kaius said, "Ruso is different than Itpy in that our amant are smaller in numbers. That makes it easier on us, but the Reding and Vading must be aware of the plans we've tried to make because they recently sent more warriors to Ruso. Despite that, the odiosom are strong. They are working against the warriors, planting traps and tricks against them and the rulers. They even have the maveor on their side."

Another gasp, this time louder.

How did they get the maveor of Ruso on the side of the odiosom? Maveor were always amant, and that fact never changed, not since the office had been implemented. Before I had time to consider my actions, I called out my very own question, "How did you get the maveor on your side when they are traditionally amant?"

Silence sprinkled down until it was heavy on me. Perhaps I should have stayed quiet, but too much could impact my way of life if this rebellion worked. If we could change people's opinions, maybe then I could go out in the open without worrying if I'd become a slave for the Reding and Vading.

"Good question," Kaius replied. "He was good friends with some of us before he became an amant. He's a kind man with many friendships that extended into his being an amant. The biggest obstacle has been his wife. She's against us more than anything else and tries to turn him away from us. I believe he's had to keep his involvement a secret from her."

I couldn't imagine that going over well. If she ever found out, she could have him sent to the dungeons or killed. She would have still been considered an amant, as would anyone that had ever fallen in love. But, if he was willing to risk his life, who else out there would do the same?

"Thank you for the information, Kaius," Leo said. "I'd like to point out their work didn't happen overnight. It took years. Kaius and his sister, Zoe, have agreed to help us, but it's going to take time and hard work. We will get our voices heard. The amant will listen to us, and if they don't, we'll change things to be in our favor. Some of you may be able to do more than others, but I expect all of you here to do the best you can. Without your help, the amant will win and our lives will get worse instead of better. Now, what concerns do you have to bring to my attention tonight? Yes, Sargon?"

A rich baritone said, "There's been rumors about the warriors looking for someone who stole something from the Reding. Is this something we need to worry about?"

Nikon's leg that brushed up against mine tightened.

"There have been rumors going around about this, yes, and we believe it's why there have been more raids than usual. It does not, however, mean there is any extra danger to us, as long as we cooperate with the soldiers and they don't discover anything of note with us."

A woman asked, "How can you be certain? The warriors will use any excuse to bother us that they can."

Leo replied with calming words, but it was hard to focus. Nikon sat tenser than I'd ever noticed him before, except maybe when I'd left the city with Zoe. Did he have something to do with what was stolen? What could it be to cause such an ordeal? And why did he feel the need to keep it hidden from me if that was the case?

Leo answered a few more questions I had a difficult time paying attention to before finally drawing the meeting to a close. Shuffling and talking grew. Words whispered about the new plan and if the jackal would be involved, whoever that was.

Nikon pulled me up next to him and placed my hand on its usual spot on his arm; the muscles were so clenched, I was afraid he would hit something—or someone.

"Nikon..." I didn't finish.

"Yes?" Despite the pressure that was barely restrained, the word came out clear and calm.

"Never mind. We'll talk about it later."

We walked a couple steps before stopping when Zoe said, "Well, what do you think?"

I opened my mouth to reply, but Nikon beat me to it. "We shouldn't have come."

"Yes, we should have," I retorted. "It was good to hear, Zoe. Thank you and Kaius both for inviting us. I had no idea that you were both so involved in things."

"That's the way it's supposed to be," she replied. "We like to do what we can, like influencing those in government, but without drawing too much attention to it. Sometimes, it can't be helped though, as we plant traps for those against us. The unwanted attention not only creates problems if the warriors catch on to it, but can cause strife within our own community if you're not well-versed in manners like Leo is."

"Both you and Kaius have impeccable manners," I replied, trying not to show my growing alarm at the stiffness in Nikon's arm. "I can't imagine anyone having a problem with you."

"You'd be surprised at Kaius's temper when it comes out, which isn't often, but does happen on occasion."

"That does seem startling. He's so quiet."

"Until you mess with someone he cares about."

Thinking of how upset Tewy got at the warriors searching for me, I said, "I can understand that."

"We should be going," Nikon said.

"Now?" I wanted to mingle and learn more about these people I was hoping to be a part of.

"Now." His tone was stern.

I frowned but didn't protest. "I guess we'll see you at the house, Zoe."

"Good. We'll have to talk about how you felt about the meeting. Hopefully, it works for you. If not, that's fine as long as you keep our secret. We'd love it if you could join and add your support and opinions. I'll let you go though. We try to leave just a few at a time, so it's the perfect time for you to make an exit."

"Thank you for inviting us," I told her. "I look forward to our discussion."

Nikon guided me away before I'd finished speaking. I would have minded, except for the fact I could tell how upset he'd become. I didn't want to make that worse. Instead, I tried to hurry along with him, to get home sooner so we could discuss everything going through his mind.

We were stopped a few times by well-meaning people trying to get to know us better, but Nikon steered the conversation to a quick goodbye, and we went up the stairs. Once we were outside, I expected him to slow down a bit, but instead, he quickened his pace. Nothing I couldn't keep up with between him and my cane. The question was, why was he so anxious?

Was he really the one who had stolen from the Reding? If so, what plans had he stolen? Was this why that woman—what was her name, Valeriana?—had come after Nikon? Did she know he'd stolen from the Reding and that was why she was chasing him? Us. She was chasing *us*—if she was still coming after us, which Nikon seemed to think she was. And if I was being hunted, I wanted to know why. No more of this sniffing around telling me it was too dangerous.

Whether he sensed my mood and wanted to get away from it, or if he wished to get around his own thoughts, he gently took my hand off of him when we got home and bounded up the stairs.

I hurried up after him, stopping at my room. A ruckus came from inside, a patter of feet moving quickly across the floor and some other noise I couldn't recognize. Tewy. I opened the door. "What have yo—"

He jumped on me, gibbering like I'd never heard before.

"You don't like being left alone, I take it?"

He popped out of my arms and down the stairs. I sighed. I'd have to deal with him later and figure out what mess he'd made of my room, because from the sound of things, I'd be shocked if there wasn't a mess. For the moment though, I wanted to talk to Nikon. I just hoped the conversation went well, and I didn't wind up back where I started—with no information at all.

CHAPTER THIRTY-ONE

I knocked on Nikon's door, and it squealed open. "What?"

"I wanted to know if we could talk." But clearly, it wasn't going to be an easy conversation.

"Sorry." He sighed. "I didn't mean to snap, it's just... Do you want to come in?" I nodded and he led me in with a, "Would you like to sit?"

"No, thank you." I'd rather hide by the wall and have a quick escape if needed. The wall was rough against my fingers as I felt my way across. Once I was partway in, I leaned my back against it. "Do you want to talk about why you're so upset over what you heard today?"

"I'm not upset." His tone clearly belied that.

How did I address what he didn't want to speak about? Might as well be blunt and get right to it. "The something that was stolen from the Reding, that was you, wasn't it?"

"Shh." The boards creaked as he hurried closer. "Don't say things like that. If someone heard—"

"But no one's here. Besides, it's true, isn't it?"

He took my left hand in his, bringing it to his chest. "Sweet

Cassandra, please don't stick your nose where it doesn't belong on this one. It's not something you're ready for."

I shook my hand from his. "Who are you to say what I'm ready for or not?"

"The person who's here to protect you."

"I think it would be better if you let go of whatever it is you're hiding. I already know about Valeriana. You've got to be involved in stealing the plans, it only makes sense. You might as well tell me everything so I'm not blundering about in things I only half understand."

"*I* don't even understand them, and don't know how to explain them to anyone else." He sounded tired.

I reached out my hand until it ran into his chest. I pressed my palm flat against him. There was no armor between us, just a thin layer of linen. At some point, he'd stopped dressing as a warrior. Likely, as soon as we'd arrived in Itpy or even before. That was probably for the best but made me worry he didn't have enough protection. "Nikon, you've got to tell me. I can help."

"No one can help." Despite his words, he moved closer. "I'll tell you, but you have to promise not to tell another person. Or monkey for that matter. And it's not something we should discuss casually. If someone should overhear us, it could be detrimental to us both."

"Because Valeriana could find us?"

"Because she and a lot of other strong people could discover us and do their best to kill us."

"Like they aren't doing that already?"

"Don't you remember me telling you they could torture you for information first? Do you want that to happen?"

"No, but whatever they think, if they capture me and realize I'm connected with you, torture is coming my way, so talk."

He sighed. "I'm sorry I got you into this mess."

"It's too late to fix that now. What is the mess?"

When he finally spoke, there was a hesitance to his voice. "I stumbled across something while working one day." I wanted to ask what his work was but didn't dare interrupt. "Though I took the papyrus and studied them, I never understood what they said. Reading has always been difficult for me. The words, they don't always make sense and scramble themselves up. Despite that, I studied them the best I could, and the more I read, the more fear grew in my heart, and I didn't dare ask for help. They were plans for something. Plans that have to do with the water and the waterfall."

Fear pinched me. "The waterfall by my home?"

"Do you know of another? Because this is the only one I know of, and I only heard rumors about its existence. Though I believe that distant rumble I heard at your home is it."

"Yes, it's there." I'd become so accustomed to the noise, it didn't even register anymore. The waterfall was one of my favorite places. I'd been there many times, but we'd gone the other way when we'd left my home, and I'd never taken Nikon through it. What plans could someone possibly have with the waterfall?

"I knew it had to be. The plans never stated what they were doing, at least not that I could tell. It seemed like the Reding wanted to research the waterfall. That there was something going on with it that he wanted to understand better. Something to do with the Govlin Wars."

"Is he trying to restart them?" He couldn't do that. The population was nearly wiped out from the last one, which had killed off almost all of the elderly. Not that anyone knew why or how the elderly had died with the wars, but that only made it more frightening. No wonder Nikon wanted to keep it a secret.

"I don't know. The Reding has always been secretive, but I thought maybe if I talked to him, he'd give me a hint as to what happened."

"You spoke with the Reding?" No one did that, except maybe the Vading and a few amant. "Are you actually an amant?"

"No, nothing like that."

"Then who were you to ask him for explanations?"

With a half growl, half sigh, he said, "Apparently, no one. Before this, I thought we had an open and honest relationship. Something that would allow me to learn and understand from him, but apparently not."

"That still doesn't explain how you were close enough to the Reding to even talk to him."

He grunted. "You're right. I'm an elite warrior, one specifically meant to protect the royalty."

I tried not to squeeze Tewy tight, though I wanted to. I'd not just been living with a warrior, but an elite warrior who could have turned me in this entire time. I shouldn't judge him though, at least not until I heard the whole of his story. "What happened?"

"When I was guarding him one night, I asked if there was anything I should be concerned about. If there was something that might affect the safety of Eppla, and the people who resided within its boundaries. He said no, but he watched me with hooded eyes. You probably would have heard suspicion in his tone. I didn't. I kept pushing. Asked if there was something going on with our water supply and the waterfall. I wanted to ask specifically about the plans I had with me, but he'd already dismissed me. Before I knew what was happening, he ordered my capture and I was attacked. That's where I got my wound and why I ran."

I slid my hand down to his and gave him what comfort I could. It was difficult to imagine being attacked for simply asking a question, but knowing what little I did about the Reding, it made sense. Didn't make it any less sad.

"I went in disguise and heard they were searching for a warrior, one who'd stolen something."

"Wait, how did you do this if you were already wounded?"

"The injury didn't seem that bad until I ran. It grew worse as I ran away."

"Then what happened?"

"I hid the plans and made my way here, and you know the rest.

I tried to get to the waterfall so fast, I stopped putting sand on my wound and wound up delirious and tied up by a beautiful blind woman."

My breath grew quiet. I didn't know how to react. What to think. How should I help him? Help us? I didn't know. If the Reding knew him personally, if this Valeriana person had been sent after him to kill him, what could I possibly do to assist him? I was just in the wrong place at the wrong time. "You don't still have the plans?"

There was the familiar, light thudding of Tewy approaching, and then he was on my lap.

"They're well hidden, but no, I don't have them with me," Nikon said.

"Just as well as I couldn't read them either. Do you think this is something the odiosom should know? Something we should bring to Leo's attention?"

"If it could start another war, no. I don't know who to trust with the information. It would be nice if you could read the papers and make sense out of what I couldn't. I'd like to think I'm overreacting, but since the Reding sent Valeriana after me, there's no doubt in my mind that whatever I came across is dangerous."

I ran my free hand across Tewy's fur while keeping my connection with Nikon. His hand held tight to mine as if he needed that bond even more than I did. "Do you know Valeriana personally?"

Silence followed by a twisted, "Yes."

"Tell me about her."

He gripped me tighter like I was the only thing keeping him anchored to Eppla. "She's cruel, doling out the Reding's dirty work whenever he needs it done. She does it with a glee unbefitting any person. She likes torturing people for fun. And now you know why I didn't want to tell you any of this. If she finds either of us, she won't stop until we're babbling incoherently, and then she'll take great pleasure in killing us."

"And to think she was so polite to me when she came to the cabin."

"I'm surprised she didn't start in on you then or that she didn't grab you and interrogate you. Though, she was probably just as surprised to find you, and she was too busy searching for me to want to drag you all the way back here. I didn't think anyone lived past the chasm. No one did."

"My caretaker took me out there herself. Said it would be a safer place for me to grow and learn away from the critical eyes of others. At the time, I thought she was right. I thought everyone would ridicule me for being stuck as an odiosom the rest of my life. But now... Now, I know she was wrong. The people here have been kind and receptive. I don't regret those years I spent there alone though, not if it meant I was to find as good of a friend as you. I'm here for you, so where do we go from here? What do we need to do?"

I expected a reply, but instead, his arms wrapped around me, pulling me to him in an embrace. Tewy chattered through it all, but I didn't mind. My two best friends were here and safe. I needed to keep them that way... I just wasn't certain how.

And then I remembered the shambles Tewy had made of my room. "You should see how little Tewy liked being locked away while we were gone."

Nikon pulled away, leaving me cold. "What did he do?"

"I don't know the full extent of it, but it felt and sounded like he made quite the mess."

"How do you put up with him?" He laughed.

Tewy squawked.

I chuckled too. "I don't know. I'd probably make a mess if I was locked away in a room without knowing why too." I sobered. "But that's not what we should be worrying about right now. We need to figure out what steps to take next."

"You're right. I've been running and hiding, but if those plans say something like we are going to cause another war, I can't stand by and do nothing anymore. As much as I don't want to talk about it, maybe we should. It seems like the rebellion here would be supportive if we told them what was going on. Or at least Leo and maybe Kaius and Zoe. It's hard to talk about after keeping it quiet so long."

"I can understand and agree. I don't think we have to go this alone. Besides, the more people know, the less Valeriana and the Reding will be able to do, right?"

He sighed. "I'd like to think that, but I'm afraid they may go so far as to commit mass murder instead. There's nothing to stop them with all the power behind them."

Not a comforting thought.

Downstairs, the door creaked open. We were no longer alone and free to discuss what needed talking about.

I whispered, "We'll figure this out."

We didn't have any other choice.

CHAPTER THIRTY-TWO

"You weren't kidding about your room being a disaster," Nikon said. "Tewy really worked a number on it."

"And I'm the lovely person who gets to clean up after him— twice in two days thanks to the warriors."

Tewy squawked angrily.

"I know. We won't leave you alone locked up again. I didn't want to lose you. Can't you understand that?" He probably couldn't, but it made me feel better to say it.

A couple thuds came from the floor, then he was in my arms. I ran my hands over his soft fur, grateful he seemed to have forgiven me.

"What happened here?" Zoe said from behind me.

I turned to face her. I knew she and Kaius had come home, and we'd stopped all conversation so they wouldn't hear it, but guilt pricked at me for not telling her more. She'd let us in on her secret of being part of the odiosom rebellion. It felt awful to keep something from her, and kind of like she knew we were hiding something. "Tewy didn't like being locked in his room."

"Bring him next time. I don't think anyone will mind."

"All right." But I wondered if there would be a next time.

Nikon's words brought a feeling of foreboding to me. There was so much that could go wrong with us staying here. On the other hand, it was nice to know we were safe in a community that included us as their own.

Still, many dangers remained for us to navigate, and I wasn't certain what the right path could be.

"I'll help you clean," Zoe said.

"You don't have to."

"I want to."

"Thank you."

"I'm going to go make something to eat, I think I'll get in the way if I try to assist you," Nikon said.

I wanted to take hold of him and not let him go. After what he'd said, I worried that any moment, Valeriana or any other warriors could come and rip us apart.

But we couldn't stop living our lives because of fear.

"As long as you make a snack for me too," I said.

"Of course."

"I'll join him," Kaius said from somewhere farther down the hall.

Their footsteps thudded away, and Zoe and I got down to cleaning. I started with my yarn until Zoe laughed. "You're mixing up the colors."

"I blame Tewy, but maybe I should let you handle this part. I don't want to make any ugly shawls." They were selling well enough and bringing in enough money, but I'd hate for even one to go to waste or to take extra time.

"The amant would probably still like them. They seem to like anything you create."

Heat rose to my cheeks. It was an exaggeration, but that didn't mean it still wasn't nice to hear. "What should I work on then?"

"Why don't you handle your clothes? I'll put them in a pile and you can fold them up," she said.

With a little shuffling, we got to work and had a system going.

I folded my few clothing items, while she asked with a note of caution, "What did you think of the meeting?"

"It was…" Hard to define scary but exhilarating all at the same time. "Good."

"I'm so glad." And she sounded it. "I knew you would fit right in, but I wasn't certain about your brother. I know he's really protective of you. I didn't want that to stop you from becoming a part of the group though."

It was the perfect time to tell her that we weren't actually siblings. There were many secrets I had from her, but this would be an easy one to reveal. Something stopped me though. "He is rather protective. I think he feels responsible for me."

"Big brothers are like that."

"You would know. Kaius seems to care a lot for you too."

A shuffling of items came from nearby. "He does. What did you think of what Leo had to say?"

"It makes sense. What were you doing in Ruso? How can I help here? I don't want the warriors, maveor, Reding, and Vading to take over our lives like I feel like they're already doing. I want control and freedom to walk the streets without worrying if I'm going to be swooped up and taken in as a slave." Why take us as slaves anyway? It seemed like sighted people would be more use. It wasn't that I couldn't do as much as a sighted person, but it simply seemed easier.

The shuffling stopped, her voice coming out low. "You shouldn't have to worry about any of those things. No one should. There's such a problem between the amant and the odiosom. If we could clear that up somehow, I know things would be much better for everyone."

"But how to make that happen is the question." I finished folding the last dress and put the clothes in my small dresser. When she didn't answer, I said, "Just because I'm blind doesn't mean I can't help."

"No, I know. It's not that I think you can't help because you're blind. That's not why I didn't answer. I didn't because I don't want to give you any advice or ideas that could wind up with you getting captured by the warriors."

"That may be true, but I want to assist you."

"Maybe you could talk to the group. I think it might help if they heard your story. What life has been like for you. After that, I'll talk to Leo privately and you can even join me. We'll find something perfect for you. The biggest thing right now is spreading the word without having any sympathizers to the amant find out what we're doing."

"I can talk to them if it helps. I'll think of what else I can do to help too. I'm afraid I don't associate with many others, so I'm not as useful there."

"But you assist in other ways so you'll be great."

I didn't know what those other ways were, but a thought occurred to me. "Was Hettie there tonight?" I hadn't seen Hettie in a few days and missed her company.

"She hasn't been introduced to our group yet. She seems willing enough, but we don't have any way to know if we can trust her for certain or not."

"I think she's trustworthy, but you're right to be cautious. I can try to put out feelers without telling her anything about the group."

Zoe said, "That'd be wonderful. We're always looking for connections with others who could be a good part of our group but aren't yet."

"I'll carefully talk to her when I can then." I felt around the smooth wooden floor, but came up empty. "Are we done cleaning?"

"Yes, we are. It looks a lot better now. Let me show you how I coded your yarn colors."

I moved over to where her voice was coming from, and she showed me each of my skeins of yarn and told me what color they were. They were each in a different place so they were easy to keep track of. "This is perfect, thank you."

"Happy to help. Should we go get a snack with the men?"

"I think I'm going to go straight to bed. It's been a long day."

"If you're certain, I'll see you in the morning then."

Her footsteps left the room and went down the stairs. I called out for Tewy, and he came running over, jumping into my lap. "I won't leave you locked in here if you promise not to destroy it again, deal?"

He gave a soft *ooo*. I'd take that as his agreement.

After getting ready for bed, I left my door open a crack so I could hear better if anyone was coming and climbed into bed. Though I tried to fall asleep, my mind twisted and turned over everything Nikon had told me, not letting me sleep.

What could the Reding have planned? Would it affect me? How would it affect the country? There had to be something we could do. Maybe Leo would know what to do after we showed him the papyrus? And if not? Well, we'd figure something out.

Nikon's familiar, subtle steps reached me. I jumped from the bed and hurried out toward him.

"Yes?" he asked.

But I didn't know what to say, not with Kaius and Zoe in the house.

He took my hand. "It's going to be all right."

I bit my lip. He didn't know that, but I appreciated the words. "If Antonia were here, she'd know what to do."

His grip tightened. "What does the Vading have to do with anything?"

"The Vading? I was talking about my caretaker." The one I'd put off finding for far too long.

"Antonia is the name of the Vading. She married the Reding about seven years ago."

Antonia wasn't a common name when I was growing up, and

the timeline fit. She couldn't possibly have been my caretaker...could she?

"It's probably a coincidence," Nikon said, but didn't sound convinced.

"It has to be, my caretaker would never have left me unless..." Unless she died or fell in love. But then why not take me with her? That answer was obvious; she'd have had to make me a slave if the Reding had known about me. But didn't the Vading have a say in what the Reding did? I didn't know, but I had always thought so. The law about taking the blind as slaves came into effect sometime around her vanishing. Realizing the law coincided with Antonia leaving, I paced the length of my room, then I stopped and turned toward the door where I thought Nikon stood. "I have to find out if it's her."

"How?"

I appreciated that he asked how instead of saying *you can't*. "There's only one way, isn't there? I'll have to go to the capitol and hear her speak."

And pray to the sands I didn't get captured while there.

CHAPTER THIRTY-THREE

"We can't go to Sirya," Nikon said. "It's not safe."

I tried to remember where my pack was as I grabbed clothes from my dresser. "*We* can't, but *I* can. I need to do this, Nikon." Though I didn't know how I'd manage without him, but I'd find a way.

"I don't know why you have to take off the *we*. Where you go, I go."

"Then you'd better pack."

A soft touch to my elbow startled me. I bumped backward into Nikon before righting myself and turning toward him. I said, "I need to do this. For years, I thought my caretaker left me or didn't want me, but maybe she got put in a horrible position instead and couldn't return to me." Though something didn't quite make sense. Wouldn't she have power, even if it was to go behind the Reding's back? Why didn't she bring me to be her slave? I didn't want to be one, but at least I wouldn't have been alone all those years. She must not have wanted to put me through whatever it was slaves went through.

"Why leave in the first place?"

I shrugged. "She often left me behind to do things." Usually, she brought back something with her like a pan or more yarn. Of course, that time, she'd taken all her things too. I just hadn't realized it until it was too late.

"All right, let's say I believe that. What's keeping her from secretly returning to you or sending a message about what happened?"

That brought me up short. I'd been so eager to find out if it was her, I didn't think about why she wouldn't tell me what happened. "It doesn't matter. I'm certain she has her reasons. The fact is, I want to find out if she's the same person. I wondered for years what happened to her. Years, Nikon. It's time I found out."

"Then we'll go, but in the morning."

He had a point. "You don't have to come with me."

"Of course, I do. You have to know though, it's going to be dangerous with the soldiers still searching for me. Or rather, for us."

That did present a problem. "Let's travel the back way again. There wasn't a wall around Sirya last I knew; has that changed?"

"It hasn't."

"Then we go the back way and figure things out when we arrive."

"Arrive where?" Zoe said from over by my door. I turned toward her. "Sorry, I didn't mean to pry. Your door is open and you were talking loudly. Are you going somewhere?"

"Yes. I think I've found my caretaker who left me years ago. I want to go find out if it's her, and Nikon's going to assist me."

"Of course, he is, but it'll be dangerous. Are you sure you're willing to risk yourself in a world that might reject you and turn you in to be a slave?"

I straightened my back. "I am."

"Doesn't Nikon know where to find her? He could go without you so you'd be safe. We'd make certain you were well while he was away."

"I need to do this for myself." And I hoped she took that as an answer because claiming the truth, that Nikon didn't know what she looked like, didn't make any sense if he was supposed to be my brother.

"Then we have to come up with a plan."

Not the response I expected. "You're coming?"

"I wish I could, but there's too much work to be done here with the odiosom. No, I have to stay, but I can help you on your way. Where are you going?"

"Sirya." I wasn't sure I wanted to tell her my guess that the Vading was my old caretaker.

"The capitol? Very well. That's going to be dangerous. The only odiosom there are either slaves or workers. They kick anyone out who isn't helping things along. Your best bet might be to go with kohl and finer linen clothes."

"You want us to go as amant?" My words were hushed. To even suggest pretending to be a different class was against the law.

"I know it will be difficult with you not being able to see, but it will make sense why you need to cling to Nikon. What's more, no one will bother you if they think you are their superiors."

"What about the amant markings? We can't fake those."

"The kohl can be used as a disguise on the base of your fingers. They won't be raised, but as long as the kohl doesn't smudge much and no one feels for markings, you should be fine."

This didn't seem like such a good idea anymore. "Nikon, what do you think?"

"The plan has merit. You'd be able to stay at my elbow and keep your head tilted down or toward me and no one would notice or bother us."

Tewy squeaked.

"I think he wants to come with us," I said.

"Wouldn't have it any other way, as long as he doesn't make a mess of things again," Nikon replied.

"He won't. The two of us had a chat."

"Good," Zoe said. "Now that it's settled, Cassandra, come with me. I have kohl you can borrow and some fine linen, but we'll have to cut it down. You're smaller than I am." A soft hand took my arm, and Zoe led me to the other room with Nikon's steps following.

"Can you put kohl on yourself?" she asked me.

"I've never tried. It's probably something I could work up to, but without having done it before and wanting to leave tomorrow, I'm not sure I should start now."

"I can help her with it." Nikon's words surprised me.

"You know how to apply kohl?" Even he had to be able to hear the surprise in my voice.

"Some amant men wear it in the capitol."

"You're not amant," Zoe said.

No, he wasn't, but he was an elite warrior. One close enough to the Reding to talk to him and steal personal papyrus. He may have gone in disguise from time to time. It wouldn't surprise me. "He's not, but he has many facets."

Zoe grunted, leaving me wondering what she thought of it all.

She said, "Let's get your alterations made, Cassandra. Nikon, Kaius may have some clothes you can have, though I think you've got more muscles than he does." There was a speculation in her tone I didn't like. Did she think he was a warrior? He did manual labor like so many other odiosom, but maybe he'd given something away.

"I'll go talk to him," Nikon said, the faint steps going into the other room.

As Zoe measured me and her dress, making adjustments to it, she said, "Are you sure you want to do this? Sirya is a dangerous place for any odiosom."

"I have to." But her words dragged me back to a time I could see, a time that my parents had taken us to hear the Reding speak. He was still quite young then. He'd stood on a platform next to a massive pyramid step, more of those giant steps behind him. Looking up, I remember thinking how strange it was that we were led by an odiosom. When I brought it up to my mother, she told me to hush up, that he was still young. And that he would find someone.

And so, he had.

I didn't know if I wanted to relive those memories. It was difficult both feeling the love for my parents despite what they did to me, and being angry at them. In that moment, I was too much of each. I needed to contain my emotions if we were to accomplish the task I'd set before us.

"There," Zoe said. "I think it should fit you now. Why don't you try it on?"

I let my old dress slide over my head and slipped on the borrowed linen one. The fabric was smooth against my skin, flimsy layers, but many together creating a dress that fit me much better than I expected. "You must have skills with a needle and thread to make this work."

"Pijo. I did what needed done."

"Are you certain you can part with this?" I ran my hands down my sides, luxuriating in the soft texture.

"Your need is greater than mine at the moment."

"Why do you have this in the first place?" I asked as I changed back into my old dress. No sense getting the new one dirty or ruined before I needed to use it.

She didn't answer right away. "There are things you don't know about me, Cassandra. Things that would be good for you to know, but I'm bound by my word not to tell you."

"We all have our secrets, and I can respect that. But, Zoe, if you ever are ready to tell me, I'll be happy to listen." If I ever came back, who knew if I'd be able to or if I'd be captured, tortured, turned into a slave, or killed? So many heinous options.

Zoe helped me pack some food for our journey with words of encouragement. I took it in stride, wondering if I should change my mind and stay. Maybe it didn't matter if I knew what happened to Antonia? Maybe I could live without knowing what of her fate?

But no, I needed to figure this out. I'd never have peace of mind now that I knew she could be out there. If I was lucky enough, I would be able to talk to her and find out what had happened for myself. Either way, there was a chance I would soon know what had become of her.

———

Goodbyes were bittersweet. Though finding Antonia would be wonderful, I wasn't ready to leave Zoe. "Please take care of yourselves."

"You're the ones I'm going to be worrying over," she replied. "Don't take any unnecessary chances."

"We won't. Tell Hettie goodbye for me when you see her?" I wished I could have said goodbye myself, but it was just as well. I knew her better that I did Zoe, and my heart already was sinking further than I wanted it to go.

"I will. And you can speak with her about what we discussed when you get back."

If I was able to make it back…

I shook myself. Couldn't chance thinking things like that. We were going to come back, and with answers. "Thank you for all you've done for us."

"Think nothing of it. Just glad we could help."

Kaius had found an outfit that just fit Nikon, and they'd somehow scrounged up sandals for us both this morning. With that and the food packed and Tewy on my shoulder, we were ready to go. Walking on foot wasn't the usual way amant traveled, but we didn't have enough money saved up for the boat ride down the river. I wasn't about to ask Kaius and Zoe for any when they'd already done so much to help us. We'd just have to do our best to blend in when we got there.

"We'll be back in a few weeks or so," Nikon said.

"We'll make sure Leo doesn't give away your rooms," Kaius responded.

I laughed, but quietly. It was still early enough that not many people should be up and we didn't want to wake the neighbors.

"Good luck finding your caretaker," Zoe said, wrapping me in a hug.

"Thank you. Good luck with everything here."

With that, we were out the door. The air held a chill that promised a cold morning until the sun fully rose. I stepped softly while I followed Nikon's lead from hanging onto his arm and using the cane with my other hand. His own footsteps were silent. I wished I had that level of control over my own, but I needed to be more grateful that at least I wasn't tripping over anything.

We wound through the city in a way that was familiar, though I couldn't have followed it myself. Zoe had informed Nikon where the ladder was that we had used to get out of town previously. Which brought another thought to mind. A dangerous one.

I whispered, "What if we run into the sphinx?"

"I'll keep you safe."

"Why are you so intent on doing so? It would be easier without me."

"Easier, yes, but not as entertaining. I like being around you, Cassandra. You're an innocent breath of fresh air. When I stumbled into your cabin, I made one of the wisest mistakes of my life. Sticking with you is the right thing to do."

"I hear a *but* in your words."

"I was trying to hide that."

"Can't do so from me," I said lightly, though inside I worried what that could mean. Did he not really want to go? Did he have reservations about this more than he'd told me? "What is it?"

"The truth is, I have some business I should attend to in Sirya. If I'm wholly honest with you, I'm going to try and retrieve the papyrus I hid."

"It's in the capitol?"

"Yes."

Where else would it be? It was hard to picture him running around the pyramid and city as a warrior, but then, it explained so much about him. It was probably just hard to combine the areas of my life and memories. The seeing ones and the blind impressions of him.

We stayed silent the rest of the way. When we reached the ladder, he went up first, gave me the all clear, and I followed after. Once we were on the other side of the wall, my nerves jangled more. It was one thing to be caught by warriors, quite another to be captured by a sphinx.

For some reason, the marauders didn't scare me. Not like they probably should, but then, I had Nikon at my side, and I doubted he'd leave me like he had before. We were more prepared this time. We'd make it through the back way, wander through the desert, and to Sirya. My desire for answers said we had to succeed.

CHAPTER THIRTY-FOUR

The longer we walked without any sign of the sphinx or marauders, the more comfortable I became. We'd be fine. Nikon would make certain of that.

We were three days into our journey. It would take longer to get to Sirya this way than if we took a boat on the river, but there would have been too many questions and we didn't have the funds. No, we were much safer trudging through the sand with our packs of clothes, food, and water.

Tewy wrapped his tail around the back of my neck as I asked Nikon, "How much longer do you think it will be?"

"If everything holds good like it has been, a couple more days perhaps."

I swung my cane ahead of us as I hung on to him.

"Do you have any plans for how we're going to hear the Vading's voice?" he asked me.

It was the same question I'd been asking myself ever since we made it out of the city walls. "I'm not sure. Does the Reding still hold an assembly once a week?"

"Yes, and the Vading is usually with him."

"That's what we'll do then. We'll go to one of them dressed as amant eager to hear his words." The thought made my stomach churn. "And then I'll only have to listen for her to speak. I'd know her voice anywhere."

"And what if she doesn't say anything?"

"Then we'll go to the next week's assembly. She has to speak sometime."

"What will we do with ourselves if she doesn't speak the first time? Where will we live and get food?"

He had to be practical. It was just as well, one of us needed to be. "We'll find a house and jobs like we did before. I still have some shawls to sell."

"The shawls are good, but honestly, I'm worried about the rest of it. It's going to be dangerous enough being there; the longer we're there, the more likely the warriors will catch on to us. Valeriana might even be there."

That wasn't good. "What do you suggest?"

"I don't know. Take things one step at a time with caution."

"I wish that made me feel better, but I can't say that it does." The sand was hot beneath my feet, the grains slipping as we walked.

"Oh no." Nikon's words made me stop.

"What?"

"There's a dust storm coming." He disengaged from me, leaving me to fend for myself.

I patted Tewy. "How far away is it?"

"Some distance, but it's moving fast."

A long-ago memory of seeing a dust storm rising in the distance above the city came to me. It was a faint memory, but enough to put me on edge. I hadn't been in one in years. They'd never bothered me back by the waterfall. "What do we do?"

"I'm setting up the tent. We'll have to hunker down and hope for the best."

"Can I help?"

"I'm almost done." Seconds later, "Got it."

He grabbed my arm, and I followed him in, Tewy jumping from my shoulder. Once I was huddled in the tent scrunched against Nikon, Tewy hopped back in my lap. I asked, "How long until the storm gets here?"

"Not long."

The air was heavy with heat and tension. It smelled of hot sand. My fingers dug into Tewy enough that he arched away from me. "Sorry, boy," I whispered to him.

The sound of wind gathered, coming closer and closer. Nikon took my hand, threading his fingers between my own. I hung on, not wanting to be torn from him in the coming storm. Tewy put his little hand on both of ours, and I wrapped my arm around him.

The wind pushed the tent against me. Outside, the sand smacked against it with a million repeated little thuds that crested into a noise so loud, I wouldn't have been able to hear Nikon if he said anything.

We clung to each other as the storm raged on around us. The only storms I'd been in before, I'd sat in my parents' house waiting it through. This was worse. So much so.

The onslaught tore through the cloth of the tent. It clawed at my hair and clothes, the tent smacking against me over and over again. I clung to Tewy and Nikon until some point when I fell asleep.

The quiet woke me. Everything was so still. When I didn't feel anything, I feared the tent had blown over and torn Nikon and Tewy away. A soft gust picked up and the tent walls gave a thwack. I stretched until I brushed against skin hardened with muscle. Nikon's thigh.

"Do you need something?" His voice was sleepy.

I ripped my hand away. "Where's Tewy?"

There was a rustling, and when he spoke again his words were clear. "He's not here."

"What do you mean, he's not here?" I searched the tent with

my hands leading me. The floor contained only sand, me, and Nikon.

When I reached him, he took my hands and clasped them together. "He's not in the tent, but we'll find him."

My shoulder was light. Too light. I wanted to call out for my monkey, but if he wasn't in here, I needed to get out first. I scrambled toward the opening and burst forward—only to discover more tent wall.

"What are you doing?" Nikon asked.

"Trying to get out."

"It's to your left. You need to turn to find it."

Grumbling, I did as he said and found the opening. I attempted to scurry out, but the sand kept moving beneath me. When I finally got to my feet, I took a couple steps and called out, "Tewy, where are you?"

A scratching sound of sand rustling against sand came from behind me, and then Nikon said, "I don't see him."

Sandblast it. "Tewy, you come out right this instant." When there was no response, I turned toward Nikon. "Is there any sign of him? Footprints or anything?"

"No."

I twisted my hands together. "This isn't like him. I mean, yes, he runs off sometimes, but he always comes back."

"Maybe it hasn't been long enough."

"Perhaps." But holding out hope was difficult. So many things could have happened during the storm if he got loose. I should have never fallen asleep.

"Let me pack up the tent and we'll go looking for him."

"What if he comes here looking for us?"

"You think about that, whether he would have come back by now, because we are not separating for one of us to stay here while the other goes in search." The soft crunch of sand followed him about as he went to work at his task.

I stayed where I was, calling out Tewy's name every so often and changing directions each time I did so. There was no response.

Nikon must have finished putting the tent back together because he came over and said, "There's a small hill just over here. If we climb it, maybe we can see where Tewy went."

"Which way?" The thought put too much hope inside me. I wanted to find him but feared the condition he'd be in when we did so.

"Behind you."

I turned around and reached out for Nikon's elbow. We hurried as fast as we could through the ever-shifting sand. When he started to climb, I grew anxious and raced ahead. I couldn't see Tewy, but maybe I'd be able to hear him playing or call out for him and have him hear me better than he could before the hill.

"Cassandra, wait." Nikon's voice was low.

I didn't know what he feared for me. There wasn't a lot out here that could harm me, but the next second, he grabbed me and threw me down. We went rolling down the hill, sand getting everywhere. The result left me dizzy and confused as I lay in the sand next to Nikon.

"What was that for?" I gave a harsh whisper.

"Marauders."

I let my head fall back in the sand. "Did they see us?"

"I don't think so. Tewy was entertaining them. Or maybe they were entertaining Tewy, it was hard to tell."

Tension rolled out of my body. "He's safe."

It was more statement than question, but Nikon responded with, "Yes."

I curled into Nikon, wrapping my arm around him in an awkward sort of hug. "Thank the sands."

"Don't go thanking me yet."

As I lay with my arm over him, his chest rising and falling rapidly with his breaths, I wondered what was wrong. Then I realized the problem that remained. "How do we get him away from the marauders? How many of them were there? Could you tell how armed they were?"

"I don't know how to get him away. It's going to be tricky without calling their attention to us. More than we already have anyway. There were about a dozen of them, all armed to the teeth."

That didn't bode well. All of my tension came slamming back into me with an aching force. An idea hit me, though it probably wasn't a very good one. I told him anyway. "Maybe we should walk in there and ask for him back."

"Are you crazy? The marauders would be on us in seconds."

"Yes, they would," a pleasant female voice said.

Nikon cursed, and I had a feeling the marauders had found us.

CHAPTER THIRTY-FIVE

The marauder ordered us up off the ground. I struggled to my feet, brushing the sand off of me. It had gotten everywhere, sticking to me from the sweat of the day. I didn't know how Nikon was faring, but I was uncomfortable both in body and mind. What were we going to do now the marauders had found us?

"What are you doing out here?" the pleasant voice asked.

"We're going to Sirya," I blurted out. "And we found you by looking for my monkey, Tewy."

"That monkey is yours?" Even for me, it was difficult to read the tone of her voice.

"He is."

A pause. "Come with me."

Nikon gave me his elbow, guiding me wherever the marauder was leading us, I presumed. His skin was hot and his arm shook. Whether from anger, fear, or some other emotion, it was impossible to tell.

"We don't mean you any harm," I said.

The woman didn't respond and neither did Nikon.

We climbed the hill and stepped back down it. The sand

shifted beneath my bare feet, trying to trip me up, but I held on to Nikon and my cane. When we were down the hill and had gone a short distance, voices came to me. Faint at first but growing with every step. By the time they were loud enough to make out, they whooped, hollered and laughed, making quite the noise.

"I've brought visitors," the pleasant voice said. "The monkey, Tewy, is theirs."

"Oh, sands. I hoped he could stay with us forever," a man said.

Did that mean they were going to let us go? The idea was unthinkable. Surviving marauders was hard.

They were vicious and cruel. They had tried to kidnap me after all. They'd sell anything and anyone they could get away with.

"You've got an interesting monkey here," a deeper female voice said.

"Tewy's a rascal," I replied.

The monkey let out a friendly *ooo* and there was a rustle of sand. I held out my arms to catch him. He jumped up them, and onto my shoulder. I wanted to run away. I had him, we didn't need to stay, but when Nikon gave me his elbow, he drew us closer to the voices instead of farther away.

I wished I could see what he did, but there was some shifting sand behind us. Maybe they were circling us? Whatever the case might have been, I was sticking with Nikon.

"What's your story?" the pleasant voice said. "I know you say you're going to Sirya, but how did you end up together? What are a couple of amant doing taking the back way to the capitol? Why do you have a monkey?"

I could have sworn she spit when she finished speaking. For such a lovely voice, I didn't think she had manners to match it.

"We're not amant," Nikon said. "We're brother and sister."

"Then why does she cling to you like a lover would?" a gruff male voice asked.

Good question indeed. Did we tell them I was blind and risk

them selling me, or was it better to pretend to be an amant? I didn't think we'd like the results either way. Thankfully, Nikon made the decision before I could finish thinking it through. "She's blind."

I held my head high. These men and women might want to try and take me, but I wasn't going to have any of it.

"Is that so?" the pleasant voice said from my right, much closer than she'd been before.

It took a lot of work not to shift closer to Nikon. I didn't want to give these people any more reason to think we were amant than they already had. "It's true."

A whisk of air brushed across my face, but otherwise all remained still.

When the pleasant woman spoke, she had lost the dangerous edge to her tone. "You have to forgive me. We've heard rumors of the blind but haven't seen any. We avoid the pyramid where they'd all be in service and have never seen any out in the wild before."

Hopefully, that meant they didn't want to take me to Sirya to sell me. I didn't want to rely on their goodwill, but if there were really a dozen of them well armed like Nikon thought, the only way we were getting out of this was if they wanted us to. "We're coming from Itpy. I've been there for some time, but we've tried to keep my presence quiet for obvious reasons." Why did I say that?

"Really? Why don't you share breakfast with us and we'll hear more about it?"

I did not like this setup. It held a note of danger, having to trust people who were untrustworthy.

"We have little to share but are happy to split what we can." Nikon stepped forward, leading me to a blanket on the ground where he sat next to me.

"Good." The pleasant woman's voice came across from us. "We will also share a little of what we have. Most of what we want is water though, as it's scarce around these parts."

Nikon's muscle tightened beneath my grip, so I slipped my hand to my lap where Tewy jumped down. We had so little water, enough to get across the desert, but not enough to share with a dozen marauders.

"We will need much of what we have for the journey to Sirya, but you are welcome to this water skin." Beside me, he shifted, presumably handing over the water skin.

As we sat there, the shifting of sand continued around us, like someone walked around the camp keeping an eye on all things. I wanted to yell at them to sit down, but instead, I tilted my head down toward Tewy as I whispered, "You naughty boy, don't ever scare me like that again."

"You have a close relationship with the monkey."

"We've been together since about the time I lost my sight."

"How did you lose your vision?" a man asked from somewhere to my left.

It wasn't something I wanted to share.

"An accident," Nikon said. "Stayed out in the desert too long without eye protection when she was younger."

Would that work? Sounded plausible enough. The sun burning out whatever controlled my sight. Best of all, I didn't have to go over the real reason. I wanted to thank Nikon but kept silent so I didn't ruin his words.

"Why are you going to Sirya?" the pleasant voice asked. She must be in charge of things.

"The woman who took care of me after I became blind went missing some years ago," I said. "I heard rumors that she might be in Sirya and would like to find her. She means a great deal to me, and I'd like to know she's well."

"Her name?"

"Aknuma Lilpyt." Nikon's words, while not true, were helpful. It was a common enough name that their minds wouldn't automatically go to the Vading, who could be a danger to them. To us all, if the truth be told.

Nikon put some dates in my hand along with a water skin. I ate as I listened to the pleasant voice say, "I don't know anyone by that name."

Was that good or bad?

The voice continued, "I feel you're not being entirely honest, but then, to be honest with a group like us is dangerous, so I'll give you a pass this one time. Your monkey has provided us with quite the entertainment this morning. We'll thank you for that by letting you go."

Grateful I was in the middle of chewing so my jaw couldn't drop open in shock, I took a pull from the water skin. Once my mouth was clear, I said, "Thank you. We appreciate the hospitality."

Why didn't Nikon say something? What was I missing?

"Just don't tell anyone we let you go," the woman said. "We'd like to keep this a secret between friends."

"I'd be happy to keep that secret for you." Especially since I still felt that marauders were a dangerous bunch who should be avoided when possible, their current kindness notwithstanding.

Tewy jumped from my lap, and the others started laughing moments later. Whatever he was doing, I was certain he thought he was a riot. I thought maybe I should leave him here with these people, not that I wanted to, but he appeared to be having a good time. I didn't want to make him come back to me if he didn't wish to. The sad thought had me wanting to get my mind on other things. "What are you doing out in the desert?"

"I beg your pardon?" the pleasant voice said.

"You don't have to tell me of course, I'm just curious what brings you out here. Is this how you travel from city to city too?" Terrorizing citizens along the way. Or not. They had been generous to us. Though I was grateful I could brush my arm against Nikon's to make certain he was still sitting there. His silence was worrisome.

"We don't usually answer to others, but since you are so naive, let me tell you a little something. Marauders go wherever they want to go. We do whatever we want to do. We don't let anyone stop us, no matter what."

I sighed. "That sounds like a nice sort of life."

"You'd be welcome to join us, though I'm not sure I'd like your brother around."

Why not? What was he doing to raise their suspicions? "Thank you for the offer. It does sound like a nice life, but I'll have to decline. Not only am I anxious to find my old caretaker, but I'm afraid my blindness might slow you down or not be as useful a skill to have." Not that I really thought that, but it was a good excuse.

"Considerate of you. More so than most are to us." She gave a soft laugh. "Off with you before I change my mind. I don't want you lingering around our camp either or I'll slit your throats. I may have given you leave this time, but if I think you're doing anything to harm us, I'll have you taken care of right away."

I rushed to my feet, trying not to show any trembling. "I understand." I wanted to call for Tewy but didn't. No, he'd come to me if he wanted to join us. If he'd rather stay where people appreciated his antics, I didn't want to be the one to stop him from that—even if he was a dear friend.

Nikon gave me his elbow, still curiously silent, turned us around, and headed back the way we came.

By the time we got to the top of the hill, I wanted to cry. My cherished friend had abandoned me for marauders. He hadn't even avoided them or been upset with them and warned us about their presence like he'd done previously with Valeriana.

No. I was alone, no longer to have my little rascal of a monkey. Would he think about me? Would he remember me? I certainly would him.

When we began our descent, Nikon said, "What's wrong?"

"Tewy didn't want to come with me." I tried to keep my voice perky but failed.

"He's right here on my shoulder."

I almost collapsed with relief. Nikon hurried and steadied me as Tewy made a little squeak. "I can't believe he's here. Can't believe they let him go."

"We were extremely fortunate in our encounter with them. I'm not counting on our luck to hold. We need to get out of here before they change their minds."

"Good point." I collected myself. "Why were you so silent at the end there?"

"One of the men held a knife to my throat. I don't think they liked my answering everything."

I hated the thought of that, but at least we'd made it out safely, and we could continue our journey to Sirya.

CHAPTER THIRTY-SIX

W e continued our journey for days, the sand never ending. I was more than relieved when we finally found some shade because it meant we were getting closer to the river again. And closer to the river meant closer to the capitol.

"The city is up ahead. There are some trees we can change behind over here," Nikon said several hours later.

"You think we need to change into our amant clothes already?" I asked.

He guided me to a place where the heat lessened. "It'd be best if we had no association with being odiosom in this city."

I bit my lip. "Do you think we can really pull this off? Maybe I was wrong to bring us here."

"You want to find out about your caretaker, don't you?"

"Yes." There was no question about that.

"This is the best way to do it then. We'll find a time the Reding and Vading are going to be out speaking and you can listen to them, and either way, you'll know if the Vading is who you think she is or someone else."

That didn't tell me what to do if the Vading was my Antonia. I couldn't imagine how we'd handle that situation; we should have worked it out on the way here. But it didn't matter. We'd figure out who she was first before we made any rash decision what to do. Nikon was right. We had this covered.

We quickly changed into our finer linen and stashed our bags by hiding them amongst the foliage except for some money we both carried. Nikon was probably carrying his sword too, but he didn't say anything about it so neither did I.

"Here are your sandals." He handed me a pair of flat shoes with lots of strappy things.

"I might need help with this." It been far too long since I'd worn shoes. "Let me give them a try and see what we come up with."

"Not a problem."

I sat down in the sand, took the first sandal, and tried to find a place to slip my foot in that wasn't covered in bands.

Nikon chuckled. "You're getting it all twisted."

"Ugh. I give up already. Will you help, please?"

"Sure. There's a strap up top you need to—no not that one, the other one. Not that one either, the next one."

I threw the shoe down in frustration. "Why do amant have such complicated footwear?" And thinking about it, Nikon had been wearing that exact type of footwear when we met. What did that mean? "Tell me the truth, are you actually an amant?"

"No! Why would you think that?" He sounded offended.

"Sorry. I was just thinking about the little I do know about you, and it seems like there's a lot of indicators that you could be an amant. For example, the shoes you wore when we first met. The closeness you seem to have to the Reding. Why would an odiosom have that kind of access? It doesn't make sense."

Tewy rustled and squawked from nearby. I wanted answers, but it didn't seem like any were going to be forthcoming. And then to my utter surprise, Nikon's story began.

"I'm not amant," the words came out of him fast, "but I am—was—able to get close to the Reding and Vading. They trusted me with their security and in time, they began to trust me with other confidences. That's why I was able to stumble across the plans I did. It wasn't a position I wanted, and in fact, I oftentimes dreaded it, but I never, ever became an amant." His fingers tucked under my chin, lifting my face. "Do you understand that? I was never one of them. The closest I've ever come to falling in love is with you, and that's not something that can happen, as we both know."

His words twisted inside me, making me wish I hadn't asked in the first place. It would have been better not to hear, at least not the end part. Not when I wanted to be his and never could be in this new world of ours that had come about since the Govlin Wars. No matter how much we both seemed to want it, no one fell in love without that first sight which I couldn't have. I didn't know what had changed to make it that way, but in my life, it'd always been so.

There was a connection between us, though not love. It couldn't be love. But there was something. And maybe if I'd had my vision, we would have become amant together.

I'd like to think, though, that it wouldn't have changed my attitude toward the odiosom. They needed relief from the oppression and work forced upon them. Their lives might be dictated by something beyond anyone's control, but that didn't mean the amant should be free to rule over them.

Realizing he waited for an answer, I said, "I understand."

"Do you? Because I'm not certain I do."

I reached up until I felt the smoothness of his cheek. He must have shaved recently. I had distant memories of knowing amant men were almost always clean-shaven. "I know there's something between us, and you would never jeopardize our friendship by lying."

He sighed, leaning into my hand. "Thank you."

I let myself have a moment to enjoy the softness of his skin. The firm line of his jaw. And then I took my hand away. Getting caught up in the moment was a bad idea, even if I didn't fully understand why. "Now. Let's get these stupid shoes on."

"Yes, ma'am."

In no time at all, he had the sandals on my feet, the pieces that needed to be wrapped around my leg up my calf almost to my knees. "Yuck. I don't know how people wear shoes all the time."

"You get used to it, just like I got used to being barefoot all the time, hanging around with you."

I grinned. "You stopped wearing shoes?"

"I do what I need to fit in."

My smile faltered. It wasn't the answer I wanted, though I wasn't certain what that was. "Because you're an elite warrior."

"Yes, because of that." His tone was sad, but then perked up for his next words. "Let's get your kohl on."

"Oh, yes, because I can't go be an amant without my pretties." I tilted my face toward the sound of his voice. As soon as I did so, the cool makeup started moving across my bottom eyelid. Instinctively, I looked up, and waited for him to get across my eye and just beyond.

Once he did both sides he said, "Close your eyes now, and I'll do the top."

I did as he requested and waited until the kohl had been applied to both my eyelids before opening my eyes again. He took ahold of my hand and a slight pressure circled the base of my left pointer finger. "How does it look?"

"Like you're an amant."

"I'm not sure if that's a compliment or not."

"In this case, it is, trust me."

Heat rose to my cheeks. I ducked away from him as Tewy chattered. "What is it, boy?"

"There's someone coming." Nikon's voice was serious.

That wasn't good. I jumped to my feet, prepared to defend myself in any way necessary. If they thought we were here as odiosom and realized we were trying to pretend to be amant, we were in some serious trouble. The kind that would get us killed or imprisoned.

I didn't know how Nikon did it, dressing up as a different class or person to get information before he stumbled into my home. It'd be a stressful job, one that would send my nerves screaming.

"We got this," he whispered to me. "We went for a walk, nothing more. Our stuff is hidden. We're fine."

I nodded, but I wasn't feeling as confident as I tried to be. As I turned to listening instead of being caught up in the moment, I heard several sets of footsteps coming this way, scratching across the sand. They'd be here before too long, and they would expect to see two amant during the middle of the day since we weren't working. Plus, we wanted to put on right from the start that we were amant, so there'd be no problems later on if they spotted us.

I stepped closer to where Nikon had spoken from. He put an arm around my shoulders, and I glanced at the ground, not wanting to give away that I wasn't looking at anything. I'd be able to give them some attention when they were talking, but didn't dare give too much and let them become suspicious that I wasn't looking right at their eyes. It was a delicate balance I wasn't certain I was going to conquer.

"Zaykai," a man said. "What are the two of you doing out of Sirya?"

"We went for a lover's stroll," Nikon said.

Tewy chose that moment to *ooo* and jump upon my shoulder that was farthest from Nikon, the one holding my cane. That'd better not give us away.

"A lover's stroll with a monkey?" The man sounded skeptical.

I leaned farther into Nikon and wrapped my arm around his back. With my other hand, I held the cane, trying to do so like it was an ornamental piece and not a needed one.

"He's our pet. We like to take him with us whenever we go out."

"I see." Though he sounded like he didn't at all. "You folks best be getting on your way. There's a lot of marauders out and though I see you have a weapon to defend yourself, it's best not to mess with such things."

So, Nikon did have his sword. Probably a few other tricks hiding on his person as well.

"Right you are. I'll take my lovely wife and we'll head back to the city."

"That'd be for the best."

It appeared that they were going to let us go. The nerves in my stomach still jangled mercilessly, but maybe it'd be all right. They didn't question us more than I expected, didn't think we were odiosom dressing up as amant. We wouldn't be losing anything today.

Nikon led me away from them. Walking was difficult with his arm around me, but I steadied myself, grateful he was going slow. I made it happen.

"Is this yours?" the man's voice from behind us asked.

Nikon withdrew his arm from around me. "Nope. Can't say that we brought any bags with us."

Sand it all. They'd found our hidden stash of things from the sound of it. How were we going to get back to Itpy without them? We'd have to worry about that later. For the moment, we needed to get out of this situation.

"Are you sure? There's two of them, just like there's two of you."

"Not ours," Nikon replied again.

"Then you won't mind if I take them with me. Looks like we have some odiosom planning on running." The man's voice grew closer. "You wouldn't have happened to see anything like that, would you?"

I had a mad desire to snort that I suppressed. I, clearly, hadn't seen anything so I honestly answered, "I haven't seen anyone about."

"Hmm."

I silently pleaded with him to buy our story, my heart pounding. If he didn't, we were heading to the dungeons for sure, and I would never know if the Vading was my Antonia. Plus, I'd be ripped from Nikon and Tewy. I was surprised that the thought of not being with Nikon any longer bothered me more than the thought of not knowing if my old caretaker was safe. I didn't think anything else could get in the way of it, but something, or rather someone, had.

"Get on with you then," the man said.

Nikon put his elbow in my hand, and I let him guide me away from the man and our things that were going to be gone before we returned. We'd never see them again. At least we didn't have anything in there that we couldn't find in the city.

As we got farther from the cluster of trees and the man bothering us and closer to the city, the more my thoughts swirled on one thing. We were off to a bad start in Sirya. It'd better better not an indication of what the rest of our journey was going to be like here.

CHAPTER THIRTY-SEVEN

The city was loud—much more so than Itpy had been. It had me wanting to put my hands over my ears. What was with these people and the shouting? It was too much, like they couldn't contain all their foul energy inside themselves.

I shook myself. That wasn't fair. They couldn't help that they were amant any more than I could help that I was odiosom, but they could help how they acted. Screaming at odiosom workers at the top of their lungs as they went about their daily business didn't seem to be the best way to do it.

As we walked, I realized we had several problems. We had no things, since the warriors had taken our hidden stash. We had no connections. We had no way of knowing when the Reding and Vading were going to hold their next assembly.

Apparently, I wasn't good at planning things out.

At least we had a little money, and Nikon was with me. With him, I knew everything would be all right. The thoughts tried to creep back in on me though. Instead of stressing over it, I followed Nikon through the crowd, people occasionally jostling me with an elbow or shoulder. The shoulders must have been from younger citizens. Since I was so much shorter than everyone else, that was the only possibility.

This worked to my advantage though, with Nikon being so large. I forced our way through tight spots. I wasn't certain whether it was him or his sword that was more intimidating, but either way, I'd take it.

At least he knew the city. I was hopelessly lost, clinging to him like he was my lifeline. If we somehow got separated, I would be found out almost immediately and taken away to become a slave if I was lucky. If I was unlucky, they'd kill me for pretending to be an amant.

With that lovely thought, I pushed closer to Nikon.

He said toward me, "We're almost there."

Almost where? Though I wanted to ask, I kept quiet. Clearly, he knew this place far better than I did.

The roaring noise let up, and though I could still hear it going on behind us, it was lessening with each step. The elbowing had stopped at some point too, but I continued to cling to Nikon, following his every lead. Trusting him with my life.

Tewy squawked. I hoped he wasn't bringing too much unwanted attention to us. Maybe it would have been best if we had left him back in Itpy with Zoe and Kaius. Then we wouldn't have had a run-in with the marauders and we wouldn't be so memorable to all these people we were coming across.

Didn't matter. I was grateful for his presence.

"We're here."

"Here, where?" I finally dared ask in a whisper, since I didn't hear others around us.

"Just a moment."

A door squeaked open and we went inside, the heat of the day abating somewhat. Nikon guided me up some stairs and into another room. Once I heard the door close again, I rounded on him. "Where are we?"

"Another moment if you will. And stay here."

He pried my grip from his elbow and was gone without another word.

I tapped my foot, trying not to feel lost or scared. The world was a dark abyss around me. Though I'd felt the sensation before, it'd been long enough that it was unsettling. Scratch that, it would probably always be unsettling. It would have been easier if Nikon had stayed with me, though I was sure he had a good reason to leave me.

I petted Tewy, who grabbed my finger and didn't let go. I let him. It was the best I could get for comfort in a moment like this.

What felt like forever later, Nikon said from somewhere across the room, "No one's here. We can talk."

"Where are we?"

"A safe house I set up a long time ago when I worked here. One of a few if I'm honest."

"There's so much I don't know about you."

"And yet, you continue to trust me." There was a note of awe in his voice that stopped further protests.

He was right. I did trust him. That didn't mean I always had to like it. "Were you planning on coming here from the beginning?"

"No. I thought we'd take a room at an inn or find housing like we did before, but I changed my mind with that warrior who accosted us back in the grove of trees and took our things. Didn't want to chance him looking for us later."

"And you think he'd do that in an inn?"

"It's a possibility. One I don't want to figure out for sure." His footsteps came nearer. "Would you like me to guide you around the house so you can get a feel for it, or did you want to explore it out for yourself?"

"I'll figure it out for myself." For some reason, I didn't want to touch him right now.

"That's fine. There's only one bedroom. I never planned on sharing this place with anyone."

I didn't know whether to feel privileged he had or upset that he needed to.

"Don't worry," he added. "I'll sleep on the sofa so you don't have to. You can take the bedroom. There's some clothes here, nothing for women, but we should be able to find something you can use to sleep in at least. There's also some preserved food. I'll go out and get a few more things to eat for both us and Tewy, along with some information."

I didn't want him to leave but didn't want him to stay when things needed to be done either. "When are you going?"

"As soon as you're comfortable."

"You can go now. I lived alone for years. I should be able to figure out this house for myself."

"If you're sure?"

"Positive."

"I'll go then, but know I won't be long."

"All right."

He said goodbye and the creak of the door opening and closing sounded. "It's just me and you, Tewy. Should we figure this place out?"

He made some chatter as I went from one piece of furniture to the next. It wasn't hard—there weren't a lot of items to maneuver around. A couch, a table, two chairs, a counter in one room. In the next, there was a bed and a dresser, all tightly packed together.

I sat on the couch. "Look at that, Tewy, I managed a tour without bumping into anything."

He oooed at me. And then we settled in to wait.

The hubbub from outside could be heard dimly from in here. A faint clutter of noises where it was hard to make out any one thing. It would have been comforting if I wasn't so scared that a warrior would come marching in any second.

I waited longer than I expected. Or maybe it just felt that way because of my fear. Either way, there was no warning before the door creaked open. I jumped to my feet, cane ready to pull apart and fight should someone make a threatening noise.

"It's me," Nikon said. "Sorry. Should have been louder coming in."

"That would have been nice."

"You'll have to forgive me. I've gotten accustomed to making a little noise around you but am going back to quiet mode while in Sirya."

"Already?"

"It didn't take much, did it?"

"Nope." I let one end of my cane relax back down to the ground.

"I brought food. We can eat and discuss what I discovered."

"Sounds wonderful. I'm famished."

I made my way over to the table, impressed when I found it on the first try. Nikon brought out food, and soon we were feasting on fish and lentils while we talked.

"We should be good to stay here until the next assembly. The warriors are out pretty densely, but they're not looking for you."

"But they are looking for you? And when's the next assembly?" An anxious shiver went through me at the thought of soon hearing Antonia's voice. What would I do if it wasn't her, though? Courting all this danger for nothing. No, I wouldn't think like that. It had to be her.

"The next assembly is in a few days. We should be able to hide in here until then. I brought enough food."

"You didn't answer my first question. The warriors are looking for you, aren't they?"

He huffed. "Why do you have to be so persistent?"

"So I learn what I need to. You gonna answer?"

"Fine. Yes, they're looking for me. Both me specifically for leaving my post, and looking for the man who stole something from the Reding."

"Will you be safe here?"

"Safe enough. They won't expect to find me as an amant."

"Unless they're looking for you, the Reding's right-hand warrior who can blend into any position." Or at least, I thought he could with the hints he'd given.

"You have to guess at everything, don't you? I'm trying to make you feel better."

"I'd rather have the truth."

"Fair enough. Yes, they're looking for me, and they know I can transform into any type of person. They won't expect me to be traveling with another person though. I always work alone."

"Until now."

"That's right."

It was hard not to feel secretly smug that I was the one he chose to break his habit with.

"My sources say I should be fine as long as I don't leave the apartment," he said.

"You have sources? Never mind, of course you do. What will you do when it's time to go to the assembly?"

"Hope that being with you and my bald head will keep everyone from suspecting it's me. I might put some kohl on too."

Not what I expected, but if it helped keep him in hiding, I was grateful for it. "What's the plan for the next few days then?"

"Keep a low profile. I think we'll be fine. The only thing you have to leave for is the outhouse that's in the back, and that will only be noticed by other people in the building. And let's just say, they want to keep their presence from being noticed too. There was a reason I picked this building to be my safe house."

That piqued my curiosity. After I took a bite of fish, I asked, "Are they amant?"

"Most of them, yes."

I tried to think of a reason an amant would need to stay away from others but couldn't come up with an answer. "Why don't they want others to know about them?"

"Different reasons that vary as much as the person. But for a few examples, they could be into drugs, they might just want privacy, or they could be working against the Reding and Vading."

"Others do that here?"

"Yes. They don't stick to just the other cities and odiosom, you know."

"I didn't."

"Oh, well, yes. The Reding and Vading often had me going to find rebels."

My food was entirely forgotten by this point. "And did you turn them in when you found them?"

"Sometimes. I did horrible, horrible things." His voice was so quiet; it was easy to hear the hubbub over him. His hand brushed against mine, linking us. "You know I would never do that now though, especially not to you."

"I do know." The peace that came with that answer was absolute.

I couldn't imagine how he'd lived with the choices he made before he found the Reding's plans and made different decisions than he had before. "How are you going to retrieve the hidden plans?"

"I'll get them on our way out of town."

"Is it on the way?"

"We'll make it so."

So that was one more thing to worry about. There was so much that could go wrong, but for the moment, everything felt right.

CHAPTER THIRTY-EIGHT

The three days we spent holed up in the apartment were idyllic, if a little boring. I liked boring though. True to his word, Nikon let me have the bedroom, even when I tried to insist otherwise. We found a big tunic of his I could wear to bed. Tewy stayed with me at night, but wandered the apartment otherwise, often going to Nikon. I'd listen to the two of them have a one-sided conversation, either Nikon telling him things and Tewy ignoring him, or Tewy squawking away and Nikon not saying a word.

Mostly, though, Nikon and I talked. We spoke of many topics that encompassed everything my heart cared about, scorned, and the things that fell somewhere in the middle. It was a good time I never knew I wanted, almost reminding me of when I'd first met Nikon, only this wasn't my home that I was free to come and go from, and Nikon wasn't tied up.

The one thing I missed was being outside, feeling the warm caress of the sun, the ghostly sensation of the breeze flowing across my skin. The sand beneath my feet, squishing between my toes.

Luckily, I didn't have to wear the sandals at least, but I did have to put them on when I needed to visit the outhouse. It was also the only time I was able to enjoy the outside, though we tried to limit these moments even though the others in the building probably wouldn't say anything to the warriors. It was the *probably* that kept us cautious.

On the morning of the fourth day, I dressed, managed my shoes with Nikon's help, and let him put my kohl on. He put some type of ornamental cloth over my head and on my shoulders, and added a the last touch, some decorations for my hair. When I had my cane in hand and Tewy on my shoulder, I asked, "Are you ready?"

"Yes, ma'am. Got my kohl on, head shaved, and this tunic that was meant for someone much more upper class than I am. I'd almost forgotten what it was like to dress a part. These last few days with you have been blissful."

I could agree to that. There wasn't a person I liked as well as I liked Nikon. Even Antonia had never held the type of appeal he had. In fact, she'd been almost rude at times, but I still cared about her and wanted to find out what happened to her. I deserved to know what became of the woman that took care of me for years.

Nikon guided me out of the apartment, making me feel a sense of loss. It'd been such a wonderful place, and I'd likely never see it again.

The pang didn't last long. There wasn't a chance for it to. The crowd was louder than before, making me grip both Nikon's elbow and the top of my cane harder than I should. I didn't care though. It was worth having something to hold on to.

We went through the crowd and I kept my head tilted down like I was watching where I stepped. It didn't take long for me to be jostled and bumped. As long as I kept hold of Nikon, everything would be fine. I would make it there and would soon discover if Vading Antonia was the same as my caretaker Antonia.

As we moved through the crowd, I tried to keep track of where we were in relation to the safe house we'd left, but counting steps and memorizing directions as we continued to turn quickly grew impossible.

Nikon and I had decided beforehand that we'd find a place in the back to listen. We'd still be able to hear, but also be able to get away if the warriors spotted us. Hopefully.

The sandals on my feet were like mini prisons as we walked. They trapped me, keeping me from being free and sprinting wherever I wanted, from feeling what was going on beneath my toes.

"Almost there," Nikon whispered in my ear.

On my other side, Tewy stayed silent. His presence on my shoulder comforted me despite—or maybe because of—the lack of his chatter.

The scent of cooked meat wafted to me, suffused with exotic spices I couldn't remember or place. The talking and bartering filled the air with its noise. Other people grew closer to me, making me draw my cane into my chest and stick to Nikon like my life depended on it. They bustled and bumped, invading my space.

I took it in stride the best I could, but was grateful when we stopped and Nikon pulled me in front of him. I pressed my back against his chest, willing to share the area with him more than the others around us as we settled in to wait.

The Reding and Vading didn't have a specific time they were coming out, just sometime early in the afternoon. Many around us enjoyed lunch on the go, but we'd eaten before we left, finishing off the fresh food that Nikon had purchased.

The crowd somehow managed to grow louder and louder until my ears hurt. People yelled to be heard over one another. The delicious scent of food got clogged down with the odor of too many people in one space. I was sure I didn't help since I hadn't gotten a chance to bathe since we'd left Itpy, much to my chagrin.

I clutched my cane, wondering if this could really be it. Would I really find out what had happened to my caretaker all those years ago? Would I find out she'd left me because she became an amant? Or would I be disappointed to discover that she was not the Vading?

Not that it would be disappointing. It would be difficult to get in to see the Vading, so if it wasn't her, that would ease one concern I had. But it'd be so good to know what had happened to her. It'd bring peace to my mind that it wasn't something horrible.

As long as I wondered if this would be the moment I'd find out, it didn't come. The afternoon dragged on, taking the remaining coolness of the day with it. The odor of too many people turned into a gagging stench.

Maybe the Reding and Vading weren't going to have an assembly today. Maybe all this waiting and risking ourselves had been for nothing?

Nikon pulled me over to my left, telling me close to my ear, "Just getting in better position."

I nodded so he'd know I understood. It wasn't about getting in good position to see, but to escape, should things come to that. Or maybe it'd already come to that and he was trying to slip us out of the crowd.

Were warriors circling the group? Were they corralling us in because they knew they had two fugitives here, and that was why the Reding and Vading weren't holding the assembly today?

Despite knowing Nikon would take care of things the best he could, I tensed. Sometimes, the best you could wasn't enough. It had to be today, but there was no guarantee that it would be. We might be going to the dungeons soon to live out the remainder of our short lives.

I shook myself away from the unhappy thought. It'd be so much easier if I knew what was going on besides the swell of the crowd. The swell that was calming down. It grew quieter by the moment until all was silent.

"Zaykai, my people, and thank you for coming," a reedy male voice projected.

Nikon gave my shoulders a squeeze, and I knew that was the Reding speaking. They were still holding the assembly after all.

"I want you to know how much it means to me and my Vading that you attend our assemblies. We love the chance to speak with you, so thank you for coming and being a part of this glorious occasion. Today, I'd like to speak on the way we can be better friends and neighbors to build up our amant community."

Nikon stiffened against my back. He didn't like where this was headed.

"We all need to be kind to each other and get to know one another. The better we know one another, the less likely it will be that we'll have infiltrators."

Ah, the Reding meant people like me and Nikon. At least we were only pretending to find out about the Vading, not to plot upheavals like others may be doing in the rebellion of Ruso or Itpy. Though I was good to do that too. Besides, they weren't pretending to be something they weren't. Not yet, anyway.

"Yes, you know of what I speak. There are some among us who don't belong. Who have not truly felt the awe-inspiring moment of falling in love at first sight. I admit, I hadn't felt it while I was leading you for some time, but you were all patient with me and trusted I would find my amant wife, and so I did. I'm a happily married person now, as I know most of you are.

"But if we are to keep the peace, to keep the odiosom in their place where they belong, it's important we snuff out any who might try to pretend to be amant. That kind is the most dangerous to us, taking resources and bounty meant for you, my people."

I tried not to feel guilty. It was only so I could find Antonia, I told myself. I wasn't trying to steal from the amant or do anything else that was nefarious to them. Then again, why should I feel guilty? As much as this was the way things had been since the Govlin Wars, it didn't mean it was the right thing.

"If you can do this, my amant, our glory and richness will

grow. We'll take care of those less fortunate than us, those who have not yet found love whether they ever will or not, by giving them jobs. By letting them see each other to give them hope they will one day join our ranks. And for those who truly fall in love, we'd be happy to have them join us and become part of our wonderful community.

"But what we should not and cannot stand for is those that try to pretend. Those that would take everything we've been chosen for away from us. It would destroy our wonderful redvadom of Eppla should we let them infiltrate our ranks."

When was the Vading going to speak? She had to have something to say about all of this? I needed her to, or all that we'd come through would be in vain.

"My people, I reiterate to you, get to know one another. Be friends who are so close that no one who is not a true amant will be able to break into our community. Make certain those who are new amant among you have been checked off by a warrior. This will make us all prosper and become better together."

The people cheered. I shook my free arm in the air and pasted a smile on my face. Despite his words making me feel sick, I needed to appear like I didn't just agree with them, but was enthused by them.

I'd never been so glad to be stuck as an odiosom in all my life. If this was how amant treated one another, I wanted nothing to do with it.

Nikon whispered in my ear, "They're going in."

"But…"

"I know." He squeezed my shoulders, and I took what comfort I could.

What did we do next? Wait around until the next assembly and hope the Vading spoke then? But maybe she never would. Maybe she always remained silent. And each day we stayed here, the likelihood we would be found out grew greater. It would be even more so knowing the Reding asked the amant to search out the odiosom pretending in their midst.

I had failed to find Antonia.

Tewy let out a great squawk followed by another and another, until he sounded like one crazed monkey. The crowd quieted down, and I imagined they were all turning toward the noise, trying to figure out what was going on.

"Hush, Tewy." I reached up to try and silence him, but he swatted at me and kept up his racket.

It didn't take long for the entire court to grow silent except for the hooting of my monkey. And then, out of nowhere, he stopped.

The air filled with nothing but a heavy silence until a familiar woman, my Antonia whose voice I'd recognize anywhere, called out, "Seize that couple."

CHAPTER THIRTY-NINE

Nikon moved before I had time to think about what was happening. He pulled me through the crowd until we met an empty street. A buzz of chatter came from behind us.

"Wait," I said. "That's her. That's my old caretaker."

"She doesn't have good intentions toward us, trust me."

"But..." Why wouldn't she have good intentions? I didn't have much of a chance to think about it or ask anything because Nikon pushed us along at a breakneck speed. I struggled to keep up, but the pounding footsteps behind us said I had to or someone would catch us.

I panted for breath as we went, pleading with the sands to not let me fall. The sands! If we could make it there, maybe the magic would help us somehow. Or we could hop on a boat and lose them that way. "Nikon. The river," I said between breaths.

"I don't think we'll have enough time." His words came out clearer than mine, though still struggling for air.

We made a sharp turn, followed by another and another, keeping a tight grip on my friend but traitor, Tewy. I lost all sense of anything except racing ahead and the clattering of footsteps after us. They seemed to be multiplying despite Nikon's best efforts to keep us away and safe.

Somehow, I managed to keep up, stumbling only a little. We turned another corner and Nikon abruptly stopped and swore. "They've blocked this alleyway since last time I was here." He pulled me into a quick but fierce hug before letting go of me entirely.

I was still trying to figure out what was going on when the faint snick of metal against metal sounded. Nikon must have pulled his sword.

"Stay behind me," he said.

Like I could see where that was. Trying to do my best, I stayed back away from his voice, twisting my cane into two fighting sticks. He couldn't keep all the warriors off forever, and neither could I, but if he thought Antonia meant us harm, I would trust him more than the woman who'd left me to fend for myself without even a goodbye.

"Turn yourselves in," a woman yelled. "The Vading demands it."

I didn't know how Nikon responded, but whatever he did had the woman calling, "You bring this misery upon yourselves."

Less than a second later, the ring of metal against metal filled the narrow alleyway, bouncing off the buildings next to us. Tewy jumped from my shoulder as I started in on my drills. They wouldn't help me when someone could see what I was doing and I couldn't, but they'd keep my sticks moving and harder to get past.

My arms moved with precision, the muscles remembering the training Nikon had put them through. This, though, was no training. This was the real thing. I didn't know how long I'd last, but hopefully long enough for Nikon to beat the warriors we needed to, and for us to get out of here.

Because we couldn't fail. Not if Nikon thought Antonia meant danger to us. To me. The thought still didn't make sense, but there was no more time to think of it. My hands tingled, magic coursing through my fighting sticks, telling me someone was headed my way and meant to harm me.

A loud thunk sounded the same time as my right stick hit the sword. I moved around, keeping the sticks going as I tried to feel for impressions that would help me determine what would work. The ground was mostly hard but had some loose pebbles or sand, something that made footing more difficult, especially in the stupid sandals.

I blocked several more times. There was a thwack each time that I felt all the way up to my shoulder and beyond. Nikon had helped me learn but had never hit this hard. Either he was holding back or my opponent was fierce. Maybe both.

A strong impression of a blade coming directly at my right with no time to parry came to me. I twisted away but not quickly enough. The kiss of steel skimmed across my upper arm. I shot out, attacking my opponent while they were opening, smacking my sticks where I suspected their chest to be.

An "umpf" came as I bashed against what I thought was a torso. Though I kept my sticks moving after that, there was no sound of anyone coming toward me, no feeling that they were coming after me. Just the fighting a little beyond where Nikon must have been holding his own.

"Are you hurt?" a man said.

Was he talking to me? Couldn't be.

"She's wicked with those things," a woman gasped out.

Grateful I hadn't answered, I kept my arms moving, wondering where Tewy went, and if he and Nikon were surviving this onslaught.

Almost the same moment I got the impression someone else was coming to hurt me, my left stick rammed against something. I swept my right one hard toward the assailant, but nothing happened except hitting air.

Cumin, limes, and sweat filled my nose as the next attack came. My attacker needed a bath far more than I did. Ugh. I focused on keeping them as far away from me as possible, which was easier to do while swinging my sticks. They moved across, up, down, diagonally, and every which way as the ringing of metal grew faster, more urgent.

"Nikon, you need help?" I called out as I tried to keep my opponent at bay. Not that I knew what I would do, but it sounded as if he was fighting off multiple people.

"Stay back," was the only reply I got.

I shouldn't distract him any more than I already had, but I was dying to know what was going on. My own opponent didn't give me much time for thinking on it, as they came at me hard. I held off their barrage, though I didn't know how I was doing it. The instinct from the magic in my sticks did far more than anything I could deliberately make happen.

When I thought there was an opening in my attacker's defenses, I swung at it, putting all my power behind it. I came up with nothing but air, toppling forward as I caught myself off balance.

"What are you doing?" a man said from nearby, on my other side.

Of course; he was on my other side. Not far, but enough that I'd missed him the first go. I whipped my sticks back into motion, attacking before he had a chance to breathe or think further. From the buzz of my sticks, he was aiming low. I blocked him with one and smacked him upside the head with the other, still using my stick sense.

A heavy thunk came. The feeling of someone attacking me left, and when I reached out with the sticks, nothing was there but air.

"Look at me. Open your eyes," the woman who'd accused me of being wicked with my fighting sticks said. "You can't let her take you down."

I focused away from the two I'd felled, at least momentarily, and concentrated on locating Nikon. There was a lot of grunting, huffing, and clanging along with the quick scratching sound of footwork.

I wanted to jump in and help but knew that was entirely the wrong thing to do.

Instead, I kept my sticks moving, and tried to stay on the defensive. I wished I knew where the walls of the alleyway were so I could back against them and not have someone sneak up behind me, but in the fight, I'd lost all sense of direction.

While I was struggling to figure out what was going on around me and how I could protect my back, there was a loud clash. It came from the ground on my right.

"Cassandra, my sword. It fell on your right." Nikon's words were panicked.

I had to get it to him. He had other weapons, but he was best with his sword. Especially if there were multiple opponents, he would need it. I switched both sticks to one hand, and in one smooth move, I bent down, grabbed the first thing I came across, and chucked it toward Nikon's voice. It wasn't until it was already sailing through the air that I realized it'd felt more like wood than metal, smooth but knobby.

I had thrown a branch instead of a sword. There must be a tree nearby—sand it all.

Nikon growled. A strange thud came again and again. It took a moment to realize that Nikon was attempting to fight off the warriors with whatever stick I'd thrown at him. I grunted, getting on my hands and knees. That would never do.

Moving was difficult with my sticks both in one hand bearing my weight, while my free hand moved in a circle, searching for the hilt of Nikon's sword.

"Interesting," the female from earlier said. "You appear to have lost something."

I froze, ready to jump up and get my sticks moving.

"How is it you can knock out my friend, but you can't seem to find your ally's sword?" she asked.

I ignored her and stretched out farther, hoping it would appear but fearing she'd already picked it up.

"Don't worry, his weapon is in good hands now."

Fear bristled through me, even as the thud and noises of fighting continued. Nikon couldn't help me, not in that moment, and especially not without his blade. I switched my sticks to have one in each hand while I slowly stood, expecting her to come at me any second.

"You're blind, aren't you?" This time, her voice came from my right.

I strained to hear her steps, but there was nothing except the fighting from my left. My throat tightened. I was going the way of the river. There was no way to make it through this. Even when my stick sense kicked in during the fighting, it felt like there were too many odds stacked against us. Why had I wanted so desperately to find the woman who obviously didn't care about me?

Didn't matter. I couldn't dwell on it. I had to figure my way out of this situation. "What do you want from us?"

"Eventually, I want you to turn yourselves in, but in the meantime, I wouldn't mind having a little fun with you." She spoke from behind me.

I reached my hand above my head and bent my elbow so the stick was protecting my back. I let my other hand sway out in front of me. If she attacked me, this way I'd have some hint of what was coming before it did so.

She laughed. "You knocked the air out of me and the consciousness out of my partner, and now you want to move around like an idiot. That's right, keep going. Don't mind me. How did you ever get ahead of us?"

Nikon wasn't coming. The sounds of fighting grew fiercer as someone cried out in pain. If it was him, I'd never forgive myself for putting us in this situation.

"No matter," she continued. "I'll finish it."

She wanted to attack. But from which direction? She had gone utterly silent. There was no way to know where she was coming from or what she was going to do. I licked my lips, concentrating on everything around me. On the power running through the sticks. I could do this. I would do it.

A split-second warning was all I got before a sword headed toward my thigh. I blocked it. She came at me again and soon, we were in a sort of dance, moving in, out, and around as she tried to get past my defenses.

She howled. "How are you doing this?"

I grinned. At least I could do one thing right, even if it was entirely the fault of magic.

That was when I tripped over something poking up out of the ground and went sprawling.

CHAPTER FORTY

A blade pierced my neck, making liquid trickle down my skin. The female called out, "Stop the fighting now or the woman dies."

The sound of a stick hitting the ground was followed by silence.

My attacker laughed. "Don't think I don't know who you are, Nikon. Oh yes, I know exactly who you are. No one else has a fighting style quite like yours. We may not have met personally, but you're a legend. I've heard so much about you, just saying your name makes me sick. To find you protecting some blind person instead of turning them in—all the rumors about you defecting are true, aren't they?"

Nikon didn't respond.

I didn't either, other than to bite my lip so I wouldn't call out in pain from slamming against the ground. Nothing felt broken, but nothing felt good either.

"We'll see what the Reding and Vading have to say about their treasured elite warrior now." The point pressed harder into my skin. "Get off the ground, blind girl."

I wanted to correct her and tell her that I was grown, but it didn't seem like the right time to do so. Instead, I got to my feet, grateful my sticks were still in hand. No one took them from me, though metal scraped across the ground, and she said, "This is a fine sword. I think I'll keep it as a prize."

Suppressing a groan, I berated myself for not finding it instead of that stupid branch. If I had, maybe this whole fight would have turned out differently.

Thankfully, she didn't request my weapons. I'd just whipped her and her partner. I wouldn't be the one to inform her of the stupidity, though.

I expected Tewy to come out at some point during all of this, but wherever he was, he stayed hidden.

The woman said, "Let's get you both to the Reding and Vading."

"Can I at least let her have my elbow? She'll go faster if I guide her," Nikon said.

That probably wouldn't happen, but I appreciated him thinking of me. Walking around in a world that held nothing but the unknown was unnerving. Having him there would make it better. I just didn't see our new captor allowing it to happen.

"That's fine," she said.

Surprises happened every day. Who knew?

Nikon slipped up next to me. I put my cane back together, held it in one hand while taking his arm in the other. If we weren't around so many warriors and if I had Tewy on my shoulder, all would be normal.

But it wasn't.

They were taking me to Antonia, my caretaker, and my Vading who seemed dangerous to me. I still couldn't believe they were one and the same. It made no sense. Why did she leave me? If she'd fallen in love, she could have told me. I would have understood.

Well, maybe not. I did have a tendency toward being overly dramatic about love about the time she left. That still didn't excuse her not telling me. I wanted to demand answers from her, but if she was taking us in as her prisoners, I wouldn't be the one to do the demanding.

And why did she want us as prisoners? Had she recognized me from Tewy's noises? Why not calmly ask for me? I wished I knew more about what was going on.

Nikon led me sure and steady through the streets. I kept expecting him to whisper some hint in my ear. A little information about how we were going to get out of this mess. Nothing ever came.

Instead, the air grew cold, and the sound of our footsteps closed in on us as if there were walls all around. But no one had said anything about going inside. Maybe we were in the pyramid. It made sense if we were going to see the Reding and Vading that we would do so there, where they lived and worked. If you could consider what they did to be work.

The ground sloped upward, rising beneath me at a steady pace. We made several turns, each one continuing the way up. I couldn't see the Reding and Vading using this way to get where they needed to go all the time. Maybe they never left the pyramid except to address the crowd? Or maybe people carried them out?

Why was I even thinking of such mundane things when I was likely going to be put to work as a slave or worse? I shivered; whether from the cold or the thoughts that were playing on a constant loop in my mind, it didn't matter. They were both bothering me.

I moved closer to Nikon, stealing his warmth and comfort. Not that there was much comfort when we were walking to our deaths or enslavement. Shouldn't even think of our deaths though. It was better than saying it aloud, but it could still invite it to us.

I missed Tewy's weight on my shoulder. His companionship would have helped in the moment, but there was no telling where he'd gone off to. I hated to think that he'd abandoned me, but maybe that was the case.

The floor leveled out, and we took one more turn before she said, "You'll wait here."

The footsteps faded, but they couldn't have left us alone. I couldn't say anything to Nikon, but then, there wasn't much to say. We'd been captured. This was it for us.

Nikon surprised me by taking me in his arms and pulling me to him. When he whispered in my ear, I realized that was why he'd done so. "There are other warriors here by the door."

I nodded my understanding.

He continued at a whisper. "Sorry. I've failed you. And don't shake your head at me, we both know that I promised to keep you safe and wasn't able to do so."

Being mindful of my words in case others were around, I replied, "I brought you here."

He squeezed me tighter. "No, I should have gotten us out of there sooner or made a different turn. Something."

"You can't change the past. Let's focus on the future. What are we going to do?"

"It depends on what the Reding and Vading want, but I don't imagine it's going to go very well for me. I have a little more hope for you. Maybe the Vading will go easy on you since you knew each other before."

Antonia had never gone easy on me, but I didn't say that. I had to leave him some hope even if there was none left for myself.

His words grew quieter, making me strain to hear them. "You still have your cane, which is great. Try to hold on to it no matter what happens."

"I will." I paused. "What do you think happened to Tewy?"

"I don't know. It surprised me he didn't stay with you."

"Me as well."

We remained like that, with him holding me, drawing me near. His chest moved with each breath, slow and steady. I leaned my head against him and listened to his heartbeat. Unlike the composure he tried to display, it beat a quick rhythm.

I wished I could calm it for him. Wished I could give him some sense of peace before the storm, but I didn't know what I could say or do that would make a difference. I wrapped my arms around him, holding tight to my cane with one hand, but with the other I pulled him close. "I just want you to know you're my best friend."

"And you are mine."

My eyes smarted, but I wasn't about to go and cry all over his amant linen and get kohl everywhere. They couldn't do anything to him. If they sent him to be killed, I would never forgive myself for bringing him here. I needed him to exist beyond this crisis. Needed him to still be around even if I was taken as a slave. I couldn't handle anything else.

"Isn't this touching?" the woman from before asked, voice sardonic.

Nikon pulled away from me, but slowly, like he didn't care what she thought. I was grateful for that. He gave me his elbow for my free hand, and I took it, ready to face my former caretaker even if she had become the Vading.

CHAPTER FORTY-ONE

Nikon guided me out of the room the way we had come, but turned right instead of left, covering new ground. We went up and up and up, like we were making circles around the building as we went, with the circles growing smaller. I grew hotter and hotter, working hard to keep up with them.

We passed a few sets of footfalls or people talking, but none made any comment to us or about us. Wherever we were going, it didn't have anything to do with these people. Though there were more footsteps behind us than there were before, so maybe they were following us. If so, they were doing it without speaking.

Voices came out ahead of us, a low rumble of speech. We moved past something, I couldn't tell what, but as soon as we did, those voices stopped and a breeze met my skin. It was a thankful change from the sticky heat that'd been grating on me while climbing up.

Nikon helped me farther in the room before we stopped. He whispered, "We're in the middle of court at the top room of the pyramid. The Reding and Vading aren't here yet."

I was grateful for him telling me without having to ask. It was good knowing what was going on.

The voices slowly grew louder. I couldn't make out many, but as they grew bolder, I picked up on a few.

"What's he doing with her?"

"Did you know he used to be the Reding's top elite warrior?"

"His disgrace is widely spoken of."

"They say she's blind."

"That must be why she's carrying that cane."

"What do you think will happen to them?"

It was the last question that stuck with me and made me ignore the rest of their words. What were the Reding and Vading going to do with us? Here, in front of such a large crowd, I'd imagine they'd want to display their power and control.

That meant no hugs of welcome, not that I'd expected them anyway, but some sort of show that she ever cared for me would have been nice. Maybe I'd still get a word of something. You couldn't live with a person for a few years without them having some feelings about you.

The noise fell silent again, quicker this time.

A woman called out, "His Royal Highness Reding Theodore and Her Royal Highness Vading Antonia."

This was it. After years of wondering what had happened to her, I was finally meeting my caretaker again. I stood straighter and let go of Nikon's elbow, though I stayed close enough that our arms just barely brushed.

Two sets of footsteps tapped through the room, followed by a man with a young-sounding voice saying, "Everyone who is not an elite warrior is excused."

There was a faint grumbling, but the crowd shifted. They must have been leaving because the noise was going with them, though not the way they came in. I couldn't imagine why the Reding kicked everyone out in that moment. Perhaps he wanted to show he had us the control he had over everyone. Whatever the case might have been, it didn't take long for the room to clear.

The voice that rang out was familiar, causing an ache of abandonment deep inside my chest. "You never should have come."

CHAPTER FORTY-TWO

Antonia's words rang in my ears. She didn't want me here. Of course, she didn't—she sent the warriors after us and left me to begin with. Despite that, deep down I'd been hoping there was something in her that wanted to see me, to know I was not only doing well but thriving. I opened my mouth to respond, but there was a sharp clang.

"Don't you speak," Antonia said. "You've caused a lot of problems for us, Cassandra. The only good thing is that you brought the worthless man with you."

I tilted my chin up and moved my head so it faced her voice. "The only worthless thing about him is that he stayed working for you both for so long."

Someone sucked in a quick breath of air, but I had no idea who. It hadn't been Nikon, and I didn't think it came from the direction of Antonia or the Reding but couldn't be certain.

"You will not speak to me in such a way." Her voice rang out with authority that was familiar and grating.

It'd been too long since I'd been with her. If I would have remembered her harsh side instead of all the good times, maybe I never would have come. It made me want to cower and get to my chores. But there were no chores here, and the last thing I wanted to do was cower.

I held myself tall and tried not to let my old insecurities out.

"Nikon," the man who I was pretty certain was the Reding said. "Why have you brought this blind girl to my assembly when you know I'm hunting you down?"

No response.

"I asked you a direct question. You will answer me no matter our past relationship. Why did you bring her?"

There was a small shift beside me. "Because she asked."

"Explain yourself, Cassandra," the Reding said.

I never thought he would directly address me. The man who was supposed to be our link to magic, and rule Eppla with peace and justice. I wanted to shrink back, but instead, I said, "It would seem Antonia already told you my name. I'm sure you heard the rest of the story."

"You will not address my Vading so informally." Despite his words, his voice held steady. "Vading Antonia has told me what I need to know, but that doesn't explain to me why you would ask my disgraced warrior to bring you to one of our assemblies. Tell me."

I wanted to refuse, but what was the point? "I wanted to know if the Vading was my old caretaker, simple as that."

"Didn't you think that maybe there was a reason I didn't tell you where I was going? That I wouldn't be back?" The venom in Antonia's voice surprised me.

"I knew being with me wasn't your first choice. I didn't realize you hated it so much." I tried to keep the pain out of my voice and thought I succeeded.

"Hated every second of it. Hated you," she spewed.

I swallowed past the poison and focused on the moment. "Why stay with me then? You were there for years before you left without a warning."

"Oh, there were warnings, you were just too oblivious to see them. You were a charge I had to take but never wanted for more reasons than you'll ever know. If you hadn't been so upset all the time, it might have been more bearable, but no, all I heard about day in and out was how you wished your parents hadn't blinded you. How wrong they were for doing so, but how you still wished they were alive. Well, guess what, Cassandra? They are."

My knees went wobbly. "They are what?"

Silence followed.

"My parents are what?" I yelled.

"Dearest, I think we'd better move on to the problem with Nikon," the Reding said.

"Very well." Antonia's words were more put together this time, but she still sounded upset.

It was nothing compared to the strange churning going on inside my chest. Did she mean...? Could she mean...? Were my parents alive?

No.

Just no.

I wouldn't allow myself to think like that. I was a grown woman with grown woman problems and issues. I didn't need to be digging up a past that had nothing to do with the now. Especially not when my mother and father had died.

But then, Antonia had been the one to tell me they'd died in the first place, the one to tell me we had to leave and go to the home we'd made by the waterfall.

My parents. Alive.

"Where are the plans, Nikon?" the Reding asked, his voice even and well-modulated.

He and Antonia were not alike in temperament. How was it the two of them were the ones who were meant to be together?

"What plans?" Nikon said.

I hoped they didn't direct the question at me. I would never be able to mimic the levelness of his voice when I knew he had them hidden somewhere.

"Don't play dumb with us," Antonia said. "We know you found them and it had to have been you who took them. I want to know what happened to them."

"Why don't you ask your High Priest?" Nikon's words took me aback.

The High Priest? What did he have to do with all this? Would his link with magic lead them to Nikon? But it hadn't. No, it was something else.

"We have," the Reding said. "However, the only direction we've gained is to follow the path the chase leads us on. All we can find on that path is you."

"Do the people understand just how little the High Priest knows?" Nikon asked.

I felt like I'd been dropped into some game I didn't understand.

"The High Priest knows far more than you ever will," Antonia said.

"The people understand our need to use him when we need to," the Reding said. "But that's not what we're here about. Where are the plans, Nikon?"

"I don't know what you're talking about."

"Then I'm afraid you leave us no choice."

Someone's fingers snapped.

I gulped, knowing that Nikon was about to be tortured, but instead of him leaving my side, hands grabbed at me, pulling me away from him. "What are you doing?" My words were more frantic than they should have been, but they were clear enough.

"Nikon's clearly grown an attachment to you," Antonia said. "Reding Theodore and I had a long discussion about it after news of your capture. With Nikon's skills, he could withstand torture for some time. We don't have the novelty of time so we're trying a new method, one in which you'll be on the receiving end of the knife. Thank you for coming and allowing us to utilize you. Maybe next time, you'll stay where I put you."

That didn't sound like they were going to kill me, but neither did it sound like they were going to leave me alone. Something tickled my inner arm on the other side from my elbow. It didn't hurt, but made my breath quicken anyway.

I tried to wiggle away, but several sets of hands held me firmly in place. I wasn't going to get out of this. Nothing could save me.

I had to hold it together though. Nikon couldn't give in and tell them what they wanted because of me. I needed to be stronger than that.

The thing that tickled turned into a sharp pain, slowly going down my arm. I sucked in a breath. They were cutting me, that much I knew. The pain was fierce and slow, bringing a feeling of nausea. Why had I put us in this situation?

A familiar squawk sounded. Tewy.

The pain let up.

"There you are, you naughty monkey," Antonia said. "I thought you'd forgotten to come to me."

"Come to you?" My voice had a dazed quality to it.

"Of course. He's trained to alert me to your presence. You didn't think I'd go to all the work of training you a monkey and then not have any benefit to me, did you?"

Stupidly, I had.

"No, Tewy here is an excellently trained monkey whom I ado — Ugh. Disgusting creature."

A hint of feces permeated the air as the snick, snick, snick of Tewy running toward me sounded.

Did he just do what I think he did? I grinned, wide and huge. "Good monkey."

"Get that foul creature," Antonia screeched.

Hands left me, liquid dripping down my arm. I was bleeding, but I didn't care. I was free from my torturers. "Get away, Tewy."

The snicks shifted from coming toward me, to moving away.

And then, a hand closed around my upper arm. So much for

being free. I was flung to the side, barely managing to get my balance.

Nikon pulled me back, hand steady. Because it was him. I'd know those calluses anywhere. I needed to stick with him, whatever he had planned. We weren't going to let this go on without a fight. We ran.

I didn't say anything though. Even through the chaos of noise shouting through the room, I didn't dare risk doing anything that might bring attention to us. I wasn't sure what Nikon had planned. We were trapped at the top of a pyramid surrounded by the most elite warriors of the Reding and Vading. We weren't going anywhere. But maybe he could do something, anything, to make it so I wouldn't have to suffer torture.

The thought made my lower arm ache where it'd been cut as we ran. It didn't matter, a little pain was nothing.

"Duck." Nikon's word came directly in my ear, barely heard over the din.

I followed his directions until he pulled my arm back up. We'd gone under something, I didn't know what.

"It's night, Cassandra, this will be perfect for getting away," was the only hint I got from Nikon, and by the tone of his voice, I wasn't going to like our escape method.

CHAPTER FORTY-THREE

N ikon had me walk in front of him, guiding me along the way. My foot moved to the left, finding an edge, making Nikon tilt me back over to the right. Wait, an edge? Where were we? What was going on?

Maybe it was best I didn't know.

The shout of voices grew quieter, but I could still hear them.

"Get that sanded monkey," Antonia yelled.

"He's going between your legs."

"No, over there."

"He's going to the exit."

"Grab him."

"Where are the prisoners?"

The last question made me move quicker, as much as I dared. I didn't know where we were or what we were doing, but it didn't feel like a good thing.

"Almost to the corner," Nikon said. "We're going to turn to our right in just a moment. You've got this, Cass."

Got what? I wasn't even sure what we were doing. But from the calls behind us and the softness of his tone, I knew we were in danger of being discovered. Maybe he knew a place we could hide until—well, I didn't know what exactly, but it had to be better than going back to those people who were willing to cut me up.

"Turn now." Nikon's voice was steady.

I turned, finding a pathway instead of the wall that had been next to me before. I didn't like the feel of this at all. I hurried forward, but after we'd gone a little ways, I stopped, turned, and whispered behind me, "Are we on the edge of the top of the pyramid?"

"Would it help if I lied?"

"Yes."

"No, we're not. We're close to the ground, we just have a narrow way to walk, and some, well, erm, some scaling to do. It'll be fine. You can handle all of it."

"I'm sorry I got us into this mess."

"I know you are, but now's not the time to discuss it. We're out of sight for now, but with our white clothes, we'll stick out against the pyramid even in the dark. We need to hurry."

I shook my head but continued forward. It sounded like we were going to climb down the edge of the pyramid, which was a bad idea with a blind girl. I wasn't about to tell him that though, not when we didn't have any other choice.

We went as fast as I could make it, trailing along the path quickly, turning to the right one more time, going a bit farther. He grabbed my arm that was injured. "We need to stop the bleeding."

A ripping sound rent the air and a soft cloth was tied around the burning pain in my arm. Then he said the dreaded words, "We're going to climb down a few of the ledges here."

"I was hoping we were going to keep circling the pyramid forever."

"Afraid we'd just be recaptured that way. Don't worry, we're not going all the way to the bottom like this."

Like that made me feel better.

I turned around, and Nikon was helping me down the ledge when there was a soft *oo oo*.

"Tewy." I kept my voice low, but it must have carried to him, because moments later, he jumped on my shoulder. "That's a good boy, Tewy."

"Very good boy," Nikon added while taking the cane from me. "I'm going to find you the best treats when we get home. But from here on out, I need you both to be as silent as possible."

"Done."

I tried scrambling down to the next ledge, Tewy jumping off my shoulder, hopefully not going far. There was nothing to hold onto until Nikon grabbed both of my hands and lowered me down. It was much farther than I'd expected it to be.

The level was taller than me. Maybe even taller than Nikon. How were we going to get down all these? I couldn't imagine. He did say we were only going partway, but it still seemed almost impossible. And to do so without getting spotted? No, it was a bad idea. We were going to get caught. The thought kept rolling around in my head as I waited on the thin ledge.

The soft pat of sandals hitting rock came next to me. How did he do that without falling over the side? Especially since he didn't have help like I did? I couldn't ask because he said to stay silent, but I was dying to know. This was a whole new side of him I'd never known before.

We went like that, over and over again. Nikon would help lower me to the next level before lowering himself. The drops seemed to get farther and farther apart, making me stretch to reach even with Nikon helping me. The different tiers of the pyramids were not at all like I'd expected. They were deadly thin and tall.

"Almost there," he whispered.

"Sing praises to the sand."

He gave a low laugh and grabbed my hands. I bit my lip like I'd been doing for the last several levels as he lowered me down, my feet swinging in the air, finding nothing but the wall in front of me. He grunted as I tried to find purchase but came up short.

"Let go," he said.

"I'll fall."

"The ledge is just below you, I promise."

I wasn't sure if I could do this, but if it was his word, I knew he meant it. I let go and landed smack on the ledge. At first, I thought I was going to be fine, but then I wobbled backward. An "eep" escaped me, much louder than I meant it to. I was going over the edge. I would be nothing but a splat at the bottom of the Reding and Vading's pyramid.

Nikon's hands grabbed me around the waist, steadying me. "I gotcha."

A flutter went through my chest.

"This way." He guided me to the side, taking me along a short distance before he said, "It's a tight squeeze through this secret entrance."

He grabbed my hand and directed me to an opening that was just bigger than I was if I scrunched up. I managed to squish myself into it. "Where does this go?"

"It's a passage to my old rooms."

"You can fit through this?"

"Not well, but I can."

I went forward, something brushing my hand. I shook it off. "I think there's spiders in here."

"I know there are."

"Lovely."

"What can I say? I know how to show my friends a good time."

I continued shuffling my way forward with my head bent down at an awkward angle. "Have you shown many friends this way?"

"You're the first."

"I feel so privileged."

"Good. Hurry up."

I smiled, but did as he asked, pushing myself faster. Going through here made me realize there was so much more to this building than I ever thought. It was huge, with hidden paths and rooms that spanned the building, halls that sloped, and all sorts of nooks and crannies. I had a feeling I just knew the smallest bit of it.

My hand hit solid rock in front of me. I felt around, expecting to find a doorknob of some sort, but came up empty. "There's nothing here. Did the Reding know about this and block it off?"

"No one knows about this. At the bottom of the rock on the right, there's a small lever. If you push it, the door will swing open."

I ran my hand along, coming across something sticky and wispy. "Ew." I wiped it on my dress and continued searching, trying not to think of what else could be in here. I hoped there were no scorpions.

Finally, I felt the floor and went all the way over to the right. Sure enough, my fingers brushed against a small thing that stood out from the rest of the door. I pressed it and there was a heavy scrape of rock moving against rock.

"Be careful getting down. You're at the top of the wall," Nikon said.

"How does no one notice this is here?" Because though I couldn't see it, I knew other people should be able to. At least, they normally saw doors.

"There's a tapestry over it that swings forward with the door. Plus, it's well made to look like the rest of the wall. I found it long after I was assigned here. You'd probably have found it on your first real search of the room, but I'm hoping no one else knows about it. Hop down."

Easier said than done. I gave Nikon my cane and crept to the edge, put my palms on the ledge, and gripped as tight as I could. Sliding off the rim into nothingness was scarier than when Nikon dropped me. There was nothing to steady me.

I fell less time than I expected, landing with a sharp thud going up my feet and lower legs.

"Are you hurt?"

I groaned. "Not permanently."

"I'll check you, but I can't do that until I'm let in. Can you move to your right? There's a space there big enough for you."

"I don't need checking." But I did as he requested and rolled over to the right.

Moments later, a soft thump came to my left, and Nikon said, "Here's your cane."

The worn wood that'd become a familiar extension of me prodded my hand, the tingle that came with it flowing through me. Tewy jumped on my shoulder.

"We should be good to talk in here if we keep it quiet. Looks like they searched the place, probably not long after I disappeared."

There was that scraping of rock against rock again. The hidden passage must have closed. "How did you find that little walkway?"

"I know a lot about this place."

Another vague and unhelpful response.

He continued on like he answered my question. "They left the place a mess, but looks like they didn't take as much as I expected. That's good. Here's a cloak. It's black so it will help hide you in the night."

Though I had faint memories of colors, they weren't vivid like I thought they should have been. It was strange to think we needed the darker material. As he slipped it around my shoulders, it pooled farther down around my feet. It must have been made for him, because there was so much material.

"There's a hood on it too. We'll put it up when we go." He tied it and then a noise rustled around off to my left.

The material was soft but strong, a tight knit on it that I wouldn't have expected from something of Nikon's. He probably got paid better than I expected being the Reding's right- hand warrior.

"What are we getting in here?"

"We're trying to figure out how we can escape the pyramid without any problems. There are some resources in here that will help. Unfortunately, a lot of my items took magic and the sand has dried out without my attention. I've a few other tricks up my sleeves and some weapons. Though if it comes to weapons, we're probably doomed."

It did smell of him in here. Well, of him and must. I wasn't surprised it was his room or that he had a stash of things we would need. "Are the plans in here?"

"No. They're not in the pyramid. We'll have to grab them on the way out of the city."

If we ever made it that far. No, I wouldn't think like that. *When* we made it that far. "What can I do to help?"

"I hate to say this, but stop touching things."

I jerked my hand away from what I thought was a table.

"Sorry, I just have some sensitive stuff in here and I don't want you to get hurt."

"It's fine. Weapons are not to be trifled with."

Tewy hooted in agreement.

"That, and they left a mess. There's broken glass on that table." He rummaged around, though I suppose the shuffling noise could have been Tewy.

"I hate to bother you while you're working, but how are we going to get out of here?"

"Stick to the shadows and hope we don't run into anyone. The secret passages I know aren't usually frequented. Some of the elite warriors might be looking for us because they know I'm aware of them, but they wouldn't want to tell everyone else about them. If we encounter a problem in the secret passages, it will be less than if we ran into a group of warriors in the usual halls."

"But they're elite warriors. That means they're highly trained, right?"

"Yes, but you're forgetting I used to be one too. One of the best, not to toot my own horn or anything." The shuffling continued.

He was one of the best. Not just with fighting, but as a person. He was one of the best I knew.

A hint of something came, a muffled sort of steps. Nikon grabbed me and shoved me somewhere, pressing up against me. "Silence."

We were about to have company.

CHAPTER FORTY-FOUR

I nodded, hoping Nikon would feel my understanding. I reached up, intending to put my hand on his shoulder and instead finding Tewy. I petted my monkey, hoping he knew how important it was to stay silent. With him, he'd probably squawk at just the wrong time.

We were shoved in some tiny space, walls all around and a curtain functioning as a door on one side. A closet maybe.

The loudest door I'd ever heard squealed open. Nikon sure had a noisy door.

"If he's here, he's sure to know we've come with that screech," a man said.

"Just look around like we're supposed to," a woman replied.

"It's not that big. I don't see him."

"Check under the bed, and I'll look behind the curtain."

Nikon tensed, his muscles bunching together, probably getting ready to move. I wished I was in a position to untwist my cane into two pieces. That would have made it easier to be prepared to fight. Instead, I got ready to move backward.

A faint rustle was the only warning I got. I shoved myself back, hugging the wall as Nikon launched himself forward. The woman swore, and the smack of skin hitting skin burst forth. The man said something muffled, and a clatter filled the room.

The fight didn't last long. When all was silent, I wanted to ask Nikon if it was safe, but stayed silent in case he had lost. Not that I thought he had, but it was good to be prepared. I'd hate to give myself away.

A scraping like something being dragged across the rock floor came to me.

"Hop out of the closet, and I'll put these bodies in there," Nikon said.

I sagged with relief, but quick enough that I could get out of the way. I wanted to ask if they were still living bodies or just body bodies but couldn't bring myself to.

As soon as I went out of the closet and moved to the side, Tewy jumped on my shoulder and the dragging sound continued, first one and then Nikon must have gone across the room and got the other. "You're so quiet when you want to be."

"Lots of training. Time to go before someone comes looking for these goons. They're going to know we were here which I wanted to avoid, but there's nothing we can do about it now." After putting up my hood, he gave me his elbow.

The hood was so low, if I tilted my head upward, it brushed across my chin. I put my chin down. I probably looked ridiculous, but as long as we weren't caught, it didn't matter.

As we moved, Nikon said, "My room is part of a lesser-used area of the pyramid, so we shouldn't run into someone right away unless they're searching this area. If we do, I want you to do just what you did before and get out of the way so I can take them down."

"I can do that."

"Thank you. We're going to go out in the hall now, so we'll have to be silent."

He guided me through a doorway, before the door itself gave that awful noise. Then we were on our merry way. Or at least, I tried to tell myself it was merry, like a game or training. This time, it was stealth instead of fighting. I could handle that.

We went some distance, this time sloping up instead of down. I wanted to tell Nikon we were going in the wrong direction but didn't dare say anything. I hoped he was right about secret passages and that we wouldn't have to scale down the side of the pyramid again. That had been one of the most frightening things I'd ever done. At least it didn't stink like the sewer.

The longer we continued up, the more the niggling feeling grew that we were going to get caught. I didn't want to go through that again. I'd had enough of Antonia, and she'd clearly had enough of me. I wished I understood the situation better. Why did she leave me alive? And then why try to capture me when Tewy alerted her to our presence?

It didn't feel like the type of thing I was ever going to have the answer to. Antonia had her ways, and no one else was to understand them, probably not even the Reding. Why hadn't I remembered how strict and unyielding she'd been before wanting to find her? And had I truly been as whiny as she said about losing my vision?

Probably. I wanted to think better of myself than that, but it felt like the truth. At least I hadn't turned whiny to Nikon when he came, I didn't think.

Nikon stopped, and the sound of rock against rock came before he helped me through a narrow passageway. Once the noise came again, he whispered, "It's too narrow for me to be at your side. Let me go first and you can hold on to my shoulder."

I squeezed against the rock as he brushed by me. As soon as he went by, I reached up, searching for his shoulder. Tewy climbed the length of my arm to switch to sitting on Nikon. At least my little monkey was staying silent, even if he did seem a bit restless. I could have kissed him for how well he had been behaving, but it certainly wasn't the time for it at the present moment.

Nikon twisted and brushed his arm against mine, moving

something. The scraping of rock against rock came again. "We're in a secret passage now but remember to be silent. Someone could still search for us in here."

We went forward, me slowing us down. I tried to go faster, but Nikon's steps remained at a steady pace that didn't allow for me to stumble. As grateful as I was for that, I wanted to run out of here. With my luck, I'd run into a wall.

Finally, the rock beneath my slapping feet began to slope downward. We'd only gone a short distance when Nikon stopped, turned around and said, "Take your sandals off, but keep them with you unless there's an emergency."

"With pleasure."

I bent down, untying them and looping them off from around my calves. They were easier to get off than on. I held them in the same hand as my cane, juggling all three and keeping my spare hand on Nikon's shoulder.

As we continued forward, my feet made far less noise. I should have done that a while ago, but I suppose it wouldn't have mattered if others heard us walking in a normal hall. In a secret passage, that was a different story.

We traveled a long ways, going down, down, down, and turning corners every so often, with each new corner taking longer to arrive. It was a journey, but I was up for it as long as it got us out of here.

Nikon lunged forward. I let him go, backing up against the wall to my left and pressing my back against it. The sound of grunts and a clatter echoed down the hall.

Someone had found us.

CHAPTER FORTY-FIVE

Nikon had said only the elite warriors knew of this place. He fought someone whose skill level probably matched his own. I didn't know what to do, how to help as the scuffling continued. I was stuck being the listener.

Tewy found me and clutched onto my ankle. Thankful he made it away from the fight, I reached down to pet him when a loud slam came like a body hitting the floor. I straightened.

It had to be Nikon's opponent. It just had to be.

A meaty hand wrapped around my throat. Nikon hadn't won. I slammed my sandals onto where I expected the man's head to be. Repeatedly.

It didn't seem to make a difference. He kept squeezing and squeezing. My cane. I dropped my sandals, keeping a hold of my cane and banging the top of it on his head. He grunted and his hold loosened for long enough for me to gasp for air. His hands tightened again.

I dropped my cane. It clattered to the floor as I pulled my hands up, searching for my attacker's face. It took precious seconds that I had little of. I ran across a thick mass of beard, rugged beneath my fingertips. I yanked on it as hard as I could, pulling the hairs.

"Sand it, girl, just pass out already," he grunted out.

That only made me want to win this battle more. As I pulled his hair, I gauged where his body was, and brought my knee up in a single, forceful jerk.

He let go with a groan. I dropped to the floor, searching the rock for my cane.

"You'll pay for that. I don't have to take you in right away. I can torture you all I want before the Reding and Vading have at you." His voice was strained.

I fumbled across the ground, coming across first one sandal then the other. I threw them toward where the sound of the man's voice had come from.

Mistake. He growled and had to be coming for me. Tewy squawked from up ahead. Hoping he was being helpful, I scrambled toward his voice, feeling my way as I went. When I got to a furry lump that had to be him, he was sitting on my cane. I brought it to my hands, twisted it apart, and flipped over on my back.

The tingle of warning came right away, pushing me to move the sticks. I whacked something several times, managing to keep out of reach of my opponent. I landed a good hit, causing him to call out.

Sweat poured down my forehead. I wanted to get off my back but couldn't do more than keep just ahead of his hits thanks to the extension magic in my sticks. There was a grunt and a thump, then silence. Nothing in my sticks gave an impression of an attack. What happened?

"Cass?" the single word from Nikon was winded.

"I'm fine." Ish.

"We've got to go."

A hand gripped my shoulder and helped me up. I didn't worry

about retrieving my sandals. They'd give us away just as much as the man who must have been lying on the ground.

"We're almost there," Nikon said.

I gave his shoulder a squeeze in understanding. It wasn't easy, but we were going to make it.

We continued down our slope, going at a quicker pace with me getting my bearings. A soft pad came from behind me, sounding like Tewy followed us. When we came to a stop, my monkey clung to my leg again. I bent down, pulling him up onto my shoulder.

"This is the exit. It goes directly out of the pyramid into a back alley. It's not ideal and there will probably be warriors, but we can take them. We've come this far, I refuse to go back."

"I'm right behind you."

"Stay in the opening with your weapon out until I tell you to come."

"I can do that."

I held my sticks at the ready, having untwisted them once more.

The crunch of rock against rock came again, becoming familiar and welcome. One step closer to getting out of there.

I hovered there, waiting for Nikon to give me some sort of signal it was safe. I strained to hear any sound ahead of me, a sign that he was searching or fighting or something, but as always, he was too quiet to hear. His skills impressed me. Maybe I should have him try to teach me. Though it would be harder for me, it might be worth an attempt.

A thin slice of metal pressed against my neck. The man from before called out, "Turn yourself in, Nikon, or I slit the girl's throat."

My pulse pounded against that tiny spot of metal.

"The Vading wouldn't like that. She wants the woman alive." Nikon wasn't close, but still could be heard clearly.

"The Reding wants you more than the Vading cares about this girl."

"I wouldn't be so sure about that."

The pressure increased on my neck. "Unlike you, I know how to earn their forgiveness. Give up."

I was going to lose my head if something didn't change. Nikon would probably turn himself in, and we'd both be goners if he did that. Taking my cane, I slowly moved it so the short end away from my hand pointed straight out. With a quick jab backward, I slammed it into the man behind me.

A sharp pain sliced into my throat the same time as the man howled. Less than a second later, the pressure was off my neck. Someone grabbed me, and I lifted my stick again, but Nikon said, "It's me."

I let him pull me forward and he scooted me to the side. The sickening sound of a wet squish sounded. I gagged, trying not to think about it. The man would have killed me or turned us both in if he could have. We had to do what we needed to survive.

Didn't mean I had to like it.

Nikon nudged my hands together. "Put your cane back together. It's clear for the moment if we go now. They must all be looking for us in the pyramid still."

Thank the sands for small mercies. I twisted my cane together and put it in one hand. Tewy climbed up my side until getting to my shoulder. Once he was there, Nikon gave me his elbow, and we hurried forward.

The trip through the city went quicker than I expected. We heard voices of others out partying for the night or on their way home, but there wasn't a hint of warriors after us. I wanted to ask how far we needed to go but kept silent.

He led me to the outside of a house before we stopped. I leaned against the stones despite them being cold. Running was exhausting. "Is this the place?"

"Yes. Hid them behind a stone here."

A light scraping came, then someone fumbling around. Nikon cursed the sand magic to the High Priest.

"What is it?"

"The plans. They're gone."

CHAPTER FORTY-SIX

"What do you mean, gone?" I asked. "The plans just can't be missing."

Silence descended. When he finally spoke, his words sounded devastated. "They are."

Footsteps fell in the distance.

"We should go." I squeezed his elbow and gently pulled him toward me.

"You're right. It's surprised me, is all. I really thought... Doesn't matter. They're gone, and we have to get out of here." The scraping of rock came again before he headed away from where we'd been. "Try to keep your footsteps light."

I attempted to do as he requested, but it was more difficult than he made it seem. Pebbles crunched under my feet as I didn't hear a noise out of him. I wanted to ask where we were going but didn't dare. Anyone could be around, and I didn't want to give us away.

We went through the streets, weaving through them in a way that left a maze in my head. Hopefully, he knew what he was doing. Without warning, he pressed me against a hard wall with bumps. Rocks maybe.

A smattering of footsteps went by. That didn't sound like warriors out searching for people, but then, maybe I didn't know what warriors sounded like.

I pushed off the wall, ready to go, but Nikon pressed me back against it.

"Warriors coming," he whispered in my ear, a warmth of breath caressing my skin.

Tension climbed through me, making me want to hide. If there was a place to hide though, Nikon probably would have found it. Instead, I moved back by the wall, making myself as small as possible. Marching sounded through the air, coming closer. An incessant banging on wood met my ears. Men and women called out.

Finally, I made out a man's voice much closer than I expected, though still muffled. "We're looking for two fugitives. A man and a woman who's blind. Seen anything?"

"No one's come through," another man replied.

"Keep a watch out. We don't want these two escaping the city."

The noises continued, but Nikon eased us back the way we came. I bit my lip, hoping we weren't caught. I didn't want to be dragged back to Antonia and learn what she wanted to do with me. My caretaker, the Vading of Eppla. How could such a thing have happened? With the way she acted, I wasn't certain I wanted to find out.

We crept some distance before Nikon said, "We're lucky this isn't Itpy or we'd never make it out with the walls. Luckily, I know an exit that has a lot of vegetation. We'll have to steal some food and water on our way out though."

I hated the thought of being a thief, but if it meant we'd live through this… "What do I need to do to help?"

"Keep doing what you're doing and keep your cane handy in case we have to fight our way out."

If it came to that, we were probably already too late.

As we continued on, we made several turns, often sticking

close to buildings. I tightened my hand on his arm, grateful for its guidance. Tewy crawled over to my shoulder, tail wrapping around my neck. It was amazing he hadn't made a peep yet. After the display he'd made at the pyramid, I wasn't sure I could ever trust him to be silent again, but one could hope.

"Found what we need," Nikon said, pulling me to a stop. "There appears to be no one home here. Let me sneak in and get supplies, then we'll be out of here. I'll be right back."

I let him go with some reluctance. There was no sign he'd left other than cool air pressing in on me where his warmth had been. Tewy played with strands of my hair as I knotted my fingers together.

Nothing marked the passage of time except my breathing. It went on, trailing through the night with no mind for my anxiousness about Nikon's safety.

What was taking so long? Had someone been home after all? Were we about to be caught? All of this had been for naught. I may have finally found my caretaker, but there was still much I didn't know about her. I didn't think I wanted to know anymore. But Nikon's plans, those seemed important. Who could have taken them? How did they know where the plans were hidden? And why take them in the first place?

None of it made sense.

A hand gripped my upper arm as Nikon said, "I'm back."

"If you hadn't said something, I might have screamed." My heart thudded in my chest despite the warning. "Did you find what we needed?"

"Yes. Let's go."

I took his right elbow, and together we headed away from the building and where we'd come from. Tewy's tail curled tighter around my neck, but otherwise he remained motionless as hurried through the streets.

There was no sound of warriors pursuing us, but then again, I couldn't hear Nikon either, only myself. The wooden staff in my hand had warmed under my touch, but there was nothing threatening coming from it.

"Almost there." Nikon's words were so faint, I almost didn't catch them.

I kept my feet moving, following his guidance as I swept the area in front of me. It was not the time to be caught unaware.

The sand beneath my feet shifted from being hard-packed to looser grains, easier to slip on. Both a good and a bad sign. We'd gotten farther from where people normally traveled, but it would be harder to walk on and we'd leave a more direct path. I'd have to hope that by the time someone found our footprints, we'd be long gone.

"We're under some trees now," Nikon said. "A ways more, and we'll be in the desert. No one is following us."

I couldn't imagine how we'd done it, but somehow, we'd made it out of the city into the desert alive. If only we had more to show for our journey.

CHAPTER FORTY-SEVEN

The sand was familiar beneath my feet, the heat welcome upon my shoulders. We walked for days and were almost to Itpy according to Nikon. He hadn't said much our entire journey. The loss of the plans had hit him hard, even if he didn't say much about it.

I was numb. Nothing had gone how I'd thought it would. I'd found Antonia, but she'd been nothing like I expected. Sure, she'd never been the kindest, but I hadn't thought that meant she hated me. She'd taken care of me for years only to despise those times. But what she said about my parents being alive, could it be true?

I wanted it to be with such a force it almost scared me. Yet, if she was lying, I'd be getting my hopes up for nothing. Why would she lie about such a thing? Then again, why did she not tell the truth about them being alive to begin with? There was no answer.

The soft shifting of sand moving beneath my and Nikon's feet was steady. I leaned on Nikon for support, both for him and me. My parents. They were alive somewhere, and yet I'd run. The fact that they were out there somewhere made me want to search for them with greater urgency than I'd ever wanted to find my caretaker.

But we couldn't search for them when we had the warriors, both elite and regular, on our trail. If we would have searched for them, we would have been dead, mummies to float down the river.

There wasn't anything I could do or say that would make things better, but I hadn't tried for the last couple of days either. I should have done so before that moment, but didn't want to bring up a sore point, plus I had my own hurts. It seemed the sore point grew worse without my interference anyway, so I said, "I'm sorry the plans were gone."

He sighed. "I should have hidden them somewhere else. Or better yet, taken them with me when I ran. I hid them thinking I'd be able to come back for them later. It doesn't matter. If there's nothing there to implicate the Reding... but then, maybe things aren't what they seem."

"They usually aren't, but I know the way the odiosom and the blind are treated isn't right."

"That's true. We'll just have to continue protecting ourselves against what we know to be wrong and doing our best."

"Our best is what matters."

He pulled his elbow away from my hand and wrapped his arm around my shoulders. "I'm grateful out of all the places I could have stumbled into when delirious, I wandered into your home."

Home. I missed my little house near the waterfall but didn't dare go back there with Antonia knowing I wasn't there anymore. Who knew what she would do with it? If she'd search for me there, anyway. Didn't matter, I'd made a new home with people I cared about. I was anxious to be with Zoe and Hettie again. They were good friends.

Realizing I had gotten lost in my own thoughts and hadn't answered, I said, "It was the best thing you've done in the months since I met you. You should probably become delirious more often."

He laughed like I wanted him to, the sound soothing my heart.

"How long do you think until we reach home?" I asked.

"I can see the wall to the city now. We'll be there soon enough. Hopefully, Zoe and Kaius will be home soon if they aren't already. It's almost dusk."

Eager to be with them, I pushed on. Catching my mood, Nikon sped up the pace. Soon enough, we were up the wall, back down again, through the neighborhood, and to the house. I stepped through the doorway and called out, "Zoe. Kaius. Are you here?"

A clomping on the stairs came soaring down. "You're back," Zoe said. "I've been so worried."

Seconds later, I was wrapped in a hug so tight, it was difficult to breathe. Didn't matter. I'd been choked and cut up, yet managed through it. This was more welcome and much easier.

When she finally pulled away, she touched the bandage on my neck. "What happened? Are you hurt?"

"Let's get all the way inside and she can tell you about it," Nikon said. "Is Kaius here?"

"He'll be down in a moment," Zoe said as we moved to the kitchen.

I spent the next while relating the tale, leaving out the part about the plans and Nikon being an elite warrior, Kaius joining us partway through. When I finished, Zoe said, "You're both lucky to be alive. I had no idea you thought the Vading was your old care-taker. If I'd have known what a dangerous situation you were going into, I would have protested."

"Which is exactly why I didn't say anything, and it turned out for the best. I learned what I wanted to know, and we're home safe and sound."

The silence that followed was heavy.

"Is there something we need to know?" Nikon asked.

A shuffle came from my right where Zoe sat, but it was Kaius who said, "They've stepped up the warrior patrols. You're lucky you didn't run into any on the way home. Things are intense. We only had one meeting while you were away. The other had to be canceled because of how close the warriors are getting to discovering us."

"Do you think they know there's a rebellion going on here?" Nikon asked.

"It seems likely." Kaius's words sent a shiver of fear through me.

I warmed it with hope. "We'll do our best, and it will be enough."

"And I'll hope you're right." Zoe sounded drained. Not just physically, but emotionally.

"You'd better get off to bed," Nikon said. "You both have an early day tomorrow, and it's grown late."

"You do too," I said, realizing my constant time spent with Nikon was coming to an end. "Work calls."

"And I'll be there, but I wanted to talk to you first."

"Then we'll get out of your way, so your brother can lecture you about not doing anything so dangerous ever again," Zoe said.

I wanted to laugh but was afraid she was too right—except for the brother part.

She gave me another hug, Kaius and she both offering their goodnights before heading up the stairs. I said, "They're good friends."

"They are."

When he didn't say anything else, I did. "What did you want to talk to me about?"

"Let me check your wounds."

I had a feeling he had been going to say something else, but I let it go for the moment. He carefully unwrapped the bandage from around my neck, and his fingertip brushed against my skin beside the injury.

"Does it hurt?" he asked.

In that moment, it almost felt good, but I knew that was just because of his touch, even if I didn't understand why it felt so nice. "Not really."

322

"When I saw that man hold a blade to your neck, for the second time, mind you, I was certain I was going to lose you. You're the best friend I've ever had, Cassandra. I don't ever want to lose you."

"You won't. I'll always be here for you." Though deep inside, something stirred, wanting me to say more. Unfortunately, I didn't know what that more was.

"Then we can agree, no more dangerous outings."

"Unless it will be for the good of the population as a whole."

He gave a sad chuckle. "I suppose that's the best I'm going to get."

"It is."

"Then I'll take it." He leaned in, wrapping his arms around me, making me feel a peace and comfort I didn't know I could possess. When we finally broke apart, I found myself immediately wanting to go back.

Tewy gave an *ooo* and prodded my hand to his back. I ran it across his soft fur. Nikon took my other hand in his, giving it a squeeze.

There still might have been much to do, but I'd manage. Life wasn't perfect, but I could handle anything that came my way. After all, I was a member of the rebellion.

ACKNOWLEDGMENTS

This is a book of my heart, mind, and senses beyond sight. Once the idea came to me, I knew I wanted to bring it into the world, but also knew it came with some unique challenges. Though I've been happy to face them, it's taken time and help from a wide array of people.

I utilized the abilities of more beta readers than usual, and they helped greatly. E. B. Wheeler had some great catches, helping to strengthen the book and giving great insights. Lorin Grace was awesome, helping me with her knowledge and pointing things out. F. Allen Roth gave me some assistance with grammar fixes, and Andie Hansen let me know her thoughts. Jordan with The Anxious Princess helped beta read and gave me new thoughts and ideas. I'm positive I'm missing some people because I had so much help it was difficult to keep track of everyone. If I missed you, I'm sorry! I'll try to do better next time!

A couple of my writers' groups have taught me a lot recently, and I'd be remiss if I didn't mention them. My Wednesday Fantasy Critique (thanks especially to Sarah Gardener, Danielle Pederson, and Alicia Morely Dodson) group helped read through the first several chapters, giving in depth feedback that I used to help the entire story. The Fellowship of the Ink has been a blast to be a part of, but also helped me learn more about writing and things surrounding writing. A special thanks to Brandon Greer and Cindy Clark, who helped me develop the blurb.

With this book presenting new challenges, I did some extra research that included watching YouTuber Molly Burke. If you haven't seen her videos, you should check them out. I've learned so much from her, and she's just plain fun.

Also, I must thank Maria V. Snyder for teaching a class on fighting (that I totally want to take three or four more times). It was beyond amazing, and I'm certain I haven't done it justice. Still, I learned so much. Beyond that, Maria was kind enough to answer some questions through email and help me develop the fighting sticks that Cassandra uses.

My developmental editor, Sotia Lazu, is one of my favorite people on the internet. Her skills are fantastic, and she used them to help me so much with this book, assisting me in expanding ideas and overall making things better.

Without my copy editors and proofreaders, my books wouldn't be readable. I owe a huge debt to them. Thank you Sara Miller for adding your thoughts and polish. Annie from just-copyeditors.com helped me proof the book, polishing up my clumsiness. The final proofread was still a task, but I was helped by Stephanie Parent. She's grand at helping cleaning up my writing!

The last, but biggest thanks goes to my family. So often they let me bounce ideas off them, support me, and love me. Tai, Xandria, and Will, Mom loves you much. Sorry if I put too much romance in my books for you now, but someday, you might just appreciate it.

Erik, my love and my heart, you are my everything. Thank you for always being there for me through it all. I can't wait to spend the rest of forever with you!